Body Moves

Body Moves

JODI LYNN COPELAND

APHRODISIA

KENSINGTON PUBLISHING CORP.
http://www.kensingtonbooks.com

KENSINGTON BOOKS are published by

Kensington Publishing Corp.
850 Third Avenue
New York, NY 10022

All Kensington Titles, Imprints, and Distributed Lines are available at special quantity discounts for bulk purchases for sales promotions, premiums, fund-raising, and educational or institutional use.

Special book excerpts or customized printings can also be created to fit specific needs. For details, write or phone the office of the Kensington special sales manager: Kensington Publishing Corp., 850 Third Avenue, New York, NY 10022, attn: Special Sales Department, Phone: 1-800-221-2647.

Aphrodisia and the A logo Reg. U.S. Pat. & TM Off

ISBN-13: 978-0-7582-2211-4
ISBN-10: 0-7582-2211-4

First Trade Paperback Printing: November 2007

10 9 8 7 6 5 4 3 2 1

Printed in the United States of America

Acknowledgments

Many thanks to Jenn Wilkins for her excellent insight on the breast-augmentation process and ensuring I didn't take too many liberties in altering details for the sake of the story. Any mistakes made in descriptions or references are completely mine.

I am blessed to have wonderful critique partners. In particular, P. G. Forte was a huge help in seeing this anthology reached the end, with no huge holes left along the way. And again I have to say a huge thank-you to Jenn. Thanks so much, ladies, for all that you do!

Special thanks to my family, who despite my best efforts not to reach that point, always get stuck dealing with an overtired crab come deadline time.

And to my editor, Hilary Sares, and my agent, Laura Bradford—I am so blessed to work with you.

CONTENTS

PRIVATE PASSION

1

Jordan Cameron sank back in his office chair and glared at the reflection of his father's profile in the eighth-story window of the New York City investment firm. For the first time in over a decade, John Cameron wore no beard, and every trace of gray in his hair had been covered with dark blond. He looked more like Jordan's older brother than his father. It wasn't right and, clearly, neither was his father's state of mind.

Jordan swiveled in the chair, curling his fingers around a brochure for the medical tourism resort his father returned from three weeks ago and had yet to stop talking about. He respected his father and never questioned his choices aloud. However, this latest decision wouldn't allow him to bottle his exasperation. "Jesus, Dad, think about what you're doing. It's a passing fad at best."

Inspecting himself in the golf green–etched mirror hanging on the wall kitty-corner from Jordan's desk, John rubbed his first finger and thumb along his clean-shaven chin. "Oh, I think about it. Every time your mother sneaks up and pinches my ass. I forgot how strong my sex drive was until I spent a week at

Private Indulgence. Thanks to that 'fad,' our marriage and love life are stronger than ever."

Jordan sighed. From the way his father talked, you would think the resort staff had restructured his entire reason for being and not just his underdeveloped chin.

"Fine. Let's say this place is the real deal and will be around for years to come; that still doesn't explain why you feel the need to sink your entire life savings in it." Not when he'd spent the last five years refusing Jordan's investment advice because he claimed the only save place for his money was in the bank.

"Split the money. Let me put seventy percent of it into annuities."

Barking out a laugh, John looked over. "Back in the day, we considered a split to be fifty-fifty."

Back in the day, there wasn't an endless supply of lowlifes coming up with every scheme under the sun in the hopes of getting their hands on an old man's money. Jordan had heard the buzz on the medical resorts—Private Indulgence had never been among those said to be taking off. Even those resorts that claimed to be doing well had yet to provide convincing proof of their longevity. "At least give me some time to check this place out. You got to know too many of the staff to view it objectively."

"Not to mention I was strung out on Percocet ninety percent of the time I was down there."

"Exactly."

His father crossed to the twin tan leather chairs opposite Jordan's desk and slammed his hand down on the back of one. "By God, son, you've gotten so stiff, you don't even recognize sarcasm anymore."

"Oh, I recognize it. I just don't find it humorous when it mixes my father with habit-forming drugs."

John closed his eyes and pinched the bridge of his nose—a habit Jordan had picked up from him. Opening his eyes, he let his hands fall at his sides. "All right. You've got four weeks. Only because I want to see you away from this damned desk for more than a few hours at a time. This place is sucking you dry, stealing your zest for life—"

"And worrying Mom sick she'll never have grandkids," Jordan finished dryly. He'd been through this song and dance too many times to count. Sorry to say for his parents, he wasn't one of those kids who lived to please only them. "She'll get her grandkids when I'm ready. Right now, I'm enjoying the zest for life you seem to think I've lost by dating whatever women appeal to me."

His father snorted. "Whichever ones are willing to come in second to your career is more like it."

"Dad . . ." Jordan warned.

"I'm leaving." John went to the door, turning back when he reached it. "Four weeks. If I don't hear convincing evidence against the resort by then, I'll be on the first flight to the Caribbean to share my investment decision with Dr. Crosby."

With the *snick* of the office door, Jordan turned his attention to his laptop. He clicked on the bookmarked resort informational page for Danica Crosby, MD, the plastic surgeon cum owner of Private Indulgence who'd somehow convinced his father to sink his money into her resort.

Calling the plain-looking, glasses-wearing redhead who appeared on his screen a surgeon was pushing it, considering she was barely out of her residency. The sudden ache in Jordan's gut told him that calling her business dealings with his father *reputable* would be pushing it even further, and in less than four weeks he would prove it.

"What in Hi'iaka's name are you doing?"

With her friend and assistant's question, Danica Crosby released her death grip on the alarm clock radio and set it on her desk. Lena stood in the doorway of Danica's office, eyeing her as if she'd lost her mind. For now, her sanity was intact. God only knew what would happen in the next few minutes.

Danica pushed aside one of several wayward envelopes and grabbed a chocolate-covered almond from the starfish-shaped candy dish on her desk. She popped the nut into her mouth, letting its soothing taste and texture work their magic on her tension before giving the alarm clock's red digital readout another glance. "Waiting. Three minutes from now, something bad is going to happen."

Lena's brown eyes flashed with hope. "You became psychic last night?"

"Wouldn't you have felt some sort of psychic friends' connection if I had?" Lena gave the expected dry laugh, and Danica continued soberly, "I grabbed my morning Pepsi out of the refrigerator this morning, only to discover there was no Pepsi to grab, even though I know there was one last night. An hour later, I almost cut my nipple off shaving."

Day-Glo pink and lime-green hula-girl earrings—what Lena claimed to be her twin talismans, since her supposed visionary powers began the day she'd put them on—swayed with the scrunching of her nose. "Ew. Your breasts are hairy? I just thought you'd given up on dating because you realized you were a lesbian and were afraid to come out of the closet."

"Not everyone's a date addict like you." Probably because not everyone had Lena's cute build, which had only gotten cuter with the recent chopping of all but the last couple inches of her hair and subsequent dye job that turned her locks from near black to dirty blond with fuscha streaks.

"I prefer 'serial dater.'"

"Whatever. I'm not one. I also don't have hairy breasts. I was shaving my underarm and fumbled the razor. It nicked my nipple on its way down." Danica winced. The memory hurt almost as much as the real thing.

Lena frowned. "A nipple ouchy tells you something bad's going to happen in three minutes?"

Danica gave the alarm clock a glance. Her stomach tightened forebodingly, so she popped another almond. "One minute now, and yes. Haven't you ever heard bad things happen in sets of three?"

"Sure, but I never knew there was a timetable."

"Well, there is. In fifty seconds, mine's due up." Judging by the fact that last almond didn't even touch her anxiety, whatever happened at the end of those seconds was bound to be a doozy.

Lena studied her so long and thoroughly, Danica thought another of her friend's questionable visions was about to strike, but then she just smiled, calling out the exceedingly cute dimple in her right cheek. "You know, most of the time you're as boringly normal as they come, and then you go and say something totally whacked like this and I remember there's hope for you yet."

The alarm clock rolled over to ten o'clock. Any amusement Danica might have found in Lena's words was forgotten in the wake of her heightened unease. "Time's up."

She looked around the office, half expecting the overflowing bookcase to fall on her, or the chaos on her desk to blow up in her face, or the bay window behind her to shatter, or . . . She swiveled in her chair, praying her customized golf cart hadn't gone up in flames.

Nope. Still there, parked two stories below.

"Looks like your timetable's off—Strike that." Lena inhaled audibly. "Trouble's headed this way. Don't look like no cowboy, but I'd know the smell of Stetson anywhere."

Danica swiveled back in her chair in time to see her friend exit her office as an unfamiliar man entered it, bringing with him the mouthwateringly spicy tang of cologne. Her belly did a slow warming, her inner thighs mimicking the intimate response as she took in the newcomer.

Lena was right. With his black power suit, which was completely inappropriate for the humid island weather, and polished Kenneth Coles, he didn't look like a cowboy. Danica still had the urge to climb up his long legs and take him for a ride.

Wow! Where had *that* come from?

She never thought of sex while on the clock and nearly as seldom while off it. It wasn't because she lacked Lena's perfectly cute everything and the natural tanned complexion of her friend's Hawaiian heritage—Danica liked her own fair complexion just fine. It was that she had too many other, more important, things to fill her days, namely seeing Private Indulgence, the elective surgery medical tourism resort she'd started up three years ago, continue to thrive in a way that would eventually allow for expansion into nonelective areas.

The guy moved into her office, assessing each inch before moving on to the next one. His measuring gaze landed on her. "Interesting place you have here."

Holy killer eyes! They matched the turquoise waters of the Caribbean Sea right down to the sparkle.

The way Danica's sex grew moist with the striking shade suggested his walking through her door might well be the third bad thing to happen to her this morning—by making her focus on something other than work. Even if she did have time for dating and he lived locally—doubtful, given his attire—and showed an interest, things would never work.

From his carefully styled dark blond hair and neatly trimmed mustache to the perfectly symmetrical divot in the knot of his gray silk tie, there was an order about him that his delectable appearance wouldn't allow her to look past. Danica and order went together like Lena and celibacy—both would be happening the same time pigs sprouted wings.

She relaxed with the knowledge they wouldn't be having sex. All but her churning stomach relaxed anyway. It was a little too coincidental he'd shown up right at ten. "May I help you?"

"I have a meeting with Dr. Crosby. I was told at the front desk that you're her."

"You *do*?" Pepsi withdrawal had to be playing hell with her memory. She didn't do visual order, but her mind usually had a firm grasp on things.

Danica stood, offering her hand over the top of her desk, along with an apologetic smile. "Sorry, this week has been hectic. I recall it now, Mr . . . ?" Shoot. So much for correcting her oversight.

His lips twitched as his gaze slid the length of her, eyeing her in a penetrating way that renewed the wetness between her thighs and made her want to squirm.

His gaze returned to hers, and he took her hand in a firm shake. "Jordan Cantrell."

She made it a point to personally greet as many resort guests as possible, shaking dozens of hands each week, many of them male. Not one of them rendered visions of strong, warm hands sliding over her aroused, nude body the way Jordan's did. Her jean skirt would allow easy access. The thin barrier of her panties barely an obstacle. She glanced at his fingers—ringless and long like the rest of him. Able to easily slide between her thighs and deep inside her slick pussy.

The increased twitching of his lips broke through Danica's reverie. Heat flooded her face and undoubtedly flushed her fair skin with the reality of where her mind had traveled. As if her thoughts weren't bad enough, he was silently laughing at her. *Mocking* would be the better word.

Damn it, she'd worked hard to see the resort gain a foothold in the fast-growing medical tourism industry and come far in the time since its launch. Too far to be made to feel incompetent by a man who didn't know her from the Easter Bunny. Yet incompetent was exactly how she felt.

"I'm here to check out the resort for potential surgery," Jordan supplied, his derisive tone making it clear how unimpressed he was so far.

She wanted to give him a tone of her own. Or forget the tone and tell him off outright. For the sake of the resort's reputation, she refrained. "Of course you are." Ignoring her damp panties, she forced a smile and rounded her desk. "Let me grab your file from my assistant and we'll get started."

Danica entered Lena's next-door office as her friend stood from behind a desk that was so efficiently organized it made Danica feel dysfunctional by comparison. Lena flashed a smartass grin. "So, is he here to repossess your villa, or tell you an active volcano was discovered in the resort's backyard?"

"Neither. He's a potential patient." *And not even close to a gentleman.* Danica ran a hand over her belly. God, she needed an almond, or maybe a handful of them. "He says he has an appointment with me this morning."

"If he's J. Cantrell, he has a ten-fifteen. He took over a late cancellation spot a few weeks ago. I was about to pull his file when you walked in." She went to the rear wall, which was lined floor to ceiling with shelves of patient files, and pulled a thin manila one from the Cs. Halfway back to her desk, she stopped on an indrawn breath and gasped out a "Whoa!" that in Lena-talk meant she'd had a vision.

She crossed the rest of the way to Danica, handing her the file and sitting down without a word. Completely unlike Lena, who compensated for her small stature by being as vocal as possible. "Well? What was it about?" Danica prompted.

Lena didn't look up. "You don't want to know."

"I asked, didn't I?"

She looked up, her lips curving in an impish smile. "A

Pepsiholic with one hairy armpit because she was too afraid to go back and finish the job."

"Cute, Lena. Very cute." Despite her follow-up groan, the friendly jab eased Danica's tension—until she returned to her own office to find Mr. Hot, Blond, and Oppressive waiting in front of her desk.

Jordan happened to walk in right at ten—fifteen minutes early for his appointment—and made her have sexual thoughts for the first time ever while on the job, but that didn't mean he was trouble. He could just be a pain in the ass.

She sat down on her side of the desk, popping two chocolate-covered almonds into her mouth before opening and quickly reviewing his file—all one and a half mostly blank pages of it. She looked up at him. Damned if a bolt of lust didn't shoot through her with the brilliance of his eyes. "There's nothing listed on what you would like to have done."

"I didn't say."

"The facilities vary a great deal depending on the type of procedure you're considering. Showing you the entire resort would require hours, possibly days."

"It's a"—he glanced down—"sensitive matter."

"A sensitive . . ." Danica's gaze landed on his crotch. For an instant, as she thought about the anatomy behind his zipper, the heated state of her body returned. Then his meaning settled and she barely subdued her gasp.

She didn't exactly like the guy, but there was no denying he was a stunning specimen of masculinity. Was it possible he could be equipped with an undersized penis?

Of course it was possible. She'd scrubbed in on several phalloplasty surgeries where the patient was bigger bodywise than Jordan yet miniscule below the belt.

The irritation in her belly let up some, knowing he was here because of body issues beyond his control—something she could relate to well. "I understand. The facility for that surgery is quite a distance from here. If you don't mind going for a ride in the open air, we can use my golf cart to take a shortcut."

"You golf?" He sounded impressed.

"Actually, I bought the cart because I live only a half mile from here and figured it a more economical choice than a car." Technically, her rationale had been the more she saved on auto expenses, the more she would have to invest in the resort. Since he actually looked impressed now, she kept that tidbit to herself. Not that she was trying to impress him. Even if she could get past the whole "order" thing, he probably had performance-anxiety issues.

How small could he be?

Her gaze strayed back to his crotch, lingering for a few seconds before intelligence caught up with her Pepsi-starved brain. "I do golf, when time allows for it."

"Same here. It's been a while since time has allowed for it," Jordan admitted, perhaps a bit grudgingly.

Danica closed his file and pushed her chair back from her desk. "Work has a way of taking over."

"That it does."

"Having a job you love helps."

He gave a noncommittal murmur. She took it to mean he wasn't comfortable with the conversation any longer. While the casual talk had lifted his oppressive air and mostly relaxed her stomach, it was time to get on with the tour.

She gestured to the door, then pointedly led him to the elevator and out into the parking lot so she wouldn't be tempted to peek at his ass.

"Have you tried a natural approach?" Danica asked as she slid into the driver's side of her golf cart.

After climbing into the cart, Jordan looked over with a frown. "Natural?"

The breeze wreaked havoc on his previously flawless hair.

The sun baking through the roof of the cart already had perspiration gathering on his forehead. He should look like an imbecile for how warmly he was dressed. Not to mention completely unappealing with that frown. Instead he looked sexy and sweaty, and he smelled downright appetizing.

It was a good thing he probably had performance issues, because Danica was aching to let passion rule her in a way she hadn't allowed in ages.

"Have you tried exercising your . . ." She sent a covert glance at his groin. "The area in question?"

"Yeah. Sure. Didn't work."

She started the golf cart. "What about pills?"

"Didn't do a thing."

"There are a lot of placebos being illegally marketed as the real deal. It's an easy mistake to make."

Jordan wanted to view the words as an insult. The reassurance in Danica's greenish gray eyes when she told him it was an easy mistake made that hard to do.

She wasn't what he'd expected. For one thing, she didn't wear glasses—not at present anyway—and for another she did play golf. Her behavior skirted from strange to skilled to sexual. She kept staring at his crotch. No way in hell could he be imagining it; his dick would know the difference and not be in the process of tenting his pants. Then there was her appearance.

The Internet hadn't done her justice. In person, her layered, shoulder-length hair was more fiery copper than dull red, her nose narrow and straight with a charming bump and even more charming freckles near the tip. Her mouth was soft pink, lush, and wide, and he had more than one idea of how she might use it on him.

Danica reached across to a small compartment in front of him. The back of her hand brushed against his knees, jetting frissons of heat up his thighs to his stimulated groin. On a sharp inhale, Jordan retracted his body into the seat. He was acting like a pubescent teen, but he didn't want to like her, and he sure as hell didn't want to want her.

"Sorry." With a sympathetic smile, she lifted a pair of wire-framed glasses from the compartment. "You don't want to ride with me when I'm not wearing my glasses."

As it turned out, Jordan didn't want to ride with her when she had her glasses on either. The golf cart had clearly been modified to go beyond traditional speed. Twice, on the mile or so ride, he'd been certain she was going to need to call 911 to come scrape his remains off the ground.

Danica halted the cart in front of a wooden footbridge surrounded by tropical underbrush and trees. "It's easier to walk from here."

He jumped out and hoofed it across the bridge, wanting the hell away from the psycho driver who had overtaken her body. The bridge opened up on the other side to reveal a number of pale gray and slate blue villas detailed in sky blue and separated from one another by a good-sized yard and towering palms. A three-story, mostly glass building loomed past the villas. He headed in that direction, guessing it to be the facility she planned to show him.

She surprised him by sprinting past, the developed muscles of her bare legs constricting enticingly. His gaze lifted to a high, round ass cloaked in a short jean skirt, and his blood heated. She could owe her body to faithful jogging. More likely, her muscles and the ample breasts filling her knit pink tank top were the result of implantation.

"In a hurry?" Jordan called after her.

"I thought you were." Danica dropped back to match his reduced pace and gave him an openmouthed smile. "I'm all yours till noon, so anything you want to know"—she looked at his crotch—"don't be shy about asking."

The glimpse of her moist pink tongue and the suggestive

words would have been enough to have his shaft hardening again after the hellish ride's deflating effect. The continued ogling of his groin had his cock stiff as a board.

He considered stripping away his suit coat and dress shirt under the pretense he was roasting his ass off—technically not a pretense but a reality he owed to the airport for losing his luggage during flight transfer—and seeing how she responded. Learning she slept with prospective patients in the hopes of ensuring their patronage would be as good of a way to start unveiling the resort as a bad investment as any.

"We have a fully equipped hospital," Danica said in a voice that sounded both professional and proud, "but the majority of our surgeries are done in ambulatory facilities, which are housed in the same building as the surgeons' offices for the associated procedure. Using these facilities is one of the ways we're able to keep our costs substantially lower than most public practices."

"Should I be worried *ambulatory* and *ambulance* sound remarkably similar?"

Her throaty laugh was as unexpected as her appearance—totally enticing, totally dangerous to his mission. "Not at all. *Ambulatory* means you arrive and leave the facility on the same day. Your phalloplasty surgery . . ." She sent him another of those damned apologetic looks that made it difficult to remember she was the bad guy, or rather woman. "I didn't mean to put it into words."

Jordan sent a pointed look around. The closest person lounged on the front porch chaise of a villa over a hundred feet away. "I don't think anyone heard."

"I'll still be more careful."

"You said same-day facilities are one of the ways the resort's able to keep costs down," he rushed on, needing to get the apologetic look off her face. "What are the others?"

"Unlike a lot of the islands around us, we're not governed by the United States."

Now they were getting somewhere. "In other words, you're able to avoid licensing fees and training staff in the latest procedures."

Danica stopped walking to shoot him a frosty glare. "All of Private Indulgence's facilities and staff are accredited and operate under international standards, Mr. Cantrell." The icy look softened, along with her tone. "The cost of living is simply lower here, which allows us to charge less overall while providing first-rate, state-of-the-art services by top-notch specialists. Many of our procedures are discounted seventy to eighty percent as compared with the national average."

Well, fuck. Instead of uncovering a skeleton in the resort's figurative closet, he felt impressed for the second time since meeting her. He couldn't stop his smile. "I'd prefer you to call me Jordan."

"Like the almond." Cheeks gone rosy, she leaned close to release another of those dangerously enticing laughs. "That probably sounded odd." Her eyes warmed as she confided in a husky whisper, "It's just that I have a nut fetish."

2

"As a physician, I have to caution you against doing this," Danica scolded herself as she adjusted the temperature of the water streaming from her bathtub faucet.

Not only was Lena due over in fifteen minutes to brainstorm fund-raiser ideas to raise money for resort expansion, but Danica would pay hell in the form of back pain for folding her body up like a human pretzel. Climaxing with the aid of a vibrator on the softness of her bed would be so much healthier, but nowhere nearly as enjoyable.

More than feeling good was at stake, she recognized as she stepped into the tub and sank down in the inch of water pooling in the blue porcelain basin. She had to get over her bizarre want for Jordan. From the way he'd accused the resort and its staff of operating below the law to the noteworthy time he'd arrived in her office, he was destined to be trouble.

One quick orgasm and maybe, if their paths happened to cross again, she wouldn't have to worry over whispering about her nut fetish.

Mortification attempted to surface with the memory of her

inappropriate words. It would have been bad saying them to a normal man. It was downright shameful saying them to a man who had issues with his genitalia.

Hopefully Jordan's nuts worked fine. Even now he could be slipping into the shower of his rental villa on the other side of the resort to treat his balls to a fondling.

The purpose of reclining back on the tub's molded floor and propping her feet on either side of the chrome faucet head was to expunge her want for Jordan. Instead, as the fast-running water connected with the folds of her sex, visions of him masturbating in his shower filled her mind.

It wasn't an undersized cock his fingers glided over, but a long, thick solid staff jutting from a thatch of dark blond pubic hair.

Relenting to the vision, Danica closed her eyes and used her fingers to spread her pussy lips. Normally, she loathed the uneven set of her hips, which made it next to impossible to find clothes that looked good on her. Now, her off-kilter frame was a blessing, placing her clit at an angle that had each of the millions of beads of water striking against it as they hammered down from the faucet.

Her cunt contracted with the intensity of pleasure blasting to her core. Warmth licked through her, increasing to a carnal inferno as she imagined Jordan standing in the opposite end of the tub, his fingers stroking over his proud member, his eyes bluer than ever with the heat of passion.

"I want you." She could almost hear him speak the words in a voice gone rough with lust. "I want my tongue on your body, my cock filling you up."

"Yes. I want that, too," Danica panted.

Did she? Of course not, but that wasn't important. This wasn't real, even if it felt too good to be anything else.

She clung to the imaginary as the pulsating water continued its sensual torment. She could come at any moment simply by lifting her hips and accepting the full force of the rushing water deep into her sex. This was the first time she'd taken for pleasure in months, and she wasn't giving in yet, to her body's trembling desire or reality.

Jordan came down on his knees in the shallow water. His muscular, hair-lined thighs hovered around her head, his fingers continuing to pet his hot, hard flesh. A drop of silky fluid cascaded from the tip of his cock to land on her upper lip. She swiped at the creamy droplet with her tongue, and his essence exploded over her taste buds.

More. She needed more.

Tilting back her head, Danica reached out her tongue and greedily lapped at the plump, purple head of his penis. So good. So male. She wanted to sink her lips down his shaft, feel his cum pummeling the back of her throat with the power of his climax.

He lifted his cock from her tongue before she could take him inside her mouth. Hands moved to her legs, more fingers went to her pussy. Opening her farther.

The increased pressure arched her hips up, connecting her swollen flesh with the cold, solid chrome of the faucet. Fingernails bit into her tender thighs, the exquisite nip propelling her ass off the tub floor. Her clit scraped against the shaft. Her leg muscles tightened. The walls of her cunt constricted with each pass of her sex along the shaft, the force of the wicked water consuming her burning flesh.

Orgasm flooded her in a pulsing rush. She screamed with its magnitude, harder as the shaft chafed against her clit. Holding herself up became too much to bear.

Gasping, she fell back into the shallow water, extending her climax with the thrust of two fingers inside her creaming, clenching sheath.

The sound of knocking filtered through the open bathroom window, overpowering the mad beat of her pulse in her ears.

Opening her eyes, Danica pulled her fingers from her body. She turned off the water and pushed to her feet, stumbling a bit with the wearing effect orgasm and the pretzel position had on her legs.

Damn. Lena was early. Only by ten minutes, but they were ten minutes she'd been counting on to come down from her climax high and get cleaned up.

Lena wouldn't care if she was clean. Considering how loudly Danica had screamed with her orgasm, her friend was bound to know what she'd been doing. As often as Lena mentioned Danica's dating dry spell, she was probably ecstatic to have overheard Danica having sex of any kind.

The knocking continued. She took a few seconds to blot at the portion of her hair that had found its way into the water. Grabbing her well-worn robe from the hook next to the sink, she quickly tied the sash and padded barefoot through the one-story villa to the front door.

She flipped on the entryway light and drew in a calming breath as she opened the door for Lena. Then nearly choked to death on that breath when she discovered it wasn't Lena waiting in the darkness, but a sexily disheveled Jordan with a smile so wickedly perceptive there was no denying he'd heard her rapturous scream.

She didn't owe him an explanation. He shouldn't even be at her villa. Still, words rushed out of her mouth. "You think I have a man in here. I don't have a man in here."

That was where she was mistaken, Jordan thought, giving her flushed, damp body an appreciative ogling that had his rock-solid dick jerking beneath his untucked shirt. It might not have been a man who'd made her shout so loudly he'd heard her impassioned cry long before reaching her door, but there was a man in her villa. Or rather there was about to be.

"Actually, you do." He pushed his way inside, taking a second to kick the door shut before he pinned her against the wall with the press of his body against hers.

Danica's eyes went wide. A gasp attempted to escape her arousal-reddened lips. He gobbled the sound up with his own lips. Sinking his tongue into her mouth, he jerked at the loose knot at her waist. The sides of her pink robe gave way, and his hands filled with warm, soft, succulent skin.

He'd come here to give her what she made clear she wanted each time she checked out his cock. He'd planned on a swift approach but never realized just how swift it would be. Or that she would be waiting, fully stimulated and mostly naked.

Or that she would taste so damned good.

Hell, he shouldn't enjoy kissing her. She didn't appear to enjoy kissing him—her tongue was lifeless against his, her body inert. That changed the instant Jordan slid a hand down the rise of her belly to cup her mound.

Heat rose off her sex. Moisture joined that heat as he fingered her slit. Her hips shot to motion, bucking wildly, her tongue licking to lusty life against his. Her fingers gripped at the front of his dress shirt, quickly moving lower, past the shirttails to find his erection freed of his zipper and already sheathed for action.

Danica's mouth stilled. Her fingers froze around the head of his cock. His ready state might have surprised her, but from the stab of her erect nipples against his chest and the dampness of her slit, there was no question that she wanted him.

He thrust into her slick pussy, fingering her core while his tongue and lips continued to render her speechless.

Wetness built with each of his strokes until her sex contracted around his fingers, her inner walls deliciously milking at them, making his cock damned anxious to get inside.

Her tongue started moving again, her lips taking his so eagerly it was as if she was starved for a lover's kiss.

Of course, that wasn't the case.

She'd probably slept with another potential resort client just last week. Maybe even last night. It was the reason Jordan was here now, to start on the path to proving her immoral, if not the resort a complete joke. Only, it was hard to remember his purpose when he pulled his fingers from her weeping cunt, lifted her up his body, and pumped his cock inside her.

He'd expected wet and loose. He had the wet part right, but Danica's pussy was nowhere near to loose.

Her sex clamped down tightly, fitting around his shaft like a second skin. She continued her eager assault of his lips and tongue and teeth while her hands gripped his back through his shirt, and she met him thrust for violent thrust.

Jordan palmed the silky roundness of her ass as he shoved inside her so fiercely the back of her head connected with the wall. He winced with the sound. She didn't miss a beat, just kept moving, taking him deep, tight, fast.

Danica tensed in his arms, her movements stopping abruptly only to restart with the clamping of her pussy. Moaning into his mouth, she came around his dick.

He moaned back as he gave in to his own orgasm, one that had been building from the moment he entered her office. As much as he would like to pretend he'd fucked her solely for the sake of verifying the unethical way she secured patients, it wouldn't be true.

He'd wanted her. Wanted her again even now.

He pulled from her body and set her on her feet. She swayed a little but then stood firm. Her robe hung open, giving him an alluring view of full, round tits and curly, damp copper hair camouflaging her sex. Arousal scented the air and ran in creamy rivulets along her inner thighs.

Jordan fought the urge to go down on his knees and lick her clean. He was here for business, to prove she was the enemy as far as his father was concerned. He would be a damned fool to forget that just because she happened to enjoy a round of golf, talked about the resort as if it really was an accomplishment to be proud of, and fucked like a champion.

"Why?" Danica's voice shook.

He met her eyes, unprepared for the shock that filled them. She had to be faking her surprise. Narrowing his gaze, he snorted out a laugh. "That supposed to be some kind of joke? You spent the morning eyeing my dick and talking about having a nut fetish."

"For *professional* reasons."

"Right. Your way of making sure I pick Private Indulgence to do my surgery."

Her breath dragged in audibly. She glared at his deflating cock, still sheathed because he had no idea where to dispose of the condom and clean himself up, and he wasn't about to ask. "I thought you were shorted in the penis department."

Jordan felt the words as a verbal punch directly to his gut. Right now his dick wasn't all that big, but when he was hard, he came in on the above-average side of things, or so his past lovers had told him. Unless those lovers had merely said so in order to stroke his ego enough to keep him in bed and away from work.

No, that was his father talking. Putting shit in his head that wasn't true. His career mattered, but he didn't put it above all else. If he did, he wouldn't be here now. "What the hell made you think that?"

Danica's gaze fell from his cock to look down at her exposed body. She tugged the sides of the robe together so quickly it almost seemed like she was ashamed of what they'd done and he almost felt guilty for his part in it.

Her glare softened a bit as she looked back at his face. "When I asked why you were having surgery, you said it was a sensitive matter and looked at your crotch. Then when I mentioned you having phalloplasty, you didn't correct me. I thought you were after a penis enlargement."

Damn. Now he *did* feel guilty. Then again, no, he didn't.

If she'd shown any sign of resistance, he wouldn't have screwed her. She hadn't resisted; from the moment he'd cupped her mound, she'd acted like she couldn't get enough of him. "I was looking at the floor, not my crotch, and I have no idea what *phalloplasty* means."

She sighed, and the last of the resentment left her face. "Why are you having surgery?"

"I don't know that I am. If I do, there are several things I'd like to change." She looked like she wanted to respond but remained silent. It was his cue to get out of here to do some serious thinking.

Jordan tucked his penis into his pants, condom and all. He would worry about the mess when he got to his place. He moved the few feet to the door and opened it.

"So that's it?" Danica asked as he was about to walk over the threshold to the rental coupe parked in a spacious yard made private by a wall of trees extending out from either side of the villa. "We're just going to forget we had sex?"

He turned back with a shrug. "That a problem?"

"No," she said, sounding like it was. "Of course not. Accidents happen."

"Sure they do." She'd covered herself up, but her ample breasts and tight pussy were ingrained in his mind. He couldn't help his lingering stare or a wolfish smile. "They just don't normally look as good as you."

She crossed her arms over her chest. A flush rose into her cheeks as she glanced away. "How did you find out where I live? Neither my home number nor my address are listed."

"Your assistant told me." That had her looking back with

the same icy glare she'd given him this morning, only this time it appeared to be all for her coworker.

Danica ignored the knocking at her front door as she pulled a baggy red T-shirt and black canvas shorts out of her white wicker dresser and tugged them on. This time her company had to be Lena. Since she hadn't arrived to hear Danica in the throes of climax, Lena wouldn't wait for her to answer the door but would knock a second time and then come inside and make herself at home.

Lena was doing as expected, relaxing on the plastic-framed couch on the villa's seaside terrace with a bag of tortilla chips on the flowered cushion next to her. She dipped a chip into the bowl of salsa balanced on her thigh, then stuck the chip in her mouth with a blissful moan.

"You're late," Danica snapped as she stepped through the sliding glass door from the living room. *And about to be dead.*

Lena jumped. The salsa tipped precariously before she grabbed it and saved the couch's fabric from a stain that probably wouldn't even show amid all the others accrued through the years.

She scrutinized Danica in the light-brightened darkness, and a slow, knowing smile curved her lips. "Ten minutes and on purpose. I saw you getting it on and didn't want to interrupt. You were way overdue."

She did *what*?

Lena had been her friend for over two years, and they'd never had anything more than temporary minor friction between them. Now, Danica felt like she didn't even know her. "Telling him where I live wasn't enough, you *watched* us?"

Lena's fingers stilled with a naked chip midway to her mouth. "Hell, no, I didn't watch. I had a vision about it."

"You had a vision of me having sex?"

"I had a vision of Jordan showing up on your doorstep

ready to do you and you answering the door looking just as ready to do him. When he asked for your address, I figured it was destined I tell him." She popped the chip into her mouth, then leaned down to pull a six-pack of Pepsi from beneath the couch's frame. "Here."

A quarter moon cast a dim glow on the beach fifty feet beyond the raised terrace. The tide was receding, leaving the sand to dry. Danica's throat suddenly felt even dryer than the sand. Her fingers curled, wanting to grab hold of the soda and drink it back can after can—she still hadn't gotten her fix for the day. Only, she couldn't let Lena off so easily. "Pepsi? You think that's enough to make up for what you've done?"

"What I've done is see that you experienced passion for the first time in eons. That's called a favor. The Pepsi's a bonus."

"I don't want it, and I sure as heck don't want or need you seeing to my sex life." *Liar.* At least the first part was a lie. She really didn't want Lena acting like her personal pimp.

"You do want it, and you're glad I sent Jordan over here." She smiled conspiratorially. "Eyes don't lie, hon. Yours are screaming happily laid and in dire need of refreshment."

Danica should hang on to her anger a while longer. If she gave in now, there was no telling who or what Lena would send to her place in the future. But they *had* been friends for over two years, and she'd never been good at holding a grudge.

She sank down on the end of the weathered couch opposite Lena, grabbing the soda and freeing a can from the plastic ring around its neck. She pulled the tab and took a long, luscious drink before sending Lena's sky blue, midriff-baring tank top and skimpy white shorts a teasingly snarky look. "Your earrings don't match your outfit."

Humor flashed in Lena's eyes. "So you tell me at least three times a week. Give it up. I'm not taking them off."

Danica smiled. "Thanks. For the Pepsi. I'm still not thrilled about your giving Jordan my address, though I probably would never have found out his cock is plenty big otherwise."

Lena paused with another naked chip dangling from her fingertips. The astonishment in her eyes said her vision really hadn't shown all—if she'd even had an honest-to-goodness vision. "Come again?"

"I thought he was checking out the resort because he was considering a penis enlargement. I spent the entire morning looking at his crotch; then I told him about my nut fetish. Hence the reason he was so eager to find out where I live. He was convinced I wanted to sleep with him."

"You did, but debating that fact's pointless now. So what is he here for?"

"He won't say, just that there are a lot of things he would like to change."

"What do you think? Is it a case of a great face and build but a freak show beneath his clothes?"

Danica stiffened. She knew Lena didn't mean anything cruel by her words, but they hit on a nerve sensitive enough to have Danica's belly rumbling for almonds. She didn't stock almonds at home, given their tendency to go straight to her waistline, or rather, a little to the right side of her waistline and a lot to the left.

Talk about a freak show.

If not for her robe covering up her sides and back, Jordan would have taken one look at her and run.

She dipped a chip into the salsa and jammed it in her mouth. She chewed slowly, letting the balmy night breeze and the salt smell lifting off the sea ease away her irritation and overcritical self-bashing. "No idea," she finally said. "He never took them off."

Lena's eyes went wide with appreciation. "Oh, man. He just pulled his cock out and did the deed. Hot."

"Actually, his cock was out of his pants and sheathed before I even opened the door." When she'd first made that discovery, Danica had been turned off by his self-assurance. Then he'd palmed her sex and dipped one of those long, thick fingers inside her body, and she could have cared less if he was arrogant, so long as he didn't stop fucking her. "But, yeah, very hot."

"Next time you'll both be naked."

Danica pulled from the hedonistic daze she'd fallen under with the memory. As incredible as it had felt to have a man's hands on her body after so much time, his cock pumping away inside her, it wouldn't be happening again anytime soon. Work was her priority. And, if she was to be completely honest, she would rather leave Jordan with the impression he'd had of her when he left the villa: that she was good to look at. "There won't be a next time."

"Sorry to break it to you, but Hi'iaka tells me otherwise."

Then it was a good thing Danica wasn't convinced Hi'iaka was sending Lena visions. Just to be safe, she downed the rest of her Pepsi in one long swig and then reached for the remaining cans for reinforcement.

3

Jordan punched the elevator button for the second floor of Private Indulgence's main offices. He'd spent the night considering Danica's response to the primal way he'd taken her up against the wall and came to the conclusion he was acting like a cynical ass. The resort could prove to be a bad investment when compared with others in the industry or all on its own. Until that happened, he had no reason to expect the worst of it or its owner.

His father was behind his cynicism. John had known Danica less than a week, and in that time she'd earned enough of his respect for him to trust her with his money in a way Jordan hadn't been able to accomplish in years.

Putting it simply, Jordan was jealous as hell.

The elevator dinged as it reached the second floor. He stepped out of the car, determined not to let jealousy play a part in his treatment of Danica from this point on. He would be open-minded, get to know her as his father had. If doing so revealed past or ongoing skeletons, hopefully they would be enough to sway his father into trusting Jordan with his money instead. If it didn't . . . It was the old man's money to invest with whom and where he chose.

He reached the executive operations suite and opened the door to an empty waiting room decorated in cheery yellows and greens, the walls lined with framed photos of the resort under construction, along with certificates of training completion for Danica and the rest of the staff housed in the suite. He moved up to the check-in desk.

Flashing a practiced smile, a late fiftysomething, silver-haired receptionist slid open the glass partition separating the administrative and waiting areas. Her gaze fell on his shirt, and amusement gleamed in her eyes. "May I help you?"

Not busting a gut laughing over his clothes would be a start. The kitschy red Hawaiian shirt, with its enormous purple and white flowers, was ridiculous-looking but preferable to sweating to death in his suit.

Jordan typically wouldn't resort to charm to get his way. Since he didn't have an actual appointment and the shirt wasn't exactly doing him any favors, he didn't have much choice. He flashed his teeth in an appreciative smile as he scanned her nameplate. "Good morning, Diane. I have a meeting with Dr. Crosby. I was here yesterday, when you had on a dress the same stunning shade of green as your eyes."

Soft pink settled over the lines on her face that said she hadn't succumbed to Botox temptation. "Why, yes, I remember now. Mr. Cantrell, right?"

He nodded. "Great memory to go with a great smile."

Diane fidgeted with the papers on the counter in front of her a few seconds before picking one up. "Ah, here's the appointment log." She frowned. "Oh, but I don't see your name on it."

If she was younger, he would add a bit of sensuality to the mix, give the back of her hand a teasing touch while he pretended to search the log for his name. Since she was his mother's age and already appeared flustered, he stuck with the smile. "Strange. Dr. Crosby asked her assistant to schedule a follow-up appointment for today. I believe her name was Lena."

She stood from her desk. "Give me a moment."

Diane disappeared through a door on the right side of the closed-in reception area. Within a minute, a grinning Lena appeared through the door connecting the waiting area to the business offices. She gave his blindingly obscene shirt a glance and her grin faltered. Like she had room to talk with those obnoxious earrings. Jordan was no fashion guru, but it didn't take one to know the hideous pink and green hula girls were no match for her sleeveless red shirt and white capris.

Her grin warmed again, revealing an attractive dimple. "Nice to see you, Mr. Cantrell."

"You, too." If she assisted him without question, the way she had last night when she'd supplied Danica's address, it would be even nicer. "I was telling Diane I have a follow-up appointment with Dr. Crosby this morning."

"Of course you do," Lena said without hesitation. "You're a few minutes early, but I doubt that'll be a problem. Why don't you follow me on back?"

Could it really be as easy as that? If so, Danica had told Lena about last night. The way Lena was grinning suggested Danica had only good things to say.

Jordan's blood warmed with the thought of getting Danica naked again, this time completely. Only, that wouldn't be happening. The plan was to get close to her in the same way his father had, and that damned well better not have included sex.

"Thanks." With a farewell smile to Diane, he followed Lena down the hall toward Danica's office. "I don't know why you're being so helpful, but it's appreciated."

"Just doing Hi'iaka's bidding."

"Hi'iaka is . . . ?"

Glancing over her shoulder, she fingered the hula girl dangling from her right ear. "The goddess who created the hula and my vision guide. I'm psychic."

Lena being gifted might explain her easy acceptance of him. Jordan still had a hell of a time believing she was serious. "You don't say."

"Danica doesn't believe me either." She stopped a couple feet from Danica's closed office door. "Wait here." At his nod, she continued to the door and knocked.

With the rap on her office door, Danica looked up from her computer monitor, where she was researching fund-raiser ideas online since last night's brainstorming session had been a complete bomb, to the alarm clock. Ten o'clock. She wasn't expecting anyone now, or for the rest of the day, for that matter. "Come in."

The door pushed in, and Lena filled the entryway, just as she had yesterday at this exact time of morning. A not-very-pleasant feeling of déjà vu settled over Danica.

Lena glanced at the candy dish on her desk. "How's the almond supply?"

"The dish is half full." She narrowed her eyes. "Or is it half empty? What's going on? You look devious."

"Nothing's going on. Just letting you know your ten o'clock is here."

"I don't have a ten—"

Lena disappeared before she could finish, and, like yesterday, Jordan took her place in the doorway. Unlike yesterday, he wasn't wearing a power suit and Kenneth Coles. Today, he had on knee-length dark blue board shorts and a Hawaiian print shirt so loud Danica's fingers tingled to tear it off and send it through her paper shredder.

Her sex joined in on the tingling with the thought of him shirtless. She hadn't seen his torso last night, but she'd had her hands on it and his back through his shirt. Both had felt very nice, as did his mustache brushing against her lips. His nowhere-near-to-miniscule cock had felt incredible pushing into her wet pussy while his hands gripped her ass.

Moisture jetted to her core, and she made a mad grab for the chocolate-covered almonds. She frowned at him as she chewed a small handful of nuts.

He smiled back. "You really do have a fetish."

God, she hated the way his smile intensified his already too-potent eyes. It made her think of Lena's omen they were destined to have sex again, maybe even this morning.

Danica reminded herself he was a potential patient and kept her voice calm while her heart sped. "We don't have an appointment today."

Jordan moved into the office. The scent of his cologne infiltrated her senses and tented her nipples. She crossed her arms over her breasts.

His attention wavered to her chest, and his smile grew as he again met her eyes. "Sure we do. Lena must have forgotten to tell you about scheduling me in last minute."

Big surprise, Lena was in on this. "She must have."

"Or maybe she had a vision about it and never actually got around to doing it in real life."

"She told you she's psychic?" What else had Little Ms. Big Mouth shared? If she'd told him they were fated to have a second screw, it wouldn't matter how much Pepsi Lena had to barter with, Danica was going to kill her.

"And that you don't believe in her abilities," he added.

What she didn't believe was that he—a virtual stranger—was standing in her office essentially calling her a lousy friend. "I never said I don't believe in her. I just have yet to see proof. Take last night. Lena said she told you where I live because she had a vision of you coming to my villa and me waiting for you at the door. The thing is, *she* sent you to my villa, and I wasn't waiting for you, but *her*. So should I buy that she had a vision or just saw an opportunity to play matchmaker and decided to go for it?"

"Do you always masturbate right when Lena's due over?"

Her pussy thrummed with his words. She guessed he knew what she'd been doing when he arrived but until now had held out hope she was mistaken.

She blew out a breath. "*Why* are you here?"

Jordan looked around her office, assessing each inch of the space as he'd done yesterday. Only, his approach wasn't quite the same. The oppressive air was gone. Now he seemed to notice the disarray had a certain feng shui appeal—all right, Danica had never considered it that way before, but Lena would appreciate the step outside of her "normally boring" box.

He looked back at her and nodded approvingly. "Organized chaos. It's never worked for me, but I have friends who swear by it."

"You haven't answered my question, Mr. Cantrell. I have a full day planned, so if it's another tour you're after, Lena will need to set you up with one of the resort guides."

"It's Jordan, remember, like the almond?" His eyes warmed to the same shade of dark turquoise they'd been last night, right before he'd pushed her up against the wall and fucked her stupid. "I do want another tour. Several of them."

"Let me get Lena to—"

"I want you."

Therein lay the problem and the reason his presence in her office yesterday precisely at ten was, in fact, the third bad thing to happen to her. Danica wanted him, too.

Another day together was bound to end on an incredibly good-feeling note with ultimately bad consequences. For once, she didn't think those consequences would center on back pain. The feral way he'd pounded into her last night had released every bit of the tension amassed in her lower spine from her bathtub masturbation session. She'd woken up this morning feeling wonderfully normal.

"I'm thinking about having a generous amount of work done," Jordan said soberly. "I don't want to rely on secondary knowledge of a procedure or the environment that procedure will be done in. I want the best person possible to show me everyone and everything this place has to offer."

"I appreciate how you feel, but I have a business to run and—"

"Surgeries to perform."

"I don't do the operations."

Surprise flickered in Jordan's gaze. "You don't?"

"I scrub in from time to time to keep up on the latest techniques and to keep from forgetting my training, but I leave the primary work to the long-time experts."

Respect shone in his eyes, quickly turning to conviction. "I intend to make it worth your while to ignore business operations for a few days."

"How?"

"Money. Name your price; I'm good for it."

Danica gave his shirt a glance. The suit he'd worn yesterday looked pricey and far more fitting to his personality. She chose to ignore that to say sarcastically, "It shows."

He looked down. "This is desperation. My luggage was lost during flight transfer, and the only shop I could find open last night after we . . ." His gaze shot up, his eyes instantly back to the intense shade that did wicked things to her panties.

Sucking in a breath, she crossed her legs against a rush of wet heat and waited for him to continue. Or to climb across the desk and kiss her until they were both panting and tugging at each other's clothes. The former was the smart thing to do, but her fluttering pussy really hoped he went with the latter.

"The only place open late," Jordan said in a raspy voice, "was Aloha Outfitters."

Danica shook off her arousal. Really, what was she thinking, wanting him, and in her office with the door open no less?

She needed the money he spoke of, and that was what her concentration had to be on. "I need to give more than a few hours of notice and arrange the appropriate staff to fill in for me to take a full day off. I'll give you the rest of the week from noon onward each day, but that's the best I can do."

"Deal." He glanced at a silver Rolex that was totally at odds with the remainder of his attire. "I'm assuming the rest of the week starts today, so I'll see you in a couple hours. Shall we meet at your place or mine?"

"My office." *The only safe place.*

Right. Safe. She'd been eager for him to climb across the desk and have his way with her when the door was open and the building full of staff. At noon, most everyone would be out to lunch. That sounded about as safe as running with a scalpel in her hand.

Two phone calls following Jordan's departure from her office had temporarily waylaid Danica from her mission. She was off the phone now and crossing the hall with murder on her mind. Fortunately for Lena, there was no scalpel in Danica's hand.

She stepped into Lena's office, slamming the door behind her. Lena's head shot up from whatever she'd been reading on her desk.

Danica glared. "You're itching for an ass kicking, aren't you?"

The surprise left Lena's face and she smiled. "I've always been a sucker for a good cat fight."

"Let me guess, a vision is behind your decision to lead Jordan into my office when you know damned well he didn't have an appointment?"

"No vision necessary. Seeing how happy you still were this morning, after getting it on with stud man last night, I knew you needed to see him again."

Danica hadn't been happy this morning, at least not any more so than usual. She'd been well rested because, for the first time in too long, her muscles had been loose enough to allow for sound sleep. She hadn't told Lena about her back issues and the resultant reoccurring pain because she didn't want her friend worrying over something that couldn't be fixed. Danica much preferred Lena focus on something she could help, like their friendship by stopping her attempts to push Jordan her way.

Not that she could blame Lena for her agreeing to Jordan's offer. Not even the need for his money had fueled Danica's decision to be his personal tour guide for the week, as she'd told herself. Impatience had made her do it.

Her frustration eased and she admitted, "You'll be ecstatic to know Jordan and I are spending the rest of the week together, from noon on each day."

Lena's expression moved right past the anticipated ecstatic to downright impressed. "Noon on. As in, you're all his for the rest of the day and night. I guess one hairy armpit wasn't a turnoff, after all."

Danica wanted to laugh, or maybe groan. Only, she couldn't get past the ominous tightening of her belly. "We didn't discuss night."

"You said noon on; including night in there would be a given."

Would it?

No, it wouldn't, since Jordan didn't want to sleep with her again. He'd said so last night. Only he hadn't. She'd asked if they were going to forget about having sex, and he'd implied as much, but he hadn't actually given her a straight answer. Instead he'd ogled her body like he hadn't just had his hands all over it and commented on how good she looked. The hot look he'd given her this morning wasn't any better. It definitely didn't make it seem he was ready to forget about him and her and soul-shaking sex.

Shoot. This could be bad . . . in a way that had her pussy swelling with liquid excitement. "I'm not sleeping with him again," she told herself as much as Lena.

Lena laughed. "Of course you are."

Danica sighed. "That's right. Hi'iaka deems it so." How could she have thought to defy the wants of a long-dead goddess? "I might as well say to hell with waiting for the fated moment and throw myself at him immediately."

Lena's eyes warmed with approval. "Like I said yesterday, there's hope for you yet, hon."

Jordan shot Danica a wary glance as they stepped out of the main office elevator a few minutes after noon and headed through the first floor of the building to the open parking lot. Yesterday, he'd been able to avoid getting back in the demonic golf cart with the excuse his villa was less than a half mile from the phalloplasty facility, and he wanted to get some exercise by walking back. Today, he wasn't feeling so lucky.

As feared, Danica proceeded toward the cart. "Since you won't tell me what type of work you're considering having done, we'll start on the far end of the resort and work our way back here as the week progresses."

He veered off the sidewalk toward his black rental coupe parked in the middle of the lot. "We can use my car."

"Taking the service drive will mean missing out on a great deal of the behind-the-scenes part of the resort. You said you wanted to see everything."

Shit. She had him there.

Jordan turned back, and the eager look on Danica's face as she jingled the cart's keys reminded him the golf cart wasn't possessed, just the woman who drove it.

He had no respect for liars. For the sake of protecting his parents' welfare, he'd had to lie to Danica about his last name and about wanting surgery. For their sake, he lied again as he made his way back to the sidewalk. "We can take your golf cart, but I'll need to drive. I have a problem with motion sickness, which is why I got out so fast yesterday. Driving is the only thing that keeps the nausea away."

The merry jingling of the keys stopped. Her lips pushed into an openmouthed sulk as she held out the keys. "Be careful. I've never let anyone else drive her."

He was supposed to regard her as his father would. Jordan hadn't managed to accomplish that this morning in her office, and he for damned sure couldn't do it now, because he was human. Any single guy with a healthy libido would take one look at her lush pink lips pushed into the evocative mew and have the vision of filling up the circle of her lips with his dick.

His shaft roused against the navy knit shorts he'd bought, along with a white and navy polo shirt, in between visits to Danica's office. "Your baby, huh?"

She continued toward the golf cart. "The one and only."

He forced his attention from the plumpness of her ass in a midthigh black skirt and continued to the cart. He climbed into the driver's side, subtly adjusting his growing erection before looking over at her. "Do you want children?"

She gasped and her gaze shot to his groin, like she thought he was making an offer to be the father.

Mom would be elated.

Jordan recoiled with the thought. He would give his parents grandkids someday, but the mother of those kids wouldn't be Danica. Not that any better candidate came to mind. It wasn't because he hadn't taken the time away from work to get to know his recent lovers either. He knew them well enough to know they hadn't appealed to him beyond a few casual fucks. A woman who kept his interest would come along when the time was right.

Danica frowned. "Why would you ask that?"

He started up the golf cart and focused out the front windshield at the many-windowed side of the building. "The resort seems like a huge responsibility. I wasn't sure if you would have time for both."

"I like kids." She sounded insulted. "If and when I have them, it will be with a man who wants to share the responsibility of taking care of both the resort and the children."

"If and when that happens, I'm sure you'll handle the balance perfectly." Jordan had said the words to appease her. But the more he learned about her and the efficiency with which she ran the resort, the more he believed they were a precise judge of her character.

He backed out of the parking space. "Where to?"

She pointed to the rear of the lot where a narrow paved path cut through the grass. He veered the cart in that direction, following the path slowly up a winding hill.

"There's no speed limit," Danica pointed out after a couple minutes.

Yeah, and he wasn't training for NASCAR the way she seemed to be. "I'm enjoying the scenery." He made a show of checking out the abundance of trees and multicolored tropical flowers. The hill crested after a quarter mile, and the lichen-covered rise of a small mountain became visible on his left. It was the rolling greens of a golf course on his right that drew his true attention, though.

His father was mistaken about the investment firm sucking the life out of him. It had, however, eaten up more of Jordan's time the past couple years than he liked to acknowledge. The last time he'd golfed was . . . Hell, he couldn't remember. With the snow soon ready to fall back in New York, he wouldn't be getting a game in this year either. Unless he took advantage of the year-round sun and warm sea breezes of the Caribbean. Playing a friendly round of golf with Danica could only aid him in his quest to get to know her better.

He stopped the cart at the head of the first hole. She looked over, and he nodded toward the tee box. "Resort owned?"

"Actually, it's not a real course." She smiled in a way that involved her whole face, her eyes going mostly gray and her mouth opening far enough to give him a glimpse of her tongue. "My father laid out a par-three, nine-hole course for practicing his game. He thought it would be a good place to build on investor relations, too."

With the flash of Danica's tongue, Jordan struggled to keep his head on the conversation and not on the unforgettable way her mouth felt moving against his. How her exuberant lips and tongue would feel even better sliding down his body to torment his cock in all the best ways. "It didn't work?"

"He died during the construction of the resort."

Christ, what an asshole. Sitting here with his dick hard and thoughts of her making it even harder while he unknowingly made her relive her father's death. "I'm sorry. You're what—mid to late twenties? He had to have been quite young."

Danica laughed. "Nice attempt at charm, but I'm almost thirty-two, and my dad died of natural causes. I was a late-in-life decision for my parents. Dad was in his early fifties and Mom forty-four when I was born."

He hadn't been trying to charm her. The reemergence of her husky laugh changed that, made him have the dangerous thought to take her out to the closest sand trap and risk getting sand in every one of their crevices.

Jordan remained seated. "Running this place is a tribute to your father?"

"Private Indulgence was my idea. Dad was the one with the money and experience to see my dream become a reality."

"Did the resort not take off as well as planned, or why do you need additional funds?"

She eyed him suspiciously. "What makes you think I do?"

"Your agreement to give me your time in exchange for my money."

"The resort is doing well." Danica looked toward the tee box. "I'm just flawed."

"Not from what I've seen." He'd only seen the majority of her front side in the buff, but it happened to be the side that contained some of her most important parts.

He'd pegged her breasts as being implant-enhanced. If they were implants, the surgeon had done an impeccable job. They looked, felt, and tasted 100 percent authentic.

Letting go another alluring laugh, she looked back at him. "I meant personalitywise. I have no idea what order is, and I'm impatient as hell. Lena helps out on the organizational end of things, but nothing can be done for my impatience. I want to see the resort expanded to include nonelective surgeries, bringing people health along with happiness, and I want it to happen now."

It was the information Jordan had been hoping for. She wanted to act rashly, and rash actions often led to failure. Proving she had a history of impulsive behavior where the resort was concerned would be the perfect excuse for his father not to sink his money into the place.

Now to clear his mind of the fact he hadn't actually felt or tasted her breasts last night . . . "Are there clubs stored somewhere around here?"

She frowned. "You want to golf? But what about the tour?"

The tour could wait an hour or two. Bonding was essential. Not the kind of bonding that joined his throbbing cock with her tight pussy either. Unless, of course, she *wanted* to sleep with him again—that was bound to be the best-feeling bad idea he ever had. "Like I said yesterday, work hasn't allowed for golfing, or for that matter play of any kind, in ages. You hinted at the same. Only in your case, you'll still technically be on the clock, since I'm paying for your time."

"Gee, thanks for making me feel like a prostitute."

"Could I pay you to have sex with me, Danica?" Jordan shouldn't have asked the question and risked their fragile connection. She'd resurfaced his cynicism with her admission to being impatient, and the words had come tumbling out.

Danica didn't bat an eyelash, just slid her hand into his lap and said in an undeniably naughty voice, "Depends how much you're offering and your kink level."

4

Maybe it had to do with his change in attire to casual shorts and a polo shirt and the carefree style the warm, salty breeze lent his dark blond hair, but from the moment Jordan looked at her private golf course as if he couldn't wait to get on it, Danica had experienced an odd sense she'd met him before. It relaxed her enough to share details of her life she wouldn't have previously told him. For the first time, she'd been comfortable with him.

Then he offered to pay her for sex.

She should have pushed his ass out of the golf cart. Only, he deserved to be treated far worse, even if it meant risking his resort patronage, so she'd put her hand in his lap with the intent to taunt him hard and then leave him stranded in the middle of the course, with only his erection to keep him company. She hadn't counted on his cock already being stiff or her sex to contract in anticipation of feeling him pumping inside her slick body.

"Does kink cost more or less?"

His sober tone was gone. Now he just sounded aroused, the

jerking of his shaft beneath Danica's palm removing any doubt. Her lips wanted to smile. She let them curve while her fingers stroked his cock through his shorts.

"Less." She lengthened her strokes. Just because the dickhead started out hard didn't mean she had to give up her plan of making him want her and then leaving him stranded. If she made herself crazy with wanting him in the meanwhile . . . It was the price one paid for playing with a fire as hot as Jordan Cantrell. "It's vanilla sex I make men pay through the nose for. I can't stand to be bored when I fuck."

The frank language quickened her heart and seeped juice onto her panties. Danica turned on the cart's bench seat, bringing her left leg under her and her right knee up to rub against his shaft with each of her finger's strokes. The angle provided him a view up her skirt to her damp panties, and his gaze took no time in wandering there.

His pupils dilated, his breathing picking up. The tight set of his lips suggested it took all of his control to keep his hands at his sides. Her miscreant pussy ached to give him the go-ahead to touch her for free.

Jordan's gaze lifted, traveling slowly up her body until he eyed her mouth so intently her lips burned for his kiss. Instinctively, she swayed toward him.

"What would twenty get me?"

Danica jerked back on the seat, feeling as though he'd slapped her.

What happened to thinking she looked good? She spent hours shopping for clothes that strategically hid her disfigured body while playing up her twin assets of naturally full, high breasts. Appearance alone had to be worth a couple hundred, right?

She narrowed her eyes. "Last night you surprised me into giving you a free fuck. Do you really think I'd sleep with you a second time for less than what a good meal costs?"

"I was talking thousands."

Thousands? Good God, when the man shelled out for sex, he shelled out for sex. It was almost impossible to feel insulted over that much cash. Almost.

She lifted her hand from his cock. "C'mon, Jordan. I'm not some whore you pick up on the street corner. If you want the good stuff, you're going to have to pay for it."

"What do you usually get?"

Now there was the way to insult her, by suggesting she made a practice of selling her body. When precisely had she stopped owning a medical resort and started owning an island brothel?

Danica resisted the urge to put her hand back in his lap to do some serious damage to his nuts. For what he was implying, he deserved to suffer to the max. She caressed the bulge of his cock with her knee. "It'll cost you fifty for a week of unlimited access."

Jordan's eyebrows shot up. "Jesus, at that rate, I would think the expansion would have happened long ago."

Ah-ah-ah. Hesitation. Couldn't be having that.

Going with vengeance, she crawled onto his lap and straddled him. Her skirt bunched up, riding higher on her bare thighs as she rubbed her sex against the hard ridge of his penis. "No way, baby. Raw materials and labor are less expensive down here, but they still aren't free." She gyrated her pelvis, and her clit scraped against his pubis. Moaning with the intensity of sensation rocketing through her, she grabbed hold of the seat on either side of his head and circled a second, pussy-flooding time. "Do we have a deal?"

"I want the terms in writing."

Danica ceased her circling. His words didn't match the lust sizzling in his eyes. They sounded planned. Who the heck was she dealing with, an undercover cop attempting to bust her for illicit behavior?

Her belly tightened with the realization he could well be a cop, or some similar law enforcer. She didn't know what Jordan did for a living, and his need to know about the resort went well beyond what should concern a patient. It would also explain why he'd been so quick to accuse the place of operating unethically.

She shut out her restless stomach to give him a feline smile. "And open myself up to libel. I don't think so."

"Then there's no deal."

If he was a law enforcer, she had nothing to hide. If he wasn't, he deserved everything he had coming to him.

She leaned into him fully, teasing her breasts against his chest as she brought her lips an inch from his. She ground against his dick, inhaling the warmth of his breath, letting him feel her own on his face. Then she eased her mouth to his ear and whispered, "That's too bad. I was going to show you my favorite move with a sand wedge. In case you're wondering, it doesn't have anything to do with golf."

Danica pushed off the back of the seat, propelling her over-aroused body to the passenger's side of the cart. She crossed her legs and eased her skirt into place along her thighs. Pretending her pussy wasn't quivering for release, her clit throbbing for his touch, she pointed into the distance. "There's a small clubhouse over the next hill. I never got rid of my dad's clubs. They should fit you fine."

Danica slid out of the golf cart, grabbed her nine iron from the bags hooked to the back, and moved onto the fairway. Jordan sank back on the seat, pinched the bridge of his nose, and groaned.

How the fuck was he supposed to concentrate on or enjoy his game when for the last twenty minutes, he hadn't been able to figure out what was going through her mind?

Would she have slept with him if he agreed to her outrageous deal? Did she regularly give prospective clients sexual benefits as he'd first guessed?

She was sure as hell acting like it.

With each swing, it became clearer she didn't care where her golf ball landed. Instead, she focused on driving him mad with the tantalizing wiggle of her ass and provocative thrust of her breasts. She was playing to his dick, and his dick was ready to play her right back.

Reaching her ball in the middle of the fairway, she lobbed what should have been an easy shot onto the green into a sand trap. "Oops."

Oops his ass. That was no accident.

He'd been around Danica long enough to note and appreciate she moved in a manner as ergonomically friendly to her body as possible, squatting to pick up items below knee level. She didn't squat to retrieve the rake lying in the center of the sand trap but bent at the waist and dipped so far down, her black skirt rose up her plump backside to expose pale purple panties.

The color was darker at the crotch. Jordan's cock twitched with the idea she was dripping wet for him. He could toss her down in the sand and be inside her hot folds in seconds. The move might prove pricey. Would the details be free? "What *is* your favorite move with a sand wedge?"

Tossing the rake onto the grass, she winked at him. "Show me the cash and I'll show you the move."

Without her signature stating she agreed to trade sexual acts for money, he shouldn't give in to a damned thing. But maybe if he agreed to this one small thing without written proof, the next time around he would be able to get that proof. And maybe, with his body rock solid and his testosterone going wild, he didn't give a shit about proving anything but how mind-blowing it felt sliding inside her tight sheath.

He stood from the cart. Pulling his wallet from the back pocket of his shorts, he thumbed through the bills. "I have roughly five hundred. Will that cover it?"

Indecision flickered through Danica's eyes. She considered the money a good fifteen seconds before lifting her gaze to his. A slow smile curved her lips, gradually becoming the open-mouthed grin that showcased her tongue and teeth and made his heart and cock hammer in tandem.

She made her way to the rear of the cart, hips swinging in seductive time with each step. She traded the nine iron for her sand wedge and then came to stand in front of him. "Normally, I would say no. I like you, and I love the way your eyes are the same turquoise blue as the sea, so just this once I'm going to say yes."

Her palm came out. Part of Jordan hoped she wouldn't accept the money, but the second he set the bills in her hand, she scooped them up. The top buttons of her short-sleeve black-and-white striped shirt came undone with the twist of her fingers. The sides parted to just above her navel. Milk-white cleavage rose generously from a bra the same shade of purple as her panties.

Flashing a brazen smile, she stuffed the money beneath the strap joining the cups of her bra. "Sure you don't want to throw in another five hundred and be the first to witness the alternative use for a three wood? It's a one-time offer at that rock-bottom price."

His dick jumped against his zipper. Things had passed well beyond the "getting to know her better" zone. If he had another five hundred on him, he knew he would be forking it over and not entirely for the sake of proving her immoral. Fuck, not even close to entirely.

Jordan nodded at the bills sticking out from above her bra strap. "I'd love to." The edge in his voice was as hard as the rest of him. "That's all the cash I have."

"In that case"—her hands came to his chest, and she shoved him back onto the bench seat—"sit back and relax. Things are about to get good."

Kicking off the golf shoes she kept stored in the clubhouse, Danica brought her bare left foot up on the side of the cart. The skirt skated an inch up her thighs. He held his breath for another five inches to follow. The skirt didn't budge. The movement of her hands more than made up for it.

Gripping the sand wedge near the top of its aluminum shaft, she ran the rubber end along the inside of her thigh, traveling slowly, sensuously higher, until the rubber grip disappeared beneath her skirt.

The subtle rasp of rubber against cotton screamed through his ears. On a hiss of breath, her eyes went wide, darkening to solid smoky gray. The rasp came a second time, and her hips arched toward him, as if seeking out his face, his lips, his tongue. Her foot slid higher on the side of the cart. The skirt hitched up her thighs.

One inch.

Two inches.

Jordan's heart beat a wild tattoo. His fingers curled and uncurled with the want to shove the skirt up to her waist and uncover the erotic show happening below.

The bucking of her hips stopped. She jerked the club from her skirt and leaned it against the side of the cart. He sucked in a hard breath. That wasn't the goddamned show. She would *not* end it so fast. Not without getting off.

Five hundred had better buy him the right to watch her orgasm.

He didn't have a chance to voice the words before Danica stepped back from the cart and removed her panties. They teased from beneath her skirt and came down her legs as a silky caress. She outstretched her fingers and stroked them along her pale, glistening skin, pushing the sodden purple lace to her ankles.

She bent fully to step free of the panties. Her breasts pressed together, one of the bills slipping to the grass and tumbling away on the breeze. It could have been a ten. Just as likely a hundred. He didn't give a damn. All his attention was focused on her breasts, waiting, hoping, praying her ample tits would pop out of the top and she would somehow work them into her show.

She straightened. Her breasts moved back into place still secured within her bra. He was disappointed for the two seconds it took for her to retrieve the sand wedge.

Her foot returned to the side of the cart, the club's rubber-coated handle between her thighs. The skirt had settled back into place with the removal of her panties, concealing even her upper thighs from his view. The skirt was no match for sound.

Jordan's blood thrummed with the slurping sound of the handle entering her pussy. Danica's chin lifted while her eyelids drooped. Her lips parted on a pant, her breasts rising and falling rapidly. "Ah . . . yeah," she sighed. "There's nothing like the feel of hot, hard rubber filling me up. Nothing like being fucked by this big bad boy."

His cock pulsated with each upward thrust of the club. Each slick sound of her cunt accepting the thick handle inside. Each deliciously throaty gasp tripping from her blood-reddened lips.

He fisted the edge of the seat, clinging for control. "Lift up your skirt."

The club stilled. Her chin came down. Their eyes met. The lust in her gaze was raw and burning. "How much?"

Whatever she wanted . . . if only he had the money. "I told you I don't have any more cash on me." The words growled out.

She considered his face a few seconds and then looked at his fisted hands. Her eyes gleamed. "Pet your dick while you watch me. Don't let yourself come until I say so, and we'll consider your debt paid in full."

Jordan sent a look around. They were hidden from view up here, and she'd insinuated the course belonged to her alone.

With a nod, he uncurled his hands from the seat, unbuttoned

his shorts, and carefully jerked down the zipper. He eased off the seat far enough to tug his shorts and boxers down his thighs. His cock sprang free, jutting up hard, throbbing, and deep purple.

Danica's tongue rimmed her lips as she eyed his erection. "Nope. No phalloplasty needed there."

Keeping her eyes trained on his dick, she removed her skirt. He caught a glimpse of fire red curls glistening with her essence in the sunlight, and then the handle of the sand wedge was hovering centimeters from her swollen cunt. She returned her foot to the cart. Every ounce of air in her lungs seemed to screech out as a throaty cry when she guided the club handle inside her pussy.

He grabbed hold of his cock out of desperation, stroking it in a method meant to ease his aching need to explode. The sight of her juicy pink folds devouring the black handle was too erotic for words. Still, he tried in a voice so thick he could barely understand himself. "Christ, you're beautiful. I would have paid triple to see this."

She tipped her hips toward his face, opening her sex as wide as her stance allowed. Far enough for him to watch the rubber taunt her clit with each pass. Far enough to seep her cream along the handle and down the club's shaft. Far enough to have Jordan's dick ready to burst despite his agreement with Danica not to come without her permission and his attempts to waylay his orgasm.

"Do you want to help me?" she purred. "I let my past customers help. It feels so much better not knowing when the shaft's going to move inside you." She shoved the club handle deeper inside, her moan punctuating the words. "Whether it's going to take you slow or fuck you so hard you can't stop from screaming." She decreased and increased the slide of the sand wedge, her pelvis shifting with each shove, her shallow cries becoming quiet shouts of ecstasy.

"How many past customers?"

She laughed loudly and huskily, in a way that said she was too far gone with passion to control the sound. "Too many to count. A place like this takes a lot of money to keep up." The timing of the club went wild. Her hips gyrated riotously, juice streaking along her thighs in a seemingly endless flood.

The heady scent of her musk filled his senses and sizzled his blood. "Last chance to help, Jord—Oooh, God. Too late."

Jordan's fingers closed hard around his dick, fighting off his climax as he watched orgasm roll through her. Rapture claimed her features, parting her mouth wide, narrowing her eyes, flushing her cheeks crimson.

Her thighs gave a last tremble, and her pussy erupted, cascading cream along the thrusting club as she screamed her elation.

He thought jealousy had made him assume the worst about her. Thought she would never be the type to sell her body for the sake of bringing the resort new patients and keeping the old ones coming back. Clearly, he'd been mistaken. Clearly, she traded sex for a profit on a regular basis.

How did the other guys react to her hedonistic show?

Jordan wanted to be disgusted. Instead he was tongue-tied and so hard and aching to fuck her, it was all he could do to stay in the cart.

Danica pulled the club from her body. Her juices caught the sunlight, shimmering on the sand wedge's black handle as she tossed it on the grass. She leaned toward him, carnal desire smoldering in her heavily lidded eyes. Her lips parted on a breathy sigh, nostrils flaring as she dug her fingernails into the front of his shirt and tugged.

Her want was primal, blatant. Too much temptation to let pass.

He forgot about his mission at the resort and relented to her tugging. She pulled him from the cart, pushing him down on his back in the grass, using the shorts and boxers wrapped around his thighs to trap him in place.

Not that he wanted to go anywhere. His cock pulsated for the hungry grip of her pussy. He opened his arms, expecting her to come into them immediately.

She stayed still, while her eyes journeyed down his body. Her gaze turned frosty as it met with his straining shaft. Venom clung to her words. "For a few minutes on the ride up here, I thought you might not be such a bad guy." She jerked the bills from her bra and threw them at him. "I was wrong. You're an asshole."

Jordan's breath hitched out as she snatched her skirt and shoes from the grass. Then she hopped in the cart and, flipping him the finger over her shoulder, sped away.

5

Danica glared at her front door, willing the man knocking to leave her resort and the Caribbean as a whole. She'd stopped to get dressed a short ways after ditching Jordan and then stopped again at the office for her almond supply before coming home to a private pity party on her living room couch. Forty-five minutes and half a pound of chocolate-covered almonds later, her stomach still felt queasy over her behavior.

The problem wasn't the way she'd treated Jordan—he'd deserved it—but rather how much she'd enjoyed masturbating with her golf club while he watched.

The knocking came again, followed by, "Let me in so I can explain."

How exactly did he plan to talk his way out of believing her to be a high-priced hooker?

Since he clearly wasn't leaving until she let him have his say, and watching the jerk grovel was her due, she pushed off the couch and stalked to the door. She jerked the storm door open, leaving the locked screen door as a barrier between her foot and his nuts. Jordan stood frowning on the front porch, his hands behind his back.

Danica smiled nastily. Subservience suited him well. Getting his despicable ass off her porch suited her even better. "I'm listening," she snapped.

He winced. "It was supposed to be a game."

"Right. A game." She laughed dryly. "Ha-ha. Let's play Danica the prostitute. Oh, wait, we already played that one. Now it's time for a rousing round of Jordan the dickhead."

"You're right. I am—was. I'm sorry." Apology dulled the sparkle of his eyes.

He both sounded and looked sincere. She groaned inwardly, wanting to hold on to a grudge for once in her life. If he was a cop, she most certainly would. "What do you do for a living?"

"I'm an investment broker."

The profession fit perfectly with the structured image she'd first had of him in her office yesterday morning. A meticulous nature would also explain his reason for wanting to know so much about the resort before taking advantage of its services. Still . . . "Got some way to prove it?"

"You can call my office and listen to my voice mail. The number's—"

"That's not necessary." Because she was a sap.

Damn it, she hated how easily the anger drained out of her. If he'd paid her to perform sex on him without thought to her pleasure, surely she would have been able to hang on to her fury. She hoped. "I don't like you, but I believe you."

"I never expected things to go so far. I probably should have stopped you, but, seriously, how many men do you know who would have?" Jordan's gaze swept her from toe to head, and the sparkle returned to his eyes as desire. "Watching your hot body creaming around that golf club was one of the most erotic experiences of my life."

God help her, she really was a sap. Danica couldn't stop her pleased smile. Or basking in the knowledge he found her body hot.

Then again, yes, she could. He only found her body hot because she'd left her shirt hooked together enough to hide her uneven sides and disfigured back. He hadn't seen the real her. The sexy grin that curved his lips in reply to her smile had her anxious to show him the real her, though, by stripping off her clothes and picking up where they'd left off on the golf course. "I don't know enough men to guess how they would've behaved. At least, not men I've been or want to be intimate with."

Regret flickered through his gaze. "Let me make up for what happened."

Her pussy fluttered a plea for her to accept the offer. After all, Lena said they were destined to sleep together again, completely naked this time. Of course, Lena's visions were likely a hoax, and sex probably wasn't even the payback Jordan had in mind.

Given the position of his hands behind his back, he was liable to act like Lena at any moment. Hell, he'd probably stopped by the office and asked her friend for advice before coming over. Danica narrowed her eyes. "Don't think you can pull a pack of Pepsi from behind your back and be forgiven."

"I can honestly say that never crossed my mind, though I'll be sure to remember it as an appropriate groveling gift for the future. As for what is on my mind . . ." All trace of regret vanished from Jordan's eyes as he slid his gaze back along her body, lingering so long on her crotch she was certain her panties would never again be dry. "What do you say I come inside and show you?"

She'd forgiven him for his ridiculous, albeit incredibly pleasurable, game. The best thing to do now would be to send him on his way tonight and arrange for another person to guide him around the resort the rest of the week. But she already knew he wasn't about to settle for another guide, and she really didn't want him leaving yet.

Nerves dancing in her belly, Danica unlocked and opened the screen door. Jordan entered the villa, pulling his arms from behind his back to reveal her sand wedge. He leaned the golf club against the wall and opened his arms to her. She'd wanted to go into them back on the course. Then, she'd been pissed off enough to deny her want. Now she didn't even try.

His arms came around her, his lips slanting over hers. He held her so loosely their bodies barely touched. His closed-mouthed kiss was almost friendly. Earlier, she would have respected that. Now she wanted pressure, heat. The passion she so rarely took the time for.

What the heck was his holdup?

She pulled her head back, freeing her mouth from his too-tender caresses. "Is this about our agreement not to have sex?"

He frowned. "I'm quite sure we never made that agreement." She'd left the top buttons of her shirt undone, and he studied the rise of her breasts above the purple lace of her bra. "Yeah. I definitely never would have agreed to keep my hands, mouth, or any other part of me off your luscious tits or any other part of you."

"Then why don't you want to kiss me for real?"

Jordan looked at her mouth. "I do want to kiss you. Lick you. Suck the sweet cream from your body. Fuck you senseless." His voice went rough as he met her eyes. "You deserve slow lovemaking for the way I behaved earlier."

Sleeping with him again was one thing. Liking him was a total other, very bad thing. But, shoot, it was hard not to like him when he not only returned her golf club but also admitted to his wrongdoing and was ready to remedy it.

Danica forgot about liking the man and focused on loving his body. She slid her hands beneath the hem of his polo shirt.

Her fingers met with warm skin over hard muscle, and her tongue ached to do the same. "I'd rather you fucked me senseless."

His eyes darkened. His lips parted. She thought he would kiss her for real and then take her up against the wall in the same forceful manner as he had last night. Instead he said, "Tell me what you want and it's yours."

She sighed. "I told you I want you to fuck me senseless. How much more vocal do I need to be?"

"Very. Tell me in detail what you want. Where you want to be fucked."

"In the bedroom."

Jordan's lips twitched as he bent and swept her into his arms. Heat simmered her cheeks with the realization he hadn't meant where in the house, but where on her body. She'd never been taken in the ass. Not that she was opposed to anal sex, just the idea of a man's attention being directly on her back. He would never be able to focus on pleasure, and she would be just as distracted.

Danica ended the twitching of his lips with the damp flick of her tongue against his ear. "My bedroom's down the hall, second door on the left." She added in a hot whisper, "Don't think I plan to use the bed either."

His cock jerked against her hip, and he hurried down the hall into her bedroom. Truthfully, she had planned to use the bed. Feeling him pound into her up against the wall was mindblowing, but her back was a bit stiff from pushing out her breasts and wiggling her behind while swinging her golf clubs. There was a chance a wall-pounding would relax her muscles as it had last night, but there was just as big of a chance it would make her stiffness worse. She wasn't about to risk that.

Doing a quick scan of her bedroom, she spotted the faded brown vinyl beanbag chair and smiled. Comfy with the potential to be naughty. Perfect.

Jordan followed Danica's gaze to the ratty-looking beanbag chair stuffed between her bed and the cream-colored wall. "You expect us to have sex on that thing?"

She looked up at him. "I do. First, I want you to kiss me with your tongue."

After the way he'd treated her, he was lucky she hadn't kicked him out of the resort. No way in hell should he be in her bedroom with the go-ahead to fuck her senseless. The thing was, the more he got to know her, the better he liked her. He liked that this resort was her dream. Liked that she truly seemed dedicated to seeing it a continual success. Liked that she hadn't put up with him when he made the stupid-ass insinuation she slept with prospective clients.

It should probably concern him that he let his like for her cloud his mind enough to suggest she call his office where she would hear him speaking his real last name. But she hadn't taken him up on the offer, so he wasn't going to worry over it.

He was going to focus on screwing her on a beanbag that looked older than the two of them combined.

Jordan had purposefully held back on the last kiss. Now he crushed his mouth to hers and parted her lips with the stroke of his tongue. Her taste was as he remembered, sweet and feminine—and something more. He recalled spotting the precariously opened bag of chocolate-covered almonds on the couch in her living room and knew it was her fetish he tasted.

Did she have other fetishes, or was the line about preferring kink to vanilla sex all for the purpose of getting even?

Danica's arms came around his neck. Her hands dove beneath the collar of his polo shirt, her nails skating with divine pressure along his nape and between his shoulder blades. Shivers pushed through him. He couldn't think of a move that would have affected his dick more.

On second thought, yes, he could.

Turning moist kisses on her neck, he groped blindly for the

beanbag. Her hands idled, and she sighed and shuddered in his arms. His cock responded with a pulsing thrust against her hip.

He grunted. Where the fuck was that beanbag?

Jordan lifted his tongue from her salty flesh to find the beanbag inches from his fingertips. He jerked it from its hiding place with the intention of laying it down and then doing the same to Danica. Only, there was nowhere to put the beanbag.

Her office was chaos. Her bedroom wasn't a whole lot better.

A dozen or so paperbacks littered the nightstand and all but hid an alarm clock and the base of a lamp. Clothes lay in a haphazard pile of multicolored material and hangers on the bed. Plants were scattered throughout the place.

He'd never considered himself a neat freak, but he suddenly felt claustrophobic. "I'm not sure there's room for sex in here."

"There's room." She nipped an impatient kiss at the corner of his mouth. "Kick over a plant if you need to; just get me down on that beanbag and kiss my other lips."

Amazing the motivation to be found in the thought of licking her pussy—just like that, a four-foot square of unoccupied sage green carpet appeared in the center of the bedroom.

Jordan tossed the beanbag down. Danica came next. He set her back on the beanbag and positioned her knees up and apart. Her skirt slid up her thighs. The dampness of her panties peeked from between her spread legs, taunting him to his knees.

"Take off my panties. Leave the skirt on." The words rolled from her mouth as a husky command and taunted him so damned much more.

He caressed her bare feet with his fingertips. Slowly, he moved his fingers up her ankles and then her legs, stroking with teasingly light pressure. "I love your kinky side," he murmured.

"I like you." He reached her knees and circled his thumbs around the sensitive pulse points at their backs. She gasped out a blissful sigh. "Oh, yeah, I like you a lot."

With a last circling, he continued his sensual journey, until his thumbs encountered the warm skin just south of the crotch of her panties. "That isn't what you said a few minutes ago."

"I've had time to reevaluate . . ." Danica stopped short with the press of his thumbs against her sex through her panties. He wiggled his thumbs, and she moaned and panted, "I changed my mind. Eat me out before I change it back."

Jordan couldn't recall the last time he'd had a lover so outspoken. There was a chance she was only talking that way because he'd told her to tell him what she wanted in detail. Regardless, he grew harder with every one of her dirty words.

He moved his fingers beneath the straps of her panties and glided the damp cotton down her legs. Her pussy lips blossomed beneath his gaze, seeping juice from their pink folds, which had his tongue swollen with the urge to savor. "Talk me through it."

"Don't tell me you're new to oral sex?"

She sounded so serious he almost laughed. His recent lovers might not have been too vocal, but they hadn't been prudes either, and he'd advanced to the oral-sex stage with a number of them. Not one of those others had made his hands shake with anticipation, though. He rocked back on his knees to give her a ravenous smile. "Just new to it with you, and I find your voice incredibly sexy. I can only guess how good your cum's going to taste."

Her breath caught as if she was shocked by the words. Then pink flared in her cheeks and she ordered, "Put your head between my legs and suck my pussy."

Planting his hands on the beanbag on either side of her hips, he bent his head to her sex. He blew on her moist folds, and they shuddered enticingly. Lowering himself farther, he licked the length of her slit.

Danica's hips arched toward his face. "Ah, yeah. Good. Lick me deep inside."

His body humming, Jordan pushed his tongue into her tight hole and lapped at her inner walls. She cried out, and a hot rush of juice coated his tongue. He moved his hands beneath her skirt. Cupping her bare ass cheeks, he opened her pussy farther, giving his tongue as much access as possible.

He consumed her cunt. Sucked, licked, and ate at her slick core. Her pelvis jerked toward his face repeatedly. Her pussy thrust against his tongue with each violent pump of her hips, forcing him to take her deeper, harder, faster, until her muscles tightened around his tongue and she cried out with her climax.

He pulled from her spasming sex to lick at her cream. "Holy cow," she panted, wriggling beneath his tongue, "you *have* done this before."

Jordan hadn't come to the resort to make friends. But learning she liked him had meant more to him than anything his past lovers had ever done or said. Hearing her appreciation for his pussy-eating skills felt damned near as good.

He alternately lapped at her cum and sucked on her clit as the remnants of her orgasm died away. Then he pulled his head free of her skirt and sat back on his haunches with a grin that probably looked as arrogant as it felt. It refused to be tamed, so what the hell could he do but give in to it?

Danica lay back on the beanbag, her face tipped toward the ceiling and her fingers clutching the brown vinyl near her hips. Her breasts rose and fell erratically, drawing his attention to the lush way the mounds spilled over the cups of her bra. He wanted her out of that damned shirt and her stunning tits out of the bra immediately.

"That's what I call a liquid lunch," he said.

Her head snapped up. Guilt passed through her eyes. "I intended to feed you once we reached the other side of the resort, but—"

"I was a dickhead." How could she feel guilty over that?

She smiled. "I was going to say we got distracted."

"Distracted? Like this?" Jordan came to his feet swiftly, lifting her from the beanbag with the intention of placing her on the bed. The pile of clothes concealing the pastel-flowered bedspread stopped him. "Where do you sleep?"

She gave the bed a sheepish look. "Right here. It's not usually so messy. I had some trouble getting dressed this morning."

"Trying to impress someone?"

"Trying to hide something."

He'd expected a sarcastic laugh for his cockiness, not the blurted words and the tensing of Danica's body.

She wriggled free of his arms. Pushing the clothes off the side of the mattress onto the floor, she climbed onto the end of the bed and lay back. She opened her thighs to him. He'd been tongue-to-pussy with her seconds ago, so he should be able to forget about the sight of her plump pink lips still juicy from her climax long enough to question the way she'd tensed and jumped from his arms. He should be able to. But his dick was stealing every last trace of blood from his brain, and he couldn't get past her shimmering sex.

She opened her arms and beckoned with a come-hither smile. "Get between my legs."

Jordan kicked off his loafers and moved onto the end of the bed. Sliding his hands up her thighs, he brought his tongue back to her pussy. He caressed her slit with the shallow stroke of his tongue and then parted her lips with his fingers and used his mustache to drive her clit wild.

Danica's hands shot into his hair. She gasped out, "That isn't what I meant."

Laughing thickly, he surrounded her clit with his teeth, tugging and twisting, torturing her to the edge of orgasm.

When her grip on his hair became painful and it was clear she would shatter, he released the bloodred pearl and kissed his way up her body, past her pubic hair and the rise of her belly to the bounty of her breasts.

He pushed the cups of her bra above her breasts. Filling a hand with one ample creamy white mound, he lashed his tongue across the erect coral nipple of the other. The flesh moved easily beneath his fingers and tongue. He'd touched enough tits in his life, both real and implanted, to know the difference—and feel damned guilty for allowing his jealousy-induced cynicism to believe hers were fake.

Jordan would make up for his skepticism, even if it meant spending the week in bed with her to do it. What a blessing of a hardship that would be.

Danica's fingers left his hair to move over his back. "Suck my nipple."

She was still giving him the details. Shit, how he loved that.

He pulled her nipple into his mouth, sucking hard. The air wheezed between her lips, and her hips bucked off the mattress. His cock throbbed savagely as it came into contact with her naked mound through his clothes.

He would love to hear more explicit words come out of her mouth. But she asked him to fuck her senseless, and the near-explosive state of his cock suggested he had best get to doing it or risk filling up his boxers.

Sucking and fondling her breasts, he used his free hand to make quick work of her shirt buttons. His lips pulled from her nipple with a pop. He sat back, straddling her thighs, wanting to see the passion roll through her smoky eyes when he freed her of her shirt and bra entirely.

Only, there was no passion in her eyes. She looked suddenly scared of him. "What's going on?"

She smiled too brightly. "We're having sex."

"I'm having sex." He fingered a lacy bra cup. "You're lying there like you're afraid of me seeing your breasts without something nearby to cover them up. I saw them last night in full detail and more than approve."

"I love my breasts. It's not them I'm afraid of." Danica winced and then smiled again. "I'm not afraid of anything. I just love this shirt and would hate to see it get ruined by accident. Let me take it off."

Some women could be odd about their clothes. Given the careless way she'd pushed hers off the bed, he didn't think she was one of them. Something else was going on. Something she wanted to move past. He should respect her wishes, but he didn't like the idea she was no longer having as good of a time as possible.

"You sure you're okay?"

"Fine. Better than fine. Take off your clothes."

Not certain he was doing the right thing, Jordan moved down the bed and came to his feet. He stripped off his shorts and boxers in unison, grinning guiltily when his cock leapt out sheathed for action as it had been last night.

She sat up to remove her shirt and bra and then lay back again. Her attention shot to his condom-wrapped penis through the vee of her thighs, and the too-bright smile became the genuine one that revealed her teeth and tongue and drove his dick bonkers.

She released the sexy-as-hell laugh. "Do you always come prepared?"

"This would be the second time," he admitted while glancing around for a place to lay his clothes. "I wasn't sure what to expect after the way you left me on the golf course. Since I was still hard, I figured it best to be ready for anything."

"You walked all the way to my villa with an erection?"

Hearing her amusement, he looked back at her and shook his head. "Just to the parking lot of your office. I drove from there."

"Slowly."

"What?"

"You drive slowly." Danica nodded at the clothes in his hand. "Maybe you do get motion sickness, but I have a feeling my need for speed scares you more. My cluttered bedroom probably frightens the hell out of you." Humor gleamed in her eyes. "Really, Jordan, you can drop your clothes on the floor. It won't hurt them or you to step out of your organized box for a little while."

His hackles went up. She thought he was afraid to drive fast? That he was some kind of organizational nerd? All right, he would admit to sticking around the speed limit, and damn it, she'd caught him hunting for somewhere other than the floor to put his clothes. But he knew fast and he knew messy, and she was about to find out firsthand on both accounts.

He dropped his clothes on the ground and jerked the shirt over his head, letting it fly as he climbed back onto the bed. He grabbed her around the waist, lifting her up and then bringing her down so that her legs straddled him and her juicy opening rubbed along his cock.

Surprise flickered in Danica's eyes, and he laughed darkly. "I wouldn't be so sure you know me that well, sweetheart. It's my turn for details."

Holding her legs in place around him, Jordan came up on his knees and moved them to the head of the bed. He pressed her back against the white-wicker headboard. Heat and awareness dilated her pupils and quickened her breath.

She was about to breathe a whole lot harder.

He grabbed her arms. "In case you've forgotten last night, there wasn't a thing slow or orderly about it. There won't be this time either. I'm going to take your wrists and trap them above your head, and then I'm going to shove my cock inside you and give you your senseless fucking. It's going to be hard and so goddamned messy we'll both be covered in sweat and cum by the time we're done."

Wrapping his fingers around her wrists, he brought her

hands above her head and pushed them back against the headboard. Her breasts thrust forward, nipples stabbing at his chest. He moved against her, taunting the hard peaks with the chafe of his chest hair.

Danica wiggled. The slide of her pussy against his cock was both heaven and hell. "Your eyes are seriously stunning when you're keyed up."

He liked that she loved his eyes, but earning compliments was not even close to his point here, unless they had to do with his stamina, speed, or ability to mess up her bed. "You have way too much focus for a woman in your position."

"What position would that be?"

"Skewered." Jordan reared back and drove his cock into her.

Her lips parted on a moan. She attempted to free her hands of his grip, but he held firm. He gave her a moment to adjust to his size and to give himself time to indulge in the carnal sensation jetting through his body with the squeeze of her pussy. Then he fastened his mouth over hers in a hard openmouthed kiss and fucked her senseless.

Or maybe she was fucking him senseless.

She met him thrust for thrust, tightening the muscles of her cunt each time he pulled back, letting them loose each time he entered her. The push-and-pull play would have been enough to send him over the edge in short order, considering he'd been hard for nearly two damned hours. But then she had to go and add those beautiful breasts to the mix.

She rubbed her tits against his chest with each grind of her pussy. Her nipples abraded his aroused flesh with every pass.

Once.

Twice.

Three times.

Danica arched her back and offered her nipples up to his lips. He pulled a hard tip into his mouth, sucking on it like it was a beer-flavored lollipop—it had been a long time since

Jordan enjoyed a beer, and he couldn't get enough of her. She flexed her wrists again, attempting to escape his clutches. He held firm and doled out punishment for her attempts by increasing the tempo of his dick, shoving up into her at an angle meant to hit upon her sweet spot.

Her breath caught. She blinked rapidly. Her hips bucked into his, her wrists joining in and nearly managing to get free this time. Still, he held firm, giving another direct hit to her pleasure zone.

Her pussy stopped the squeeze-and-release game to clamp down tightly around his cock. The nipple in his mouth jerked. Her head crashed back against the headboard, thumping in time with the pump of his hips. Orgasm sizzled through her in a tidal wave of heat and pressure he felt even before her juices flooded him.

Taking her mouth with his, he pushed into her again and again, letting her ride out all but the tail end of her climax before giving in to an orgasm so intense it broke his mouth and hands away from hers and temporarily blinded him.

Vision returned to reveal a blissfully smiling copper-haired hottie on his lap.

"You win. It was fast." She glanced down at the juices seeping from their joined bodies. "Definitely messy. In fact, I think you owe me a new bedspread."

"What about Tylenol? Your head has this way of punishing whatever's behind it when we have sex."

"Next time we'll have to try the beach. Nothing to hit there but sand."

Was there going to be a next time?

Danica seemed to come up with the question at the same time he did. The amusement drained from her expression, and she lifted from him to lie on her back, off to the side of the bed. "We should eat," she said soberly.

There was going to be another time, and another and another, Jordan decided with the loss of her hot, wet body around him. Now that things had progressed this far and they clearly enjoyed each other's bodies, why not indulge for the remainder of his stay?

He glanced at the beanbag on the floor and licked his lips. "Already did. I highly recommend the crème de Danica."

A small smile curved her mouth. "More than that."

He considered suggesting seconds of the same but then realized she probably brought up food for her sake as much as his own. "Are you hungry?"

"Not really. I had some nuts."

He laughed. "I saw the bag on the couch. In a hurry to get in?"

"There's a reason it's called a fetish." She yawned. "I should have sex more often. I'm beat."

"Good. I was thinking I was getting old for a while there." Technically, he wasn't tired. The thought of curling up with her warm, soft body in his arms was too tempting to let pass.

Reclining on his side, he reached out an arm with the intention of rolling her over and spooning her back against his front. Danica batted at his hand. "I can't get comfortable that way."

Really? Or did she just not want to be held, the way her cool tone seemed to indicate? Maybe mentioning another round of sex had been an accident, and in reality she was hoping he would take her yawning as a cue to leave.

Too bad if that was the case, because Jordan wasn't going anywhere.

He rolled over next to her. Coming up on an elbow, he brushed a kiss across her lips. "Night, good-looking."

She frowned. "What about the tour?"

"It can wait until later today or tomorrow." He would like to say it could wait indefinitely. He might not know what was going through Danica's head right now, but he did believe she wasn't the type to rob someone of their money. Unfortunately, she *was* one to act rashly. Then there was the resort staff and the odds of longevity for the place. Until he felt comfortable with each of those things, he wasn't about to forget his mission and give his father the go-ahead to invest.

Danica woke from one of the most erotic dreams of her life ready to ravish her bed partner. Leaving her eyes closed in the hopes of keeping the dream fresh, she felt for Jordan. Her fingers came up empty again and again. She opened her eyes to discover the bedroom lit by the lamp on the nightstand. The alarm clock was too covered in books to tell the time, but the parted curtains showed twilight settling in.

Where the heck was Jordan? Had he woken up and left without saying good-bye? Really, it wasn't like he owed her a good-bye. They hadn't shared anything more than an early afternoon screw. Still, she'd hoped he would stick around for a second course.

Two thumps sounded behind her. She rolled over to discover Jordan hadn't left. He stood nearly up against the wall, fully dressed and wearing a disgusted look on his face that told her exactly where his attention had just been. On her back.

Danica's arousal vanished with the roiling of her belly. Heat swamped her face. She'd convinced herself it would be okay for him to see the real her, right up to the point where he started to remove her shirt and doubt had kicked in. She'd been right to doubt. Jordan hadn't been prepared to learn she wasn't good-looking. That she was a freak show beneath her clothes.

Foolish tears pricked her eyes. She sniffed them back and steeled her gaze.

He squatted to the carpet, straightening with his loafers in his hands. "Sorry to wake you. I dropped my shoes." He glanced at the door. "I have to go. I have a meeting. A teleconference. It's a different time zone back home."

No, it wasn't. His file said he was from New York, which was in the Eastern time zone, same as the Caribbean.

Negative as she could be about it, she honestly hadn't thought her body looked *that* bad. Bad enough, yes, but not so repulsive he would lie to her to get away from it.

Her belly hurt a little more. She wanted to crawl under the bedspread. It was too warm for covers, so she comforted herself with the knowledge there were almonds waiting for her in the living room.

Jordan moved around the end of the bed and came up to the side she lay on. Relief sighed out of her as he leaned down to kiss her. Maybe he didn't find her repulsive after all. Maybe he didn't even live in New York anymore.

Or maybe he did.

His mouth didn't come over hers but brushed her cheek, quickly lifting away. He straightened to flash a smile that looked painfully forced. "Night."

What? No calling her "good-looking" this time?

Spite had Danica wanting to ask the question, but she wasn't up to the answer. She was barely up to the thought of facing him again for his tours. If she was lucky, her deformed body would scare him away forever. She wouldn't have to worry over his tours or the absolute way he stole her focus off of work and onto thoughts of losing herself to passion with his long, luscious body.

6

Diane slid open the glass partition of the administrative area for the executive operations suite. Her smile wasn't the practiced one of yesterday but a genuine one that crinkled lines around her green eyes. "Good morning, Mr. Cantrell."

Unfortunately, it wasn't a good morning. Jordan had spent the night tossing and turning and feeling like a dickhead all over again. He couldn't work up the energy to smile back, let alone lay on the charm. "Morning, Diane."

Her smile vanished with his mellow tone. "Dr. Crosby asked not to be disturbed till noon."

"I'm here to see Lena. She said I should come by this morning." He was going out on a serious limb guessing Lena would assist him after the way he'd left Danica last night. If Lena truly was psychic, he hoped a vision had provided her with the insight to see that helping him would be a good move.

Diane went through the door on the right side of the administrative area. A half minute later, Lena opened the door connecting the business offices with the waiting area. A bright orange sleeveless sundress flirted with her knees and almost proved a good match for her gaudy earrings and the streaks of neon pink in her cropped blond hair. Her smile wasn't so bright.

Lena gestured to come inside. After closing the door, she guided him down the hall, stopping midway to Danica's office to face him. "If you want to see her now, it's up to you. Personally, I'd recommend coming back later."

"Pissed at me?" Like he had to ask.

"Is she?" Crinkling her nose, she gave him a scrutinizing look. "Maybe you *are* the problem. She's definitely upset about something." She shuddered. "She's cleaning her office."

Lena made this sound comparable to Danica jumping face-first out of her second-story window. Jordan thought about mocking Danica's chaotic ways as she'd done his orderly ones. If she was speaking to him, he might do it. Not only were the odds of her speaking to him slim, but it also sounded as though she wasn't even talking with her friend. At least, she hadn't shared what happened last night with Lena.

He kept his voice light. "Does it look like my coming back later would help?"

"How should I know?"

He smiled optimistically. "I thought you might have had a vision."

"Oh." Her brown eyes warmed with the implication he believed in her gift. "Nope. Nothing new on this end." She resumed walking down the hall, stopping when she reached Danica's closed office door. "Want me to take you in?"

"Thanks, but I don't want her mad at you, too."

Lena went into the office across from Danica's. Jordan waited for her to sit behind an efficiently organized desk and then knocked on Danica's door. The disgust he'd felt upon returning from the bathroom last night to find her nude, sleeping body curled into a ball and her back toward him reared up.

He'd been annoyed with himself for allowing his jealousy to

skew his judgment and believe her a fraud and the majority of her body fake. Seeing her scarred, misshapen back had self-loathing eating at his gut and him ready to beat the shit out of himself. He'd planned to crawl back into bed and pretend he hadn't noticed, to make up for his shortsightedness over the course of the next few days. But then she'd opened her eyes and looked at him like he'd crossed into a serious no-trespassing zone.

Leaving had been his solution to stepping away from that zone and settling her unease. In hindsight, leaving probably hadn't settled a thing but had made Danica assume he'd been turned off by her body. He hadn't been turned off by a little misshaping, the raised pink scar that ran from just below her neck to just above her backside, or the smaller, diagonal one slashing over the left side of her lower back. Nothing could detract from the blazing hot temptress beneath her skin, and he was here to prove it.

Jordan waited another half minute for her to respond to his knocking. When that didn't work, he twisted the doorknob. The door inched inward, and he poked his head through the small opening. He could live without an eye if she chose to lift something off her desk and throw it at him. He wasn't about to risk his other organs.

Danica stood in front of a wooden bookshelf topped with an ivy that trailed nearly to the floor. Yesterday, the bookshelf looked ready to collapse with its overabundance of journals and magazines. Today, it and the rest of her office looked like they'd been paid a visit by Mr. Clean.

She appeared mesmerized by the transformation, so he took a moment to appreciate the view of her profile. Yellow slacks hugged her shapely rear end. A white top with yellow trim fitted her breasts snugly and the rest of her body loosely. He recalled her saying how she dressed to hide something. Now that he knew what that something was, he could see the way the shirt fit a little sideways across her torso, the slight bulge of her spine pushing out from her lower back.

What happened to her? Did it hurt? Had *he* hurt her when he'd taken her aggressively not once, but twice?

Passion had gleamed in her eyes, not pain. Guilt and sympathy still welled as Jordan opened her office door the remainder of the way. He slipped inside and locked the door with a soft *snick*.

Danica glanced over. Hurt flared in her eyes that had nothing to do with physical pain. She quickly masked it by moving to the chair behind her desk and sitting down. "You're early. It's only"—she glanced at the alarm clock off to the right side of her desk and visibly tensed—"ten o'clock."

The wheeled black chair that had been propped against the wall and covered with paperwork now sat empty in front of her desk. He considered going to it and sitting, then caught the anxiety in her eyes and remained standing in front of the door. "I didn't want to wait till noon to talk to you."

She turned toward her computer monitor and started typing. "Don't worry about it, Jordan. You don't want to continue with the tour. I understand."

"You're right, I don't." Her fingers stalled on the keyboard with her gasp. He moved to the side of her desk and placed a hand on her upper arm. "I have something better in mind. Will you be my girlfriend?"

Danica's gaze zipped to his face. "*What*?"

"You made it quite clear you aren't one to take sex lightly. With the sizzling chemistry between us, I don't believe we can turn off the heat when we're in public. I also don't want anyone guessing you're sleeping with me and assuming the worst."

Her lips curved in a malicious smile. "You mean like thinking it's my way of making sure you pick Private Indulgence to do your surgery?"

"I was stupid to say that."

"Being stupid appears to be your forte." He winced, and her smile grew for a few seconds before falling flat.

She shook off his hand and reached for the starfish-shaped candy dish next to the alarm clock. Tossing a chocolate-covered almond into her mouth, she swiveled in her seat to face him. Her gaze narrowed as she slid it slowly along his body. Jordan wasn't much on modesty, but she made him feel damned naked and not altogether certain she approved of what she saw.

Her attention drifted lower, idling on his groin. His mind might not be certain if she liked what she saw, but his cock was positive, stirring to rock-solid awareness.

Danica looked at his face. She raised an eyebrow as if to say she'd noticed the hardened state of his dick. "What's in this whole girlfriend proposal for you?"

"Other than the obvious, it would give me the best chance possible to get to know the workings of this resort and its staff. People act and talk differently when dealing with a client than with a friend of a friend."

"Do you really think you're going to uncover anything I can't tell you? I realize surgery is serious stuff, but it is just surgery you're after here, right?"

"Actually, no."

"It's not?"

"Nope." Gripping the arms of her chair, he leaned over her. Her eyes widened, her lips parting with surprise. He leaned closer, bending toward her, all but touching his lips against hers.

This time, he wouldn't give in to the ache of his cock and take her wildly, with her head pounding against the wall or an equally hard headboard. This time, he would ensure all she experienced was pleasure. "What I'm after right here, right now, is a morning quickie with the most beautiful redhead I know."

She tensed and pushed at his chest. "You know damned well I'm not beautiful."

He moved closer, brushing his mouth against hers. He slipped his tongue between her lips. The heady taste of chocolate and Danica flooded his senses. She relaxed some with the stroke of his tongue. He let go of the arms of the chair to knead her thighs. She went soft in his arms, her lips pliant, her tongue caressing his with hungry little licks.

Jordan lifted from her mouth when he was nearly out of breath and discovered she was in the same winded state. He pulled in a few calming breaths and risked entering her no-trespassing zone. "You're confusing beautiful with perfect. Your body might not be perfect, but it is beautiful."

Some unnameable emotion passed over her face. She opened and closed her mouth a couple times before finally asking, "Why should I believe you? Your body's both perfect and beautiful, yet you think you need cosmetic surgery to enhance it."

He couldn't tell her the truth of his reason for being at the resort, but damn, how he wanted to. "I don't need it."

"All right, then you want it."

"I'm not sure I want it either. I'm still in the considering phase." He went to his knees and moved his head into her lap. Pulling her thighs apart, he nuzzled her mound through her clothes, inhaling her musky feminine scent. She moaned and he smiled—definitely no pain there. "At the moment, I'm considering how impeccable your legs are going to feel wrapped around my neck."

"I don't like you anymore," she bit out.

He glanced up at her face. The gray shade of her eyes assured him the heat in her words was all about passion. Hooking his fingers around the tab of her zipper, Jordan gave it a tug. "You will in a few minutes."

He slid his hands under her ass and lifted her hips up to pull her slacks and panties down her legs. Danica stiffened and looked at the door. "We shouldn't—"

"It's locked. . . .And I'm ready for seconds."

Taking her ankles in his hands, he brought her legs up onto his shoulders and jammed his tongue into her pussy, swirling it inside her hole. She sighed. Her sex went moist and then juicy wet. He released an ankle to finger her clit while he lapped at her cream.

Her sex fluttered. She whimpered and clamped her thighs around his head. He could quite likely suffocate, but what a way to go.

Rubbing his thumb across her clit, back and forth, he increased the play of his tongue. Her thighs clamped tighter. A husky moan left her lips. He forgot about breathing and devoured her pussy, licking and sucking at her lush body.

Orgasm shook through her in the next moment, and he turned his teeth on her clit. He rasped the engorged edges again and again, until she was shivering a second time, shuddering beneath his tongue, filling his mouth with her salty-sweet cum.

Jordan tongued the last of the juices from her body. Placing her feet on the ground, he sat back and smiled at the sensual picture she made. Her hands were in a white-knuckled grasp around the arms of the chair, her fiery hair a wild halo around her flushed face, and both sets of lips deep pink and puffy.

"That wasn't a quickie." Her lips remained parted.

He wanted to move back over her, slide his tongue in her mouth and share her essence. If he did, he was liable to end up with his dick back inside of her as well, fucking her hard and rough. He wouldn't take her that way again, not until he knew for certain the only thing the primal pounding made her feel was ecstasy.

He came to his feet. "You got off quick, didn't you?"

"Yes, but quickies generally involve two people climaxing."

"Until you start liking me again, you're going to be the only one coming. I still owe you for yesterday afternoon and for giving you the wrong impression by leaving so hastily last night."

Danica considered his face for a long while and then looked

at his groin. Her tongue came out, lashing over her swollen lower lip. His cock jumped as if she'd made contact with his hard flesh. She looked back up with an approving smile. "All right. I'll be your girlfriend for the week . . . on one condition."

Danica crossed the decorated conference room in midnight black and regal gold silk pantaloons with sewn-in bells swishing decadently around her legs. Humid night air snaked through the room's open windows, and the lights had been dimmed to add to the sultry harem theme of the staff Halloween party. She moved past tents fashioned of pastel sheets and spilling out the spicy aroma of Middle Eastern food, and a dance floor covered with sand and crowded with genies and sheiks and Lena getting her groove on.

Laughing at her friend, she continued to the scaled-down papier-mâché replica of an Arabian castle she'd told Jordan she would meet him in front of after being pulled into a private discussion with a couple of the resort surgeons. He stood with his back to her, an empty beer bottle dangling from his fingertips as he visited with Jezi, the camel tied to a stake at the castle's entrance.

Jordan's black costume pants were baggy everywhere but in the ass, which they hugged to mouthwatering perfection. If she hadn't given in to his gifted tongue this morning and accepted that he was attracted to her despite her physical flaws, Danica probably would have done so now, just to get her hands on his rear. Since she had given in and they were operating under the pretense of dating, she gave in to her urge to pinch his ass.

He jumped and spun around. The sides of his gold and black vest parted an inch, flashing a tantalizing view of dark blond hair curling over a deliciously muscled chest. His mouth curved in a slow, sensual smile. "We were just talking about you."

How could she have possibly believed him oppressive? The

only waves he gave off now were the sexual kind that dampened her pussy and made her regret forgoing panties for fear
they would show through her pantaloons.

Pinching his ass in a room full of employees and colleagues
she could get away with. Pushing him up against the castle wall
and relieving her growing desire with the slide of his cock wasn't
liable to go over so well.

Danica nodded at the camel. "Tell the truth. You were really
discussing Jezi's portfolio, weren't you?"

Jordan's gaze fell to her cleavage, pushed up and nearly out
of a black halter with long gold fringe strategically covering her
lower torso. His smile went from sensual to sizzling. "Only if it
includes a top designed to bring a man to his knees."

So much for reining in her libido with nonsexual talk. Her
nipples strained against the halter top, begging for the wet heat
of his mouth. Her sex grew a little moister with each second he
ogled her breasts. She thought to tell him to save his hot looks
for after the party when a familiar male voice asked, "Did I hear
portfolio?"

Jeff. Thank God. A nice guy with a bad habit of talking until
she was certain her ears would bleed, he was just the distraction
her pussy needed.

He appeared next to her in a black and white robe and matching mantle that made his slender frame look fuller and hid his
prematurely receding hairline. She smiled a greeting and then
gestured at Jordan. "I don't believe you two have met."

Jeff held out a thin-fingered hand to Jordan. "Jeff Dartmouth.
The resort's client account specialist and the guy Danica relies
on to invest her money wisely."

Jordan took his hand in a shake. "Jordan Cantrell. Danica's
boyfriend and the guy she relies on to make sure she goes to
bed happy."

Warmth rushed up Danica's torso and into her cheeks. She

wanted to believe it was embarrassment but knew better. Every word out of Jordan's mouth, no matter how inappropriate, had the fire in her core stoking higher.

He released Jeff's hand to smile at her. Teasing sparkled amidst the turquoise of his eyes. The contentment of his smile registered even as pangs of longing rushed through her. He'd cringed when she'd brought up the costume party, saying he hadn't celebrated Halloween since he'd been eight and wasn't sure he wanted to change that tonight. She told him he would have fun, and she'd been right. "You're having a good time. Told you so."

"Obviously my tastes have changed over the last twenty-five years." Eyeing her breasts, he ran his tongue over his lower lip, leaving it shiny. "When do I get my treat?"

Anytime he wanted.

She couldn't help herself; Danica swayed toward him. One little suckle of his tongue. One quick press of her sex against his.

Jeff gave an indiscreet cough. "What's up with the portfolio chat?"

She straightened without making contact to cut Jeff a scathing look. Then remembered he was doing his job by stopping her from making a scene so graphic she would never be able to live it down. "Jordan's an investment broker."

"You don't say." Jeff looked at him. "Know much about PIMR?"

Hot stocks were a sure way to get Jordan talking. Everything else fell to the shadows of his mind as he discussed the pros and cons of investing in a mover. He wanted to say women didn't fall into that "everything" category, the way his father claimed, but he realized now, until these last few days with Danica, they had.

Danica didn't fall to the shadows but made it damned hard

to concentrate on anything else. Even now, the sensual promise shining in her greenish gray eyes and the succulent press of her tits against the halter top had his body rock solid. He'd spent the first hour of the costume party meeting Private Indulgence staff members and their significant others. He wanted to find a quiet corner and spend the next hour pumping his cock inside Danica's hot body.

Until she confirmed she'd forgiven him for last night by saying she liked him again, the only parts of him that would be fucking her were his tongue and fingers.

Jordan responded in a dry tone, hoping Jeff would figure out his presence wasn't welcome, "Can't say I do."

"It's going places fast." Jeff's voice rang with excitement. "This time next year, Danica's going to have more money than she knows what to do with."

"You have all of her money invested in one stock?" He didn't want to chat with the guy, but he didn't want some wannabe stockbroker losing Danica's money either.

Jeff gave a noncommittal shrug. "It's around."

Danica grabbed Jordan by the vest, bringing his attention to her face and stopping him from asking additional questions. Good humor shone in her eyes. "Lena's channeling Hi'iaka."

Jordan looked to the sand-laden dance floor where Lena turned her hips and swayed her arms to the Moroccan beat of "Arabian Nights." Her belly undulated with each of her suggestive shimmies, purple and pale blue translucent scarves fluttering around her low-riding pantaloons. Her torso was bared below her purple-and-blue sequined bra, and a Day-Glo pink and lime green hula girl to match the ones dancing at her ears dangled from her navel.

Jeff snorted. "Lena's channeling something, all right."

"She looks sexy," Jordan said truthfully.

Past the music, he thought he heard Danica huff. Her hand

returned to his vest, grabbing hold and spinning him to face her. Her hips started in on the same, slow-thrusting, side-to-side rhythm as Lena's. She released his vest and slid her hands beneath the material, her warm palms pushing the sides up and away from his chest and making him damned glad he'd commented on Lena's hula show. Where her friend looked sexy moving to the sensual beat, Danica looked scorching.

The gold ring piercing his left nipple winked in the low lighting. Smiling like a cat about to pounce on a fat, juicy mouse, she brought her mouth to his chest. She'd done her face up to go with her costume, surrounding her eyes with black kohl and painting her lips fuck-me red. Those seductive lips closed over his pierced nipple, her tongue flicking the nub to hardness before taking the ring between her teeth and tugging.

The lipstick appeared to be working its magic. Erotic sensation shot to his dick, and his urge to drive inside her reached dangerous limits.

She freed the ring to give him a lusty look. "You're the sexy one."

Her teeth returned to the ring, tugging again, harder.

Jordan sucked in a sharp breath as pleasure bordered on the kind of pain that wasn't good. He seized her hips in his hands, slowing them. "Careful, sweetheart. It's too fresh for rough play."

Danica went still. She released the ring to eye him with disbelief. "Fresh? You *really* got your nipple pierced?"

"It was your condition."

Horror took over her expression. "My condition was for you to wear a fake piercing along with the sultan costume. I didn't want to scar you for life."

He laughed at the words. He realized what she'd said then, how she truly was scarred for life, and cut the sound off short to explain, "I had a piercing when I was in college that I let

close up after graduation. When you brought up nipple pierc-
ings this morning, I remembered how stimulating they are and
decided to get repierced."

The horror left her eyes. She looked back at his chest, giving
the ring a gentle, testing tug with her fingers. Pleasure returned
as an exquisite wave arrowing to his groin. His cock jerked and
he groaned.

She looked positively elated. "You're nothing like I first
guessed."

"Neither are you." *Thank God*.

His liking her wouldn't matter beyond this week in the physical sense. It would, however, make it easier to accept his father's
decision to forgo Jordan's advice to invest in a stable annuity
and put his money into Private Indulgence, should it come to that.

The music ended on the dance floor, and a request for the
unmarried slave girls to report to the marketplace sounded over
the speaker system.

Danica glanced back at his nipple ring. Her lips formed an O
as she lifted her fingers away. "Guess that includes me."

His mind wanted to roam with thoughts of the gratification
to be found in the circle of her lush lips. He forced his attention
from her mouth and gave her backside a soft swat. "You have
all night to torment me. Get going."

Jordan watched her walk away. Her round ass swayed with
each of her steps in a way he knew she was doing for his sake
alone. His dick appreciated the effort, bobbing a temporary
good-bye.

"How long have you been going out?"

He turned to find Jeff still standing there. Jesus, did the guy
have no life? "Long enough," he said shortly.

"It's strange that she's never mentioned you. We do lunch on
Mondays."

Shit, he hadn't realized Danica was so close with Jeff. It

wouldn't go over well acting like an ass toward him. "We met on the Internet quite a while ago. We finally met for real a few days ago and discovered the chemistry was even better in person."

"I can't remember the last time I saw her so happy."

The implication she was happier since he'd arrived sliced through Jordan. How would she feel when he returned to New York in a few days? How would he?

His gut felt suddenly hollow. He remembered the beer bottle in his left hand and brought it to his lips only to discover it empty. Hell, he needed a distraction from his thoughts and from Jeff's expectant look.

Jeff nodded toward the marketplace—a stage at the front of the conference room made up to resemble the slave markets of the ancient Middle East. "Looks like the sale's about to start."

Jordan breathed a sigh of relief . . . then discovered the first slave girl up for sale was Danica. Unlike in the olden days, she didn't remove her clothes as she rose up on the auction pedestal. He envisioned her naked all the same, her killer curves on full display along with the rest of her perfectly flawed body.

Buying her time reminded him of his stupid-ass move on the golf course. This time his money would go to a genuine cause. All auction proceeds would benefit families from the neighboring islands whom barely had enough funds to live off of and for whom celebrating the holidays was out of the question without aid.

Danica could have easily designated the money to go toward resort expansion. That she hadn't told him she wasn't as impatient as she'd led him to believe, just passionate about seeing her dreams become a reality.

"Break out your checkbook for this one, folks," the unseen announcer blared over the speakers. "Not only is she the boss to most of you, but she comes with her very own camel as well."

Laughter echoed through the conference room. Jordan glanced at Jezi. The camel lay so passively on her belly she could be asleep as easily as dead. Not exactly the animal you wanted to be paired up with in a bidding war.

"What do you say we start the bidding at fifty dollars?" the announcer asked.

A hand shot up across the room. "I'll give you fifty-one."

Jordan glared at the hand. Christ, was the guy kidding or just plain blind to make such a measly offer?

"I've got fifty-one. Do I hear fifty-two?"

"Seventy-five," Lena called out a short distance away from Jordan.

Thank God, Danica had someone on her side. Actually, she had two someones, but he wasn't stepping into the bidding at this lame stage.

"Ninety," a young black-haired guy who looked like he was wearing only a bathrobe called out. The room fell quiet and the guy beamed.

Twenty seconds passed without another bid. Another ten went by and the announcer said, "I've got ninety going once. Going twice. Did I mention the camel?"

Laughter went up from the crowd. Danica shifted on the pedestal, looking incredibly uncomfortable. She probably thought everyone could see her disfigurement past the halter top's fringe from their vantage below her and were dissuaded from buying her because of it.

Maybe the closer bidders could see her uneven frame. Jordan couldn't see a thing but her striking face and those awesome tits. Even if her tits weren't part of the deal, the three hours of her time on the auction block were worth a hell of a lot more than ninety dollars.

He opened his mouth to shout out a bid when a sultry smile curved Danica's fuck-me red lips and she started moving on the pedestal, shifting her hips in the same carnal way she'd been doing in front of him moments ago. She swayed her arms at her sides and thrust her pelvis suggestively forward.

A whistle went up over the crowd, followed by a shout of, "Two-fifty."

Danica brought her hands to her sides, coasting them up along her body, over the outer swells of her barely contained breasts. Caressing her fingers back down again, she moved her hips in a swift circling that tinkled the bells sewn into her pantaloons. The sound broadcasted through the speakers and sped Jordan's heart rate.

He was ready to shout his offer a second time when Lena yelled, "Five hundred. A thousand if you show us your hairy armpit."

Odd looks were exchanged amongst the bidders. Up on the stage, Danica laughed out loud. The husky sound came through the speakers. Her laugh hardened his body at a normal volume level. Amplified ten times, it had his balls snugging tight and his dick ready to explode. His dick took over his mouth, which barked out, "Three thousand!"

With a wink his way, Lena said loudly to the woman next to her, "Guess he has an armpit-hair fetish."

The crowd laughed again, while the announcer shouted into the speaker, "Sold!"

With the precarious state of his body, Jordan didn't dare look at Danica again just yet. He turned to Jeff. "Do you have a cell phone handy?"

"Sure thing." Jeff reached into the V-neck of his robe and pulled a small silver flip phone from a place Jordan didn't want to question. "Calling in my stock tip?"

"Something way hotter."

Jeff's eyes glinted. He handed Jordan the phone, then rubbed his palms together excitedly. "Care to share, one investor to another?"

"Not on your life." Danica was his alone. At least until

Monday, when he would be back in New York, putting in fifteen-hour-plus days at the investment firm with edgy clients he couldn't work fast enough to keep happy.

The hollow feeling returned to Jordan's gut. Not about to diagnose it, he fisted the phone and went in search of a quiet place to call in a cash transfer.

7

Danica rode Jezi around the dimly lit conference room for fifteen minutes before determining Jordan wasn't in it. He probably realized what a bad investment he'd made and got the heck out of there. Either that, or her spark of immature jealousy over his saying Lena looked sexy had registered and worried him enough to send him packing.

She turned Jezi toward the dance floor. Lena was giving belly-dancing lessons, and she had to admit her friend looked even more attractive than usual moving her body in such a seductive manner. As if she felt Danica's gaze on her, Lena stopped dancing to look over. A knowing smile curved Lena's lips, and she mouthed "Jordan" and pointed toward the exit doors.

After mouthing back "thanks," Danica guided the camel through the costumed partygoers and tents of food and out into the faintly moonlit night. She veered Jezi off of the sidewalk and onto the grass. Jordan seemed to come out of nowhere, stepping from the shadows and directly into the camel's path. Surprise flickered over his face. He planted his feet apart and braced for impact.

"Whoa!" Danica shouted, tugging back on the camel's reins. Jezi lurched to a stop a foot away from toppling him. Danica's heart pounded into her throat. "Are you trying to die?"

"After shelling out three thousand for the pleasure of your company?" He pushed an unsteady hand through his hair.

She followed the move of his fingers, and her panic disappeared as her hormones took over. His hair and skin appeared darker in the night. The sides of his vest and his baggy black pant legs caught in the gusting wind, whipping around his virile body. The arousingly spicy tang of Stetson didn't fit the image, but otherwise he looked 100 percent the sexy sultan.

Her stimulation had faded during her time away from Jordan. It returned now as a deluge of wetness in her pussy. It took all her self-control not to jump off the camel and into his arms. She focused on his words, wincing at the outrageous figure for the twentieth time since Jordan had bid it. "You could have had me for five hundred and one."

"That's what you think. The guy next to me was ready to go five grand." He glanced over his shoulder toward the beach a couple hundred feet away. "Had to drag him out into the water and hold his head under until he agreed to forget about it."

Danica fought a smile. "Liar."

His lips curved sheepishly and he blinked. "Me?"

Her heart warmed with the unexpectedly boyish response.

God, he was just too much. Amusing, sweet, sexy, and, yes, if she was being completely honest, a dickhead who acted without thinking at times. She'd been so certain he was destined to be trouble given the time he'd shown up in her office. In a way, he was bad, since thoughts of him kept her mind off work. But in most every other way, he was good. Too good to hide her smile a second longer.

She smiled blissfully. "I thought you'd regretted your bid and took off."

"Not a chance. I was waiting for a cash transfer to go

through." Jordan replaced his sheepish look with a wolfish grin. He gave her an ogling that started and ended on her breasts. "The money's all set, and you're all mine." His grin fell flat as his eyes snapped back to hers. "I didn't mean to make it sound like I want you to sleep with me because I paid for your company."

"Then I guess you don't care to hear where I want you to fuck me." She glanced over her shoulder and down at her ass.

He followed her gaze and groaned. "Did I say 'want'? I meant *expect*. I don't *expect* you to sleep with me, but I definitely *want* you to."

Laughing, Danica toed the camel's sides. "Koosh," she instructed, and Jezi came down on her belly in the grass. "Sorry, no magic carpets, but I'd still love to take you for a ride." He gave the camel a doubtful look. "C'mon and get on," Danica urged. "I seriously doubt motion sickness applies to camels."

With another wary look, he climbed on the saddle behind her. She commanded Jezi to stand. The camel obeyed and Jordan's breath whizzed out beside Danica's ear as his arms wrapped around her waist in a vise grip. "I take it you've done this before?"

"We've used Jezi for various functions in the past. Let your body move with her natural gait and you'll be fine."

However, she might not be fine, Danica realized minutes later as she guided the camel down the moonlit beach, toward the lights of the resort's pier, which featured a handful of rental bungalows. The tide slowly washed in, and the damp sand sank beneath Jezi's weight, increasing the swaying effect of her gait. With each step, the inside of Jordan's thighs rubbed along Danica's outer ones. The subtle caress she could have ignored. The nonstop slide of his erection against her bottom not so easily.

Her backside tingled with the knowledge she wanted to feel him pumping inside of it. Until Jordan, she'd never considered anal sex an enjoyable possibility, thought her lover could never move past her unsightly back long enough to experience pleasure. Jordan didn't find her back unsightly. When his hands and mouth moved over her body, he made her want to forget about her disfigurement as well.

Where his cock seemed to grow increasingly harder, the man himself was relaxing. His arms left her waist. One hand slid past the fringe of her halter top to cup her right breast. She sighed with the dip of his fingers beneath the built-in bra cup, the stroke of his fingertips along her sweaty skin.

His left hand tunneled into her hair, lifting the shoulder-length layers away from her neck. Moist lips brushed her ear in a hot caress. Shivers coursed through her, swelling her sex with fresh cream. "Are you wearing a condom?"

He nibbled on her flesh, asking in between bites, "Why?"

"Your dick is poking me in the ass, and I know how you like to be prepared."

His tongue sank into the shell of her ear. Little bursts of pleasure rippled through her body and deep into her core. "I wasn't planning on fucking you on a camel."

"But you are now?" The words sounded more like begging than an actual question.

Jordan obviously heard her tone. Amusement joined the lust in his voice as he said, "Of course not." The hand at her breast lifted, journeying downward to cup her mound through the pantaloons. "Not with my cock anyway."

One finger pushed lightly into her slit. Silk taunted her sensitive pussy lips, flaming her folds and rushing heat up her torso. His finger moved deeper, plying her aching flesh. She fisted the camel's reins and writhed against his hand. "I'm not wearing panties."

"That's my kinky girl."

He cupped the side of her face and turned her head, slanting it back to stroke his tongue into her mouth. Fire scalded her body with the hot male taste of him, mellowed only the tiniest bit with the subtle flavor of beer. The stroke of his fingers stopped, and he found her clit with the silk, dragging the filmy material across the swollen pearl as he sucked at her tongue and stole her breath.

The camel moved up an incline. Danica's mouth pulled away, and she lurched backward with the change in Jezi's gait. Jordan's cock rammed against her ass. He groaned, and she wiggled her bottom, grinding against his shaft with purposeful pressure. He taunted her back, pushing two fingers into her pussy, the silk easily moving with them, torturing her cunt with delicious friction.

She moaned and reflexively yanked on the reins in her hand. Jezi responded with a jerky shift and a backstep. Unprepared for the rapid change in motion, Danica fell toward the camel's neck, her breasts crushing around the saddle's hard pommel, her butt lifting off the seat. Panic skipped through her, barreling a scream up her throat. Jordan wrapped an arm around her waist before the sound could come out.

She thought he would tug her back into place on the saddle. Instead he held her forward and slipped a silk-covered finger into her pussy from behind. Panic turned to anticipation and then the need to explode as he thrust his finger into her slick body again and again. Pressure balled in her belly, working its way quickly to her loins. The breath panted between her lips. Her back gave an achy twinge of protest.

Releasing Jezi's reins, she palmed the sides of the camel's neck, holding herself more upright, relieving some of the tension from her spine. Jordan's finger slid from her sex. He took her clit between his first two fingers and pinched. Wicked sensation rocketed from the tips of her nipples to the walls of her cunt.

His fingers pinched a second time. Her hips arched up in response, and she cried out. But, damn it, not from the pleasure scorching her inside and out. The lower right side of her stupid freaking back was on fire with pain.

"Wait!" Danica tried to press herself back into the saddle. "I can't do this. I mean I can, but if I stay sitting at this angle a second longer, my back's going to feel like hell the rest of the night. I don't want to feel like hell. I have plans for you."

Jordan released her clit. He used the arm around her middle to ease her back against him and secure her in place. "I got a little carried away." Apology rang past the desire in his voice. "Does it hurt a lot?"

She retook Jezi's reins and turned the camel around on the beach. The painful knot of tension began to ease. "Once a week or so it'll ache like a dull arthritis sensation, generally more on one side than the other, which results in me standing off-kilter and making it worse. Then a couple weeks out of the year I'll have a bad flare-up that starts over something as simple as bending wrong to grab a piece of paper, and I'll be convinced I'll die from the pain before it gets better."

The arm around her waist tightened, and he pressed a kiss to the back of her head. "You poor thing."

His sympathy warmed her through. Danica appreciated it, but it wasn't the kind of warmth she wanted to experience with him tonight. "This conversation really isn't sexy."

"Does it have to be?"

"I want to be sexy for you." His cock was back to prodding her in the ass, and her butt cheeks were back to tingling with the want to feel him sliding between them. "I know you were having fun at the party, but I'd like to go to my villa now. Do you mind?"

"Are we taking the camel the whole way?"

"Nope. My golf cart." She heard his intake of breath and smiled. "I know how many drinks you had tonight, so don't even think about suggesting you drive."

"What if I get sick?"

"Better being sick over my driving than dead over yours."
His snort suggested that was a matter of opinion.

Danica returned to the living room where she'd asked
Jordan to wait for her while she checked on something in her
bedroom. Rimmed in black kohl, her eyes looked smokier than
ever as she took his hand and led him through the villa. Whether
it was the cloak of darkness or he'd drunk more than he thought,
her driving hadn't made him fear for his life tonight. Then again,
it was probably neither of those. It was probably the fact his
dick was so hard with wanting her, he hadn't been able to pull
his eyes from the way she filled out the silky, sexy slave girl costume long enough to notice how fast she was going.

They reached the bedroom door, and she pulled him inside.
Gone were the plants and clothes and every ounce of clutter
from the floor. A dozen freshly lit exotic-smelling candles sat
throughout the room, perfuming the otherwise lightless area,
and a tent fashioned of orange silk canopied the white wicker-
framed bed. The nightstand was freed of books; in their place
was a bottle of massage oil.

"You decorated."

Danica let go of his hand to turn around with a siren's smile
curving her lips. "You're not the only one who likes to be prepared." She sidled back toward the parted sides of the tent. The
bells sewn into her black and gold pantaloons tinkled as she
eased herself down on the bed in a slow, sensual move that
ended on a whimper. Ache flitted through her eyes. She fell
back on the mattress, murmuring, "I suck."

"Then I'm a lucky man."

She laughed, which had been Jordan's intention, and he
climbed onto the bed next to her. "Take off your clothes and
lay on your stomach."

"Your sympathy overwhelms me."

He moved over her. Placing a hand on the mattress on either

side of her, he held his weight off of her as he skimmed her lips with a kiss. Her breasts brushed against his chest, and his gaze fell on them. He'd been damned anxious to get his tongue on the generous, milk-white mounds from the moment she arrived at his rental villa in the risqué halter top. He was going to have to be anxious a while longer. "I'm going to give you a massage."

"Oh." Approval warmed her eyes. "In that case, thank you."

He moved off her and she came to her feet, undressing in a manner that told him sensuality was the last thing on her mind. Danica returned to the bed, lying down on her stomach with her arms folded beneath her head and the lush expanse of her backside inches from his face. His cock pulsed with the memory of the taunting way she looked down at her ass and let him know she wanted him inside of it.

With an inward groan, Jordan shut out the memory and straddled her upper thighs. He placed a hand on her back, and she went board-stiff. "Relax. It's just you and me, and we both love your body exactly as it is."

She relaxed a little, then a little more when he poured rose-scented massage oil onto his palms and placed his hands on her shoulders. He worked the oil into her shoulders, the friction activating the lubricant's natural heat.

She went utterly soft beneath his touch. "Holy hot oil."

Applying more oil to his palms, he brought them down on the raised pink scar that ran the length of her back. He massaged the area lightly, unsure how she would respond or if his touch would do more harm than good.

Danica lifted her head from her arms. "Don't be afraid to touch me, Jordan. My back has metal rods in it, so it's stronger than a normal person's." He increased the pressure, kneading his fingertips along her misshapen spine. She sighed and her head fell back to her arms. "Much better."

He wanted to ask what happened to her, or at least point out she was normal—probably more so than most of the population—but he feared doing so would tense her up again. And, really, it was none of his business.

Jordan kneaded at her spine a while longer and then brought his hands to the curve of her ass. He massaged oil into each supple cheek, making her skin glisten in the twinkling light of the candles. His thumbs brushed near the rear of her pussy, and she sucked in a loud breath and arched toward his touch.

Blood pounded between his temples and throbbed in his dick as he slid his hands lower, dipping the tips of his thumbs into her folds. Juices seeped out to greet him. The scent of her arousal mingled with the rose scent of the oil, lifting and curling in the humid night air.

Her pain was clearly gone. The time for pleasure had arrived.

"What do you want, Danica?"

She didn't miss a beat but answered in a throaty voice, "Your fingers inside me, fucking my pussy, sliding into my asshole."

The throbbing of his dick turned savage with her dirty talk. He wanted to bypass the fingering and get right to the part where he filled her with his cock. But he hadn't heard those three magic words yet, and he wouldn't move into her until she was dripping wet with orgasm.

Jordan guided her up to her hands and knees and then followed her order, sinking a finger into her plump pink folds from behind. Pumping inside her tight, wet sheath, he bent his head and kissed and tongued the sweaty flesh surrounding her asshole.

"Ah . . . so good." Danica writhed against his mouth, contracting the muscles of her sex with each push and pull of his finger. He peppered her sensitized flesh with damp, open-mouthed kisses and then lashed his tongue up the seam of her ass. She bucked back hard. "Put your tongue in me now!"

His balls snugged tight, gathering tension at the base of his spine with the urgent command. He plunged into her asshole and loved her with the thrusting stroke of his finger and tongue in unison.

Orgasm shook through her in seconds, trembling her limbs and leaking her cream onto his hand. "Oh, God!" she shouted. "I might have to make you my boyfriend permanently."

Jordan's body thrummed with the words and how much he wanted that same thing. It wasn't a possibility, but keeping this moment ingrained in both of their minds would be a worthy second.

He drew his tongue from her body. Sitting back on his knees, he pulled his cream-coated finger from her pussy and eased it into her asshole.

"No," Danica panted.

Disappointment flashed through him, but he wasn't about to take her in a way she wasn't comfortable with, even if she had taunted him with the idea. He pulled his finger from her hole and was ready to return it to her weeping sex when she ordered, "Your cock! Put your cock inside me. Fuck my ass."

Sighing his relief, he moved off the bed. His hands shook as he pushed off the vest and then the baggy sultan pants. He hadn't come prepared with a condom on his penis, but he had several of them in his wallet. Grabbing one, he tore into the wrapper and rolled the condom on in record time.

His shaft jerking toward her lush backside, Jordan climbed back onto the bed. He went up on his knees and took her hips in his hands. Candles flickered around them, their lights mirroring off the sheets tenting the bed and centering on her buttocks. Juices shimmered from the lovely rosette of her ass.

Words hissed between his lips. "Tell me you like me."

"I like you . . . so much it hurts."

His heart hammered with the words. He released one of her hips to take his cock in hand. Pre-cum oozed from the angry purple head as he guided it to her asshole and eased inside her tight, damp passage a fraction.

They cried out in unison. Raw needy sensation grabbed him by the throat and balls. He released her other hip to fondle her erect clit and swollen folds, allowing them both a chance to prepare for his next move.

Danica pushed back, taking him a little deeper inside. She ground out, "All. The. Way."

He closed his eyes and fought for control, knowing it was pointless, knowing one deep push would have him coming. Gasping for breath, he fingered her pussy back to the point of explosion. When her thighs were trembling and the breath raging from her lungs as wildly as his own, he gave in to her command and the painful tightness of his balls and pushed his dick into her ass, past her sphincter muscles and beyond.

"Yes!" she screamed, her hips pumping in time with his, her fingers clawing at the bedspread as climax tore through her body. "Oh, God, yes!"

"You're beautiful. Every inch of you," Jordan growled, and then climax took him over as well.

Spasmic waves of pleasure shook through him, gripping him to the core and telling him he liked her so much it hurt, too. Only, he had a feeling Danica meant her ache in a physical way eased by orgasm. His hurt wasn't physical, and it didn't end with his orgasm but grew that much stronger.

8

Seated in the buff at her aged kitchen table, Danica and Jordan shared a breakfast of scrambled eggs and bacon. She lifted her morning Pepsi and took a long drink from the can.

From a seat away, Jordan sent her a disgusted look over the rim of his coffee mug. "You're a sick woman, wanting Pepsi over coffee in the morning."

If anything about her was sick, it was her ability to sit so close to his naked, virile body without ravishing him. Truthfully, if it wasn't for the well-loved ache between her thighs and the famished state of her stomach, she probably wouldn't be able to contain herself. "It gets my brain started."

Amusement shone in his eyes. "Should I hold out hope it'll get moving enough to remind you to shave your hairy armpit?"

Setting the soda can on the table, she laughed. "That's an inside joke between Lena and me."

"I gathered as much." Jordan looked to her right underarm, which was too incredibly close to her breast for her nipple not to notice his gaze and tighten in response. "Your underarm and I got quite close last night, and I don't recall a trace of hair."

Thoughts of all the many ways they'd been close last night flooded Danica's mind until her nipple wasn't the only part of her body aroused. She forked up a bite of scrambled eggs in an attempt to waylay the moisture gathering in her sex. It might have worked if Jordan didn't push back his chair and stand to reveal his cock standing at full mast.

He took his empty plate to the sink and set it inside. Her mouth watered with the taut play of his ass muscles. He turned back around, and his shaft twitched under her gaze. Her pussy tightened, cream trickling down her thighs.

Apparently, he hadn't been so far off with his insinuation she was a whore. She sure felt like a slut for wanting him again so soon. "I'm not going into work today."

He sank back down in his chair. "You must have an incredible boss to get a Thursday off."

Danica's eyes were glued to his cock, standing so long and thick and firm from the dark blond thatch of his pubic hair. She attempted to pull her attention to the safety of his face but failed. "She's amazing"—passion turned her words throaty—"but actually, most of the resort staff don't work a typical Monday to Friday workweek. Sometimes I do, but just as often I schedule my days off around meetings . . . and sex."

"Unless you plan to have it right now, I suggest you stop looking at my dick like you want to devour it."

Oops. Caught in the act.

"I was considering how good it's going to feel sliding inside my mouth when I blow you out on the terrace." It took more self-control than she knew she had, but she finally managed to lift her gaze to his face. As it turned out, that area wasn't safe either. The want smoldering in his eyes only made her pussy ache more. "You won't be getting your blow job for a while." She forced the words out and made herself stay seated. "I'm not going into the office, but I still need to do a little work."

"Anything I can help with?"

The hunk she was desperate to fuck gave way to the orderly Jordan she'd first met. She thought his methodical ways would never allow them to make a good match, but Danica had come to appreciate that side of him, and she found now, she wanted that side, too. For the sake of the resort's welfare, it was a very good thing he was going home the day after tomorrow. Her own welfare didn't look so sunny.

No other man had made her feel comfortable enough about her body to be naked with him when sex wasn't a factor, or for that matter, nearly as often when it was. No other man had made her feel beautiful despite her disfigurement.

Sorrow threatened with the idea she would probably never see him again after Sunday morning. Then again, maybe he would come back to have his surgery. Or surgeries. He still wouldn't tell her what he wanted to have done. Having spent the night getting to know every inch of his body, she couldn't find a single part in need of enhancement. He was all long lean lines and hard defined muscle she'd taken great pleasure in running her hands, lips, and tongue over.

Danica's sex fluttered and she sighed. She had to stop thinking about Jordan's naked body and focus on her morning plans.

Grabbing the last piece of bacon off her plate, she set her fork on the plate and pushed it toward the center of the table. She took a bite of bacon and chewed it slowly, giving her stimulation time to settle. "Maybe you can help," she finally responded. "Lena and I have been brainstorming ideas for a fund-raiser to generate money for the nonelective surgery expansion I told you about. So far we've got nothing worth repeating."

He grabbed his coffee mug off the table and brought it to his lips, taking a drink before responding. "You said your father thought the par-three golf course would be a good place to build on investor relations. Presuming you have the investors in question, why not ask them for more money?"

"I don't want to be greedy. The loan route doesn't appeal to me either. I have enough stress in running this place without needing to worry over being up to my eyeballs in debt."

Jordan set his mug back on the table. He brought his hand to his nose, pinching the bridge as he closed his eyes. He released his nose and opened his eyes after nearly a full minute had passed. "How much of the island do you own?"

"Four miles. Roughly thirty percent." Danica's excitement rang in her voice. He obviously had an idea for a fund-raiser, and the conviction in his eyes said it was a winner.

"Will the expansion eat up all of the vacant land?"

Would he get on with revealing his idea already? She felt ready to wiggle out of her chair with anticipation. "There's a quarter mile of property that starts a couple acres from the right side of my villa. I know the resort is literally in my back-yard, but I don't want it so close even the trees can't block out the buildings and noise. I love the place, but I like to leave it be-hind from time to time, too." She waited three seconds for his response and then gave up. Really, she'd warned him of her im-patience, so he ought to know better than to drag things out. "What are you thinking about?"

"A five-hundred-dollar-a-ticket raffle."

Her excitement died down with the amount of the figure. She glared at his coffee mug. "If this involves me and a sand wedge, you're about to eat that mug."

Jordan tossed back his head and let out a hearty chuckle.

He'd been so polished that first day. Now he looked carefree and happy and . . . naked.

Her miscreant gaze fell to the gold nipple ring she'd taken great pleasure in tormenting him with last night and then to his cock. Her pussy squeezed. Would it be so wrong to forget about fund-raising for a few more minutes?

"No sand wedge," he said. "I was thinking you could take a waterfront chunk out of the property next to yours and build a villa on it. It doesn't have to be huge, just a nice seaside getaway shack. Play up the cruise port I noticed on the other side of the island—the quaintness, the year-round sunshine, and the mixed ethnicity of the Caribbean are some other obvious draws. Then maybe you have five or ten secondary prizes of a free surgery of the winner's choice up to a set value. It seems like a lot of your past clients and your employees' friends and family would want to buy a ticket or two."

Danica's mental excitement rekindled with the suggestion. She lifted her gaze to his face and smiled her approval. "That's good. Different. I really like it."

"I like you." Jordan's gaze heated as it wandered down to her breasts. His fingers flexed as if they wanted to do some wandering of their own. "Want to see?"

"I was planning on spending the morning letting my mental wheels spin, but since you already did the work for me . . ." She pushed back her chair and leapt onto his lap, straddling his thighs as she devoured his mouth.

"Danica!" Knocking followed the female shout into Danica's open bedroom window.

Recognizing Lena's voice and figuring her friend would track her down in the bedroom if she didn't respond, she lifted Jordan's arm from her waist and crept out of bed. Smiling at his nude body glistening in the afternoon sunlight and the soft snores leaving his mouth, she hurried into her robe. She stepped out of the bedroom and nearly slammed face-first into Lena.

"I have to tell you something about Jordan," Lena blurted.

Danica pulled the bedroom door shut and gestured for Lena to follow her out to the living room. "Is it bad?" she asked when they reached it.

"Potentially."

"Then quit yelling. He's asleep in the bedroom."

Lena's brown eyes went wide. She slid her gaze over Danica, seeming to notice for the first time she wore only a robe and probably smelled of sex and had a major case of bed head. Lena smiled faintly and said in a much quieter voice, "Sorry. It's probably nothing, but I had this vision last night shortly after the two of you rode off into the sunset on your camel." Her dimple flashed. "Very abnormal thing to do, by the way. I'm impressed."

The sun had already set by the time they'd taken Jezi for a ride, but that was a moot point. Probably so was Lena's supposed vision. Only, the sudden tightening of Danica's belly made her wonder otherwise. "You had a potentially bad vision about Jordan that could affect me and are just now telling me about it?"

Color rose into Lena's cheeks. "I ran into Akeave right after I had it. He was at the party alone, and I was there alone, and you know what a weakness I have for him. Besides, you don't even believe in my visions."

"I *do* believe in them." Liar. "All right, I want to believe in them and will when I see some proof. What is this one with Jordan about?"

"He was getting on a plane and leaving."

Lena hadn't supplied any proof, but the tightness of Danica's belly still became a queasy sensation. She wanted to rub it away or retrieve the bag of almonds she'd stashed in her cupboard after Jordan walked out on her the other night. She stayed where she was, refusing to let Lena see how much the words bothered her. "That's going to happen. He's only here for a couple more days."

Lena eyed her pitifully. "You were watching him fly away with tears in your eyes; then you mouthed 'I love you' as the plane disappeared in the sky."

"No worries there. I don't love him." That much was the truth. She didn't love the man, just his body and the sense of comfort and happiness he instilled in her.

"You're sure?"

Danica smiled reassuringly while her mind pondered exactly how far off loving the way he made her feel was from loving him in general. It had to be a long ways, because Private Indulgence and New York City were thousands of miles apart, too far to be in love with Jordan. "Sure, I'm sure. I like him and will undoubtedly miss having a sex life that involves another person after he's gone, but it's nothing a few days of focusing on work and some hands-on time in the tub won't take care of."

Inhaling long breaths meant to calm the frantic beat of his heart, Jordan held Danica against his sweaty chest and stared at her bedroom ceiling.

Would sex with her always be so good?

He frowned at the question. His mission here was complete, and sex with Danica was almost over. Tomorrow morning, he would fly back to New York and report to his father that Private Indulgence was indeed a great investment. Today he would spend with the resort's owner, making memories that damned well better last a lifetime because the ache in his gut told him his expectations would be so high from this point on, no other woman would be able to meet them.

He tightened his hold around her, silently urging her not to pull free of his shaft anytime soon. "Why was this place your dream?"

"Isn't it obvious?" The movement of her lips tickled his chest as she spoke.

He loosened his arms to run a hand along her spine. "This?"

"Yes. I can't change my flaw, but I can help others feel better about what they deem to be theirs."

"Why here? I know the cost of living is lower, but that can be said for a lot of places. Like New York City, for example." He snorted quietly, too aware what complete bullshit that was.

"I picked the Caribbean to make it feel more like a vacation—time away in the island sun, or at least being waited on hand and foot inside a villa while watching the sun set over the water through the window."

"And?"

Danica came up on her forearms, pressing her chin against his chest as she eyed him. "What makes you think there's an 'and'?"

"Experience."

"With other women?"

Was that jealousy in her voice? He thought he'd heard the same at the costume party when he'd commented on Lena looking sexy. Then the noise level had been too loud to be certain. Now it sounded a hell of a lot like it and quickened his heart. "With you. So what is the other reason?"

"People mean well by saying you look good as is, that beauty comes from within so you shouldn't worry about your appearance. It's true that inner beauty is more important than looking good, but in the case of most of our patients, they didn't feel truly beautiful on the inside until they were happy with how they looked on the outside. A lot of people don't understand that, but I do. The staff here does. By having the resort where it is, our patients are able to get away from their well-meaning friends and family members under the pretense they're going on a tropical vacation. People might notice a physical change when they return or they might not. By then, it will be too late for those well-meant words, which unintentionally hurt, to make a difference."

"Are you happy on the inside even though you can't change the outside?" Would she be happier if she had a man in her life permanently? It was a pointless question and still one Jordan wanted to ask damned badly.

Danica bent her head, giving his nipple ring a playful tug with her teeth as she squeezed her sex around his shaft. "Parts of me are very happy."

Sensation arrowed downward from his nipple, and his deflating cock began hardening again, like she was his personal answer to Viagra. He didn't feel nearly as happy as his dick. "I was being serious."

"I know." She sobered. "I am happy. Could I be happier? Well, who couldn't? Everyone has something they'd like to change."

"I don't."

Her smile returned in full detail, elation filling her eyes. "You're not going to have surgery?"

Guilt cruised through him stronger than anything he'd known. She was thrilled to think he wouldn't be giving her resort money by having surgery done at it. If he had even a fleeting thought that his father's money was unsafe with her, it died in that moment. Jordan ached to come clean with her, but doing so now would be futile and would only serve to destroy their last afternoon together.

Grinning, he moved his hands down her nude body. He squeezed her butt cheeks and clarified, "I meant I wouldn't change a thing about this moment."

Danica's smile faded for an instant and then returned, bigger and brighter. "I would. I have a meeting in less than an hour, though I'd much prefer to spend the afternoon in bed with you." She rolled from his arms to the side of the bed, coming to her feet in one fluid move. "Unfortunately, I have to get showered and out the door."

Her expression didn't match her words. She looked happy to be sacrificing a chunk of their last day together for the sake of a meeting. He wanted to ask what the meeting was about, but that was no more his business than learning what had happened to her back.

She pulled khaki capris, a white tank top, and a white lacy bra and panty set from her dresser. Tucking the clothes under her arm, she came up on the side of the bed for a lingering kiss. Jordan's hands moved to her breasts out of habit.

Danica jerked back, laughing. "Hands off the goods until I get back. I honestly don't know how long this will take, but you're welcome to stay and make yourself at home."

"Thanks, but I need to call in for a meeting of my own and don't want to run up your phone bill." Shit, he hated adding one more lie to the growing number of lies between them. But then, it was better than admitting he didn't want to spend any more time in her villa than necessary for fear he wouldn't be able to leave. Once he'd stopped ogling her body long enough to check out her home, he'd discovered it wasn't chaotic, but cozy and lived in, nothing like his utilitarian apartment back in the city. "Drop by my rental when your meeting's over."

"I'll be there with bells on." She went to the bedroom door, turning back with a suggestive smile. "Nothing else if you're lucky."

Would she? Her smile suggested so, but the sudden hollow feeling in Jordan's gut made him wonder otherwise.

He shook his head at the thought. His gut didn't know a damned thing . . . unless Lena's visionary powers had rubbed off on him.

Danica no sooner sat down to prepare for the meeting of her dreams than a quiet male voice drifted in through her office door. She looked up from her desk to find a blond man standing outside the door with his back to her. His elbow came out as he reached a hand to some part of his face.

The gesture was so familiar. It looked almost like he was squeezing the bridge of his nose.

Jordan?

He couldn't have made it to the office so quickly, with her taking a shortcut in her golf cart and him using the service drive in his rental coupe. Not to mention he'd been naked in bed when she left the villa. This guy wore black jean shorts and a burgundy knit sleeveless shirt.

The man turned to reveal his profile and that he spoke on a cell phone. Since hanging up from the phone call of her life last night, Danica had felt wrung out with nervous excitement—too much to share the call with Jordan for fear of jinxing the potentially incredible news it brought. Now that excitement died as anxiety took over. From this angle, she could tell he wasn't Jordan but a man who looked like an older version of him. Too much to be coincidental.

She made an impulsive grab for the candy dish, scooping up a small handful of almonds and popping them into her mouth.

The man stopped talking. He slid the cell phone into the holder hanging from his belt and entered her office with a wide, friendly smile. "Sorry about that. I was just about to come in when a call came through I couldn't ignore."

"John?" My God, without the beard and gray hair, she hadn't recognized him.

John Cameron was a man she couldn't forget. He'd come to the resort for a chin augmentation almost two months ago and during his stay had charmed most of the staff and convinced Danica to share her expansion dreams with him. She thought she would never hear from him again. But then he'd called last night to say it was time for her expansion to happen, that he had the money she needed and was ready to invest it in Private Indulgence.

Yesterday morning, she'd told Jordan she didn't want to ask her current investors for more money, and she felt nearly as strongly about accepting it from a new investor. But John had sounded so eager. He said the resort had all but turned his life around, and he wanted to help see it do the same for others. Danica knew that enthusiasm firsthand, and she couldn't say no.

And she couldn't look at John without seeing Jordan.

John glanced at the brown-leather-banded watch on his wrist, frowning when she remained silent. "We agreed to meet at one, didn't we?"

Danica nodded, searching for words, finally finding them. "Yes. Of course. You just look . . . different."

With a whoop of laughter, he dropped down on the chair in front of her desk. "I hope that means better."

"You looked good before and now—do you have a . . ." *What?* Son? Jordan couldn't be his natural son with a different last name, unless he'd taken his mother's name for some reason. "Do you know Jordan?"

John's humor died. He sat forward, banging his fisted hands on the edge of the desk. "Has my son been bothering you?"

His son.

The breath snagged in Danica's throat. Her heart felt ready to pound from her chest. White, hot fury raged through her with the realization Jordan had spent this last week lying to her. But, no, she didn't know that. "He *is* your son?"

John sat back in his chair with a sigh. "I don't think I want to own up to it right now, but yeah, he's my son."

"Did you send him here? To look into the resort?" *Please say no.* Not that it mattered. Jordan was all but out of her life. Only, it did matter. She wanted him to fly away leaving a happy memory behind.

"I agreed to give him time to come here and check the place out, but whatever he found wasn't about to skew my investment decision. I just wanted him to get the hell away from his desk and remember how it feels to live."

Danica's belly cramped. She ran a hand over it, letting the words sink in slowly. Jordan *had* lied to her. Why? Had he slept with her for the same reason? Had he been pretending all those times he called her "beautiful" and "good-looking" when in truth her disfigured body appalled him?

That last question was too much. Tears pricked her eyes. She sniffed them back.

Damn it, she'd known he'd been bad news when he walked into her office Monday morning right when something bad was due to happen. Something bad like breaking her heart. Only, he hadn't broken it. It just felt that way.

"What does Jordan do?"

Sympathy filled eyes the same shade of stunning turquoise as his son's—the color should have been a red flag from the start. "He's an investment broker."

At least Jordan had told her some truth. A truth she'd never considered in detail. Danica sent the candy dish a longing look as she let the details unfold in her mind.

She wanted to keep the venom from her voice because this was his father, and even if Jordan hadn't been nice to her—at least not for the right reasons—he had been looking out for John's welfare. The venom still came through. "He doesn't think helping to fund the resort expansion is a good investment?"

"As I said, I don't care how my son feels about my choices."

"Sadly, I do." That was the bitch of it. She did care, even now.

Her belly roiling over what she was about to lose, she stood on shaky legs and offered her hand to John across the desk. "Thank you for flying down here and for your sincere interest in the resort, but I can't accept your money. I'm sorry."

He stood to give her an understanding smile. "Can you accept an offer of a late lunch with an old man?"

All she wanted to eat was a truckload of chocolate-covered almonds. But after John had come all this way and made such an altruistic offer, the least she could do was forgive him for raising a dickhead and share a meal with him.

Letting her hand fall to her side, she forced a smile. "That sounds—"

"Dad?"

Danica's blood ran cold with the too-familiar voice. What it sounded like was the devil had arrived, and all she wanted to do was kick him in the nuts.

9

What the fuck was his father doing here?

Jordan didn't need to ask the question; the betrayed look on Danica's face told him everything.

She stood behind her desk, lips pushed into a tight line and her hands balled into fists. He wanted to pull her into his arms and tell her the lies he'd told hadn't meant a thing. That everything he'd said that mattered had been the truth.

His father turned, disappointment clear on his face. "What did you do, son?"

Fell in love with a woman who hates me. Even if she didn't hate him, they lived worlds apart, or at least close to it.

"*Why* are you here?" Jordan couldn't keep the accusation from his voice.

"We had a deal. Time ran out."

"Tomorrow. Time runs out tomorrow." Today he was still supposed to have Danica in his arms.

John smiled sadly. "Better check your calendar again. You had four weeks starting from the time and day you asked for them."

"It doesn't matter." Danica sounded wooden. "Your father already wrote the check . . . and I refused it."

"You *what*? Why?" Jordan dragged a hand through his hair. Jesus, he'd never imagined things coming to this. Never wanted to hurt Danica. He wanted to place that blame on his father's shoulders for arriving today. Jordan couldn't, because he'd hurt her more than once this week all on his own and all because he was a jealous asshole who couldn't stomach the idea that his father might want to trust his money with someone other than him.

"I'm not about to take your father's money, only to have something unpredictable happen to the resort. I like *your father* too much for that." Her lips wobbled into a smile as she glanced at John. She looked back at Jordan, and her gaze turned frosty, her smile wicked. "I doubt you were serious when you came up with the fund-raiser idea, but I'm going ahead with it. It will make for a good start to generating the money I need for the expansion. I'll have to be patient until I have it all."

"You're rotten at being patient." Jordan spoke the words lightly, wanting to somehow turn this thing around, wanting to prove to her he had been listening, had been caring. Had been falling for her from the moment he walked into her office and she checked out his cock. He smiled with the memory.

Loathing flashed in Danica's eyes. "You're just plain rotten, period." She rounded the desk to ask John, "The lunch offer still stands?"

"I love you." The words blurted out of Jordan's mouth.

She stiffened, blinking a couple times and giving him hope. Then her frosty look returned. "Is that what you were trying to prove when you called me a whore?"

John's breath drew in sharply. His gaze narrowed on Jordan. "If you ever hope to gain back my respect, I suggest you don't speak another word."

Jordan swore under his breath. He hadn't called her a whore—

implied as much, yes, but he'd repented for that sin days ago. Obviously, she thought his apology as much of a lie as so many of the other things he'd said to her this week.

He turned a pleading look on his father. John was pissed at the moment, but he knew how atypical Jordan's behavior had been this week. He had to see that truth, had to help him in easing Danica's fury and showing her he wasn't such a bad guy.

Only, it appeared his father didn't have to do any such thing. Without so much as a good-bye, John took Danica's arm and guided her out the office door.

At the roar of a rapidly ascending plane, Danica looked up from her terrace couch where she attempted to lose her thoughts in a book. Cruise liners were prevalent in the islands, but only a handful of planes flew over on any given day. Jordan would be on this one. John would be with him.

John she liked, respected, would love to go into business with. Jordan she loathed, disrespected, would love to spend the rest of her life with.

Happily-ever-after had never been in the stars for them.

Danica had known they had no future even before she discovered Jordan did, in fact, have a small penis and it was located between his ears. Still, the tears leaked down her cheeks as the plane became a tiny speck of silver shimmering in the Caribbean sun. And still she made Lena's vision come true by mouthing, "I love you" as it disappeared from sight, taking with it the man who could fulfill her expansion dreams and the man who filled her dreams nightly.

Jordan had met his fair share of assholes. Until he'd become one, he'd never stopped to wonder how they got anything accomplished.

Maybe the rest of the assholes didn't suffer from guilt and heartache. The two, coupled with the stricken look on Danica's face when he walked into her office to find his father there, ate at his gut until he couldn't concentrate enough to work. He tried anyway, picking up the phone to make a client call he should have made a week ago.

Knocking sounded on his office door before he could get the number fully punched in. He set the phone back on its base. "Come in."

The door pushed inward, and his father poked his head inside. "Are you busy?"

Jordan's pulse sped with relief. "Not for you."

The plane ride back to New York had been damned painful. His father barely spoke to him. The silence had continued the week and a half since they'd been home, and Jordan was nearly convinced his jealousy had cost him two people he loved.

John pulled out one of the two tan leather chairs in front of Jordan's desk and sat down. He bridged his knuckles together on the edge of the desk and looked at Jordan, his expression unreadable and not one word coming out of his mouth.

Seconds turned into a minute and then two. Jordan didn't want to be the first to talk—his father had clearly come here to say something, and Jordan feared saying the wrong words would be enough to send his father away without speaking.

Another minute passed and finally John asked, "Why?"

"That question could pertain to a lot of things."

"What did you think to accomplish by going down there and breaking that poor girl's heart?"

Jordan's pulse beat a little faster. Had Danica told his father he'd broken her heart? "Did I?"

John sighed. "Hell, son, if you don't know that answer, you're an even bigger numskull than I realized."

He didn't have a single problem with being a numskull, so long as it meant his father was talking to him again. Getting back the old man's respect would be even better. The truth was his best hope. "I wanted the resort to prove a bad investment so you would trust me with your money instead of Danica."

His father's eyebrows came together in surprise. "I trust you, Jordan. But investing in stocks, bond, annuities, whatever, isn't my thing. I went down to Private Indulgence and found my thing. Then you went down there and took that thing away."

The words were like a punch to the gut. Jordan never realized his actions had hurt his father. Never even took the time to consider it through his eyes.

When the hell had he gotten so shortsighted? Probably around the same time he'd let the investment firm suck the life out of him and started driving at or below the speed limit. "I'm sorry, Dad."

John nodded. "I know you are. I know you were sincere when you told Danica you love her, too." He came to his feet. "I suggest you figure out how you're going to get her to forgive you and accept my money. Then you'd best put your notice in here. You got back your zest for life down there. It's where you belong."

Even if Danica didn't hate him, Jordan had thought they could never work out because they were thousands of miles apart. But his father was accurate once again. The hectic pace of both the firm and city living had long since lost their appeal. He'd scoffed at his father for sounding like the resort had reshaped his entire reason for being. Maybe it hadn't done so for his father, but the resort and its remarkable owner had done exactly that for Jordan.

In the Caribbean with Danica was where he belonged. "You were right about my putting work before everything else."

"I know that, too, though hearing my son tell me I'm right never gets old." John went to the door. He turned back before leaving, flashing a wide smile. "Get your ass to work on winning back that girl. Your mother's already picking out gifts for the grandkids."

Kids with Danica. Jordan had once vetoed the idea. Now it sounded like everything he'd ever wanted.

How in the hell were they supposed to get from not speaking to making babies?

The resources he'd come to rely on to find his solutions were those at his fingertips: his keyboard, computer, the Internet.

The icon for NASDAQ's home page flashed on his laptop screen. He'd accrued a sizeable chunk of cash putting his money into climbing stocks and pulling it back out when they peaked. Would investing that cash in the resort be enough to prove to Danica how he felt? Her own investment funds couldn't be all that big, considering she hadn't pulled the money out for her expansion, but maybe he could help to turn a better profit on them, too.

Her friend Jeff might make a superior client account specialist, but he hadn't exactly come off as the guy Danica should be relying on to handle her investments, as witnessed by the way he'd sunk all of her money into one rising stock.

PIMR, Jordan recalled the stock symbol. At the time, he'd been too distracted by the generous cleavage revealed by Danica's skimpy halter top and thoughts of burying his dick in her to wonder if he'd heard of the stock. Now he was nearly certain he had.

He clicked on the flashing NASDAQ icon. The Web site popped up, and he did a search on the symbol, swearing when the information for PIMR came up.

Einstein Jeff hadn't just sunk all of Danica's money into one stock. He'd sunk it into the stock of one of Private Indulgence's biggest competitors.

A month and a half ago, the find would have thrilled Jordan by giving him an excuse for his father not to invest in the resort. It thrilled him now, as well, by giving him an excuse to get close to Danica and convince her to listen to him.

* * *

Danica's office door burst open, and Lena dashed inside. Seated behind her desk, Danica eyed her friend. Only one thing made Lena move that fast. "Let me guess, you had a vision?"

"Yes!" Lena's blue-sandaled feet moved relentlessly on the carpet, sending the neon pink and lime girls dangling from her ears into a mean hula. "Of Jordan. He's here, Danica!"

Danica's belly turned and her hand shot on autopilot to the almonds in the candy dish. "Why would he be—"

"Because I have news that could make or break the future of the resort, and I knew you'd never listen to it over the phone."

Jordan's voice slid over Danica, waking sensations he had no right to awaken. She stuffed a handful of almonds into her mouth, chewing them for several seconds before looking toward the door. He wasn't the oppressive Jordan he'd been that first day but dressed in a casual black short sleeved shirt and jean shorts and looking back at her through the most striking pair of turquoise eyes she'd ever seen. Her sex fluttered with awareness.

"I swear I didn't know he was here," Lena declared. "I mean, I did, but not because I saw him. I mean, I did see him, but not in person."

"I believe you." Danica had come to terms with Lena's gift while watching Jordan's plane take off and silently confessing her love. Her friend really was psychic. And Jordan really deserved to have his ass kicked for daring to show up in her office.

Beneath the cover of her desk, she crossed her legs against the dampness his presence stirred. She took a moment to gather her composure while she smoothed her skirt along her thighs and then narrowed her eyes. "I won't accept your father's money."

"That isn't the news."

"Do you want me to stay?" Lena asked.

She gave her friend an appreciative look. "Thanks, but if anything too bad was destined to happen, I'm sure you would have foreseen it. Besides, I have my scalpel handy."

Lena left, closing the door behind her. Danica was considering shouting at her to reopen it when Jordan said, "I thought you didn't operate."

She wished he hadn't spoken the words. They made it sound like his stay here hadn't been solely for the sake of swaying his father away from the resort, but that he'd actually been listening to her when she spoke. "I don't, but you never know what kind of lowlife is going to walk through your door."

He winced. "Can I sit down?"

She'd been so upset since he'd left she'd done the unthinkable and kept both her home and office clean. Taking advantage of her sorry state of mind, she nodded at the empty black chair on the opposite side of her desk. "Go ahead. I'm as good as armed."

Jordan crossed to the chair and sat down. Leaning his elbows on the front edge of the desk, he nodded at her computer. "Pull up a Web browser."

Sure thing, just as soon as she rescued her senses from his mouthwateringly spicy scent.

Stetson infiltrated Danica's nose and she further dampened her panties. She'd missed his scent. Missed him so much more. And that was too damned bad. He'd lied to her, and for once in her life she was going to hold a grudge.

She clicked on the Internet Explorer icon on her desktop and bit out, "All right."

He leaned closer. "Do a search for 'Philippine International Medical Resort' and click on the first link."

Blocking out his scent and the wetness of her sex, she followed his orders. She frowned when a site popped up. "It's a Web site for another medical tourism resort. Why do I care?"

"Because that's where Jeff has your money invested."

Danica jerked her attention to his face. "*What?*"

Sympathy shone in Jordan's eyes. "Sorry, but it's the truth. Jeff told me about it at the costume party, right after you mentioned I was an investment broker. Not the name of the place but the stock symbol. I checked it out earlier this week and knew you couldn't have any idea."

"No. I didn't." She looked back at the computer screen, scrolling through the index page. The tightness of her belly for once had nothing to do with Jordan. "This looks really bad for Private Indulgence. Why would he think to invest in the competition?" She didn't wait for his answer but picked up the phone and ordered Jeff into her office.

Jeff's office was just down the hall, and he shuffled in fifteen seconds later all beanpole thin and receding hairline. "What's going on?"

Danica didn't believe he would do anything malicious on purpose. Still, she couldn't keep the anger from her voice. "You tell me. Why do you have my money invested in our competition?"

"You mean PIMR?" She looked to Jordan for clarification. He nodded and Jeff grinned. "That resort chain is hot. They have facilities popping up left and right. I've already doubled your money."

"And made me look like a fool who's bound to sell out her resort any day."

"No way. I invested using your father's old account. No one's ever got to know it's your money."

"Not until you sell the stock," Jordan pointed out. "Come tax time, it's going to look rather suspect when Danica's late father doesn't report his earnings."

Danica frowned from one man to the other. This day had been looking so favorable. Two good things had happened and the third was due to take place any second. Maybe learning Jeff didn't know squat about investing was the third thing. But did the news really have to come at the cost of seeing Jordan again?

Frustration ate at her. She looked back at Jeff and took it out on him. "I want my money out of there now!"

Jeff's grin disappeared. He focused on his feet, looking like a mopey little kid who had his favorite toy taken away. "It's almost five. The market's closed for the day."

"Then first thing in the morning. Never mind, I'll take care of it myself. Just get me whatever paperwork you have immediately." He started to shuffle from her office. She could hold a grudge against Jordan, but she'd known Jeff for years. He was a nice guy, just clearly a little too overzealous at times. "Jeff?"

"Yeah?" he asked without turning back.

She urged warmth into her voice. "I know you didn't do this on purpose. I value you as a friend and employee, just not as my stock broker."

Jeff gave a silent nod and left the office, closing the door behind him.

"Do you know anything about the market?" Jordan asked.

Danica had too much to worry over for his presence to affect her now. Or so she wanted to believe. The reality was nothing appeared great enough to distract her body from wanting his. She looked back at the computer monitor and absently flipped through the Web site. "No. And obviously neither does he."

"I can help you get the stock put under a legal name and then sell it and find something better to invest in."

No matter how badly she wanted him gone, she needed his help. Because, stupidly perhaps, she believed she could trust him to fix this mess without allowing anything to leak out. "Okay. Fine." Keeping her expression neutral, she looked at him. Apology burned in his eyes and hurt her chest. "You can help with the legalizing and sale of it. I'm not putting it back into the market, though. Jeff said the money has doubled. Between it and what I earn off the villa fund-raiser, I'll have enough to make a good start on the expansion." She stood and nodded at the door. "Come back tomorrow and I'll set you up in a temporary office."

Jordan came to his feet but otherwise remained in place. "I was thinking of long-term investment help. Even if you do use the money from the sale of the stock, as soon as the expansion is up and running, you'll have new money to invest. And, frankly, I quit my job and could really use a new one."

Had he quit it to be with her? Danica pushed aside the question and the unwanted hope it gave her. It didn't matter if he wanted to be with her. Not even if he loved her.

She dropped back down in her seat and reached for the almonds. "That's not a good idea."

"Why?"

Because all it took was the thinking he might love her despite his past actions and she wanted to go on an almond binge.

Damn it, she was stronger than this. She could resist temptation. She lifted her empty hand out of the candy dish. "You know why."

Jordan gave her a look that said he didn't, but then went to the door and disappeared from sight. Danica sank back in her chair, inhaling deeply.

So what if her chest felt ready to explode from the pain caused with his leaving? Time and distance had begun to ease the ache he'd left behind last time, and they would this time, too.

"Do these help?"

The question snapped her attention to the door, and a sigh of relief shot between her lips. A two-liter bottle of Pepsi hung from one hand and a can of Jordan almonds from the other. Damned if she didn't laugh. He laughed, too. Humor glinted in his eyes, doing wonderful things to their already consuming shade and making her feel good all over. And that just sucked.

She couldn't give in so easily. No. She couldn't give in at all. "I can't do this, Jordan. You—"

"I hurt you, and I've lived with regret every day since." Soberly, he came to her desk and set his bartering gifts down on the edge. "I hate lying, Danica. I didn't feel like I had any other choice with you."

"You were looking out for your father's welfare."

"I was jealous as hell and trying to prove the resort a sham." Self-loathing filled his voice. "I've tried to convince my father to let me invest his money for years. He didn't even seem to consider it, and then he comes down here for a week and all of a sudden he's gung ho to sink his money into this place."

Compassion reared its head against Danica's desire not to let it. She'd never considered he might be affected by his father's decision. "I'm sorry."

Jordan smiled weakly. "You don't have a reason to be. I'm the sorry one. The one who stole my father's thing away. The dickhead who messed with your mind until you couldn't tell the truth from the lies. I lied to you about my last name and reason for being at the resort, but most everything else was the truth. You are beautiful, Danica, and I do love you."

The tension let up on her chest with the sincerity in his eyes. She wanted to say to hell with one more grudge. She looked back at the computer screen. "What is your father's thing?"

"Investing in this place. He wanted it so badly, and I made you stop it from happening." He came around the side of the desk, bringing his scrumptious scent and delectable body inches from her. "I considered giving you my money to fund your expansion, but that wouldn't make my father happy. Pulling your money out of the market for the resort won't accomplish that either. You need to accept his money. This place has become his dream almost as much as yours."

"All right. I'll consider it." Even as she said the words, Danica knew there would be no considering about it. John was a wonderful, selfless man, and she would call him first thing tomorrow morning and give him back his thing.

"What about us?" Jordan came down on his knees beside

her chair. "Will you consider giving us another chance? I love you just as you are, and I'm not going to give up on convincing you of that until you understand it's the truth."

Danica's heart beat faster. She fought back a smile. God, she really was a sap for him, occasional dickhead ways and all, and she was going to give in to one more grudge. "The first day you walked into my office I was having a run of bad luck. First, there was no Pepsi in the fridge, and then I almost cut my nipple off shaving."

He frowned. "You don't have hairy breasts."

She sighed. Sometimes the man really did remind her of Lena. "I wasn't shaving my breast. I was shaving my underarm and fumbled the razor. The point is, bad things happen in sets of three, and three weeks ago you arrived just on time to be the third bad thing. I also believe good things happen in sets of threes, and it just so happens you arrived on time today to be the third good thing."

"What are you saying?"

"Folding myself up like a human pretzel in the name of orgasm isn't cutting it. I want to have real sex with a real man, and I want that man to be you."

"Just sex?"

The disappointment in Jordan's voice was nearly tangible. She could ease his frustration now, but he deserved to pay a little for making her cry and, worse, for making her clean. Danica shuddered just thinking about that hellish act.

Forgetting about the tidiness of their surroundings, she moved to the front of her chair and parted her legs. The skirt slid up her thighs. His gaze shot to the damp yellow cotton exposed at her crotch, and his breath drew in. That she affected him so completely was too great an aphrodisiac to allow for the punishing surface kiss she'd planned.

Grabbing his shirt by the collar, she bent her head and

jerked his mouth to hers, savoring the delicate scrape of his mustache along her upper lip for an instant before devouring him with her kiss. She tongued his mouth with urgency. He kissed her back just as recklessly. She needed so much more.

She wanted him inside her body yesterday. Every day since he'd been gone. Every day from here on out.

Yanking Jordan's shirt free of his shorts, she pushed it up his chest. Hard packed muscle greeted her fingertips, but it was the nipple piercing that had her pussy throbbing.

She lifted her lips from his to come down on her knees on the floor in front of him. She stroked her tongue across the nipple ring. His hands gripped her sides. She bit down on the ring, giving it a tug harder than she'd dared when it had still been so fresh. He moaned and arched against her mouth. "Is this your way of saying you missed me?"

"This is my way of saying I'll give you a job and a spot in my bed. You can work your way to better things from there."

Danica flicked her tongue back across his nipple. He sighed, and then went still. "So basically you're going to pay me to work for you and sleep with you. That really does feel cheap."

"Sure does." She released his shirt to unfasten his shorts and push her hand past the open vee of the zipper. "Makes me want to break out my sand wedge." Her fingers moved beneath his boxers to wrap around the hot, hard flesh of his shaft, and her pussy contracted. "I'd much rather feel your cock inside me."

She pumped his erection. Groaning, he pulled her hand from his pants and brought her down on her back on the carpet. Her heart raced with the primal move. Faster as he straddled her thighs and popped open the buttons of her shirt.

Jordan pushed up the yellow lace cups of her bra, freeing her breasts to the heat of his gaze and then the warm, wet lash of his tongue. "I'll give you an orgasm"—he flicked her other nipple—"but I'm not sticking my dick in you and getting off myself until you've decided you like me again."

"Maybe I do like you. Suck my nipple and we'll see."

He pulled her nipple firmly between his lips, sucking, twisting, tugging. Carnal sensation zinged to her core, increasing her wetness until she wanted to forget about making him pay a while longer and tell him the truth of her feelings immediately.

He moved to the other nipple, biting down hard. Her hips shot up, meeting with the hard ridge of his cock trapped behind his boxers. She panted, "Mmm . . . not sure yet. Better give me more to work with."

Working damp kisses up her chest to her shoulder and then her neck, he lifted her up his body and placed her on the desk. Nibbling on her ear, he pushed the shirt down her arms. Shivers shook through her as he unhooked the back clasp of her bra.

His fingers touched down on her scar, and he lifted his mouth from her ear to ask her soberly, "What happened to you? I've always wanted to know but never felt it my place to ask before this."

For the first time, Danica didn't have to mentally remind herself not to tense beneath his touch. For the first time, she answered the question with a smile. "Nothing happened, like an accident or anything. I was diagnosed with scoliosis when I was teenager and had surgery to stop the curvature from getting worse and pressing my spine into my lungs. That was a long time ago. I don't have any leftover body issues because of it. You made them go away."

The sobriety lifted from Jordan's eyes. His fingers went to the front of her skirt, and he returned her smile. "You brought back my zest for life." His smile became a wicked grin as he popped the skirt's button. "Made me realize what my job was doing to me." The zipper came hissing down. "How much I missed the nipple ring." His hands moved to her hips, grabbing hold of her skirt. "How much I love going fast." Her entire body trembled with desire as he worked the skirt and her panties down her hips. "How much I love you."

Danica couldn't play the "make him pay" game any longer. Not when her body was quaking for his to be inside of it. Not when she loved him beyond question. Grabbing hold of his shoulders, she lifted her butt off the desk. He swept the skirt and panties down her thighs, and the cool wood of the desk kissed her naked ass.

Bringing his mouth over hers, he slipped a finger inside her body, caressing her pussy and tongue, making her burn for so much more.

She let his strokes take her to the edge, and then she lifted from his mouth and caught his hand in hers, stilling his finger. "Not like this."

Concern filled his eyes. "Am I hurting you?"

"Of course not." He didn't look convinced, so she took his hand and brought the finger that had been inside of her to her lips. His attention fell on her mouth. She pulled his finger inside, running her tongue around its thick length as she sucked at her salty cream. "Doesn't taste like hurt to me."

He closed his eyes on a pained-sounding sigh. "I missed my kinky girl."

She smiled. "I missed you, too, but I don't want you to fuck me with your fingers. I don't like you, Jordan . . . I love you."

His eyes popped open. "You're serious?"

"Do you think I'd lie?"

"No, and neither will I ever again."

She glanced at his nipple ring, shiny wet from the stroke of her tongue, the nipple pink and erect beneath. Her clit tingled and she licked her lips. "You might not lie again, but you better lay me right this second, or I'll change my mind about liking you and call Jeff in here to do the job."

To the sound of their laughter, he pushed his shorts and boxers down his legs and sheathed himself with a condom from his wallet. Then he returned to her, lifting her hips off the desk as he crushed his mouth over hers and pushed his sex into hers, right where Danica planned to keep him for the rest of the day. All right, so maybe she wouldn't keep him in her office all day, but she did plan to make love with him for the rest of the day. Or week. Or month.

Make that years. Many, many long happy years to come.

PRIVATE FANTASIES

1

Breasts. Boobies. Titties. Ta tas.

Call them what you will, in little more than a week, Logan Delaney was going to have a set worthy of cupping.

Logan glanced in the mirror mounted over her bedroom dresser and cupped her current rack. It was a lot like palming a flaccid penis—warm to the touch but nowhere near too exciting. Not that she'd palmed a lot of penises, flaccid or otherwise. The last few years, she'd had her hands on a grand total of one. And she had the depressing feeling that if she hadn't been smashed that night and didn't care that her bed partner looked like he fell out of the ugly tree and hit every branch on the way down, she wouldn't have gotten her hands on that one. Or at the very least, she wouldn't have wanted to get her hands on it or her body wrapped around it.

"I'm heading out, honey." Jim Delaney's booming voice echoed up the stairs to the second floor of the house and through Logan's bedroom door.

"'Kay. Have a good time, Daddy," she called back, then

winced with the realization her sixty-two-year-old father had a better chance of getting lucky than she did.

Not that she thought he would rush Sarita, whom he was going out with for the third time tonight, between the sheets, with Logan's mother's death still so fresh. Then again, her mother's death from ovarian cancer really wasn't that fresh. Hard to believe as it was, almost three years had passed. Three years since Logan had returned to Cristos Island to live and work alongside her father in an attempt to help fill the void left behind from losing his wife.

It was very possible that living under her father's roof was the reason for her pathetic lack of a sex life—she wasn't quite comfortable screaming her ecstasy over a raging, quaking orgasm with him in the bedroom next door. More likely, the reason she couldn't attract a guy with the charisma and sex appeal to set off her va-va-voom meter was the rest of her body resembled her chest—they both had all the eye-catching curves of a stick figure. And her profession . . . Let's just say the hunks weren't standing in line to do a female mechanic who preferred jeans, T-shirts, and a ball cap to short skirts, tight shirts, and the buttloads of makeup and sprays women put on their face and into their hair in the hopes some guy would come along and mess it up for them.

Logan couldn't exactly move out of the house tomorrow, leaving her father alone without forewarning, and she loved her job, so that wasn't about to change. However, her figure was. She'd scrimped and saved the last few years—totally cutting out her tri-daily trek to the island's only Starbucks for a Mocha Frappuccino—and she finally had the cash to make an investment on herself, in the form of grade A, first-class, just-gotta-get-your-mouth-on-'em breasts.

Soon, the hunks *would* be lining up to do her, to hurry her back to their place where they would barely be able to make it inside before they had to have their hands on her luscious body.

Soon, she would be spending next to every night screaming and quaking and climaxing until she couldn't come a drop more.

Logan gave the mirror another glance, plumping up her miniscule breasts in a loving hug that—my God—actually made it look like she had cleavage. She grinned over the fantasy that would soon be a reality. Just over a week to no-plumping-necessary cleavage and just over a month before the first day of the rest of her sex life.

A month was still a hell of a long time.

Orgasm didn't have to be so far off. Her father was out for the night, and her favorite vibrator, which never failed to set off her va-va-voom meter, was stashed beneath her underwear in her top dresser drawer, conveniently within grabbing distance.

Thinking about the pink, rubber-coated vibrator buzzing away inside her had her inner thighs tingling with warmth. That warmth was nothing compared to the heated sensations that shot through her when she stripped off her shorts and panties, lay back on the bed covers, and touched the spinning head of the dildo against her pussy lips.

Moisture pooled within her sex with that first touch. Moisture that grew exponentially, along with the heat spiraling in her belly and working its way up her torso as she closed her eyes and imagined the hottie who had ruled her fantasies for weeks now.

Light green eyes. Thick, curling chestnut hair. A tall, leanly muscled build created for wrapping her legs around and scraping her nails over . . . if she actually had nails.

In her fantasy, Logan had nails to envy. In her fantasy, she was already curvalicious.

God bless Rob for delivering her this fantasy. A coworker at her father's garage, Rob was the lone doable candidate to show a sexual interest in her since her return to Cristos. Not that it had made a difference. Minutes into their date, they'd realized his sister, Isabella, had been in Logan's high school class and shortly after that discovered Isabella had slept with one of

Logan's past lovers. Rob wasn't about to go where someone who'd done his little sister had been, and Logan was pretty well icked out by the whole scenario, too.

Rob didn't let her famished libido down completely. When he'd learned she would be having breast augmentation done at Private Indulgence, a medical tourism resort on a neighboring West Indies island, he'd let her in on a secret. A resort tradition in the form of a Don Juan employee who picked a new female patient every week or so and made her stay more pleasurable by gifting her body with his oh-so-skilled hands and a cock celebrated for its size and aptitude.

Rob had learned of the guy through his friend Vivian, who'd gone to the resort to have the side effect of too much Ben & Jerry's sucked from her thighs and ended up experiencing Don Juan's talents firsthand. Logan knew just enough about the guy to make her dangerous in her ability to track him down and convince him she should be his next lucky resort-guest lover. To make him the first in a long line of hotties who would soon be spending naked, hot, and juicy time alone with her.

"Tanner." Logan mouthed Don Juan's name on a throaty sigh as she slipped the big pink vibrator fully inside her.

Moving a hand between her bent legs, she parted her labia and rubbed her engorged folds against the textured shaft of the dildo as she thrust it in and out of her passage.

Her wetness intensified with each pump until it wasn't a vibrator inside her but Tanner's legendary cock. Tanner's adept fingers spreading her slick folds. Tanner toying with her aching clit. Circling. Rubbing. Pressing without mercy against the highly aroused pearl.

Logan's belly tightened. Her heart pounded. Heat blistered through her body. She fought to keep her eyes closed.

Tanner rewarded her efforts, licking his gifted tongue over her plump pussy. He ate at her with masterful sucks, forceful laps, searing nibbles of his teeth upon her hypersensitized flesh.

His tongue speared into her cunt, and she nearly came off the bed with the violent arching of her hips.

Raw, needy, aching, she pumped against his face, forcing his tongue deeper inside her hot, wet body. Forcing him to give no less than everything. And he gave it—oh, wow, did he ever.

She bit her lip to quell her scream of release, but it wouldn't be stopped. "Yes, Tanner! Oh, God, yes!"

Her sex exploded with cream, drenching Tanner's tongue and spilling over into his mouth. Still, he licked, sucked, ate, devoured her whole.

Logan rode out the toe-curling orgasm, basking in sensual bliss for long seconds after the breath-stealing spasms ended. Then she opened her eyes and came down to the hard reality of a buzzing dildo fucking her with programmable-plastic precision.

With a groan, she lay back on the bed and tossed the vibrator aside. "How pathetic are you, coming with the first lick? And it wasn't even a real lick!"

Obviously, really pathetic, or at least really horny. All it took was the reemergence of Tanner's imagined sexy smile to have her grabbing the vibrator, twisting it on, and shoving it back between her thighs for yet another screaming, quaking, raging fantasy orgasm.

"Remember, I won't be around the next couple weeks." Logan had hoped to remind her father about her impending absence without having him recall the reason.

The disapproving look on his sweat-flushed face as he rolled on a dolly from beneath an old blue Chevy truck said he remembered all too well why she would be gone. He sat up and gave his head a shake. The top of his head was apparently as sticky as the rest of him from working in the garage's trapped heat, as his gray-blond hair didn't budge. "Still have that nonsense in your head about needing to look more girly?"

"It's not nonsense, Daddy." How could it be when clothed in her work uniform—shapeless gray cotton coveralls—it was nearly impossible to tell her apart from the guys? "But, yes. I'm going to have the surgery."

"Fine. It's not nonsense. It's a crock of shit. You're perfect as is—a near replica of your mother. She didn't need fake knockers to win my heart, and you don't need 'em either."

Logan struggled to hold in her grimace. They should be talking carburetors and fuel lines, not about her boobs, or lack thereof. "I don't want to win some guy's heart. I already have yours," she added in the hopes of turning things light and soothing him in the meanwhile.

His hard look gentled, easing the lines time and the Caribbean sun had etched into his face. He let out a boisterous laugh. "You're as much of a tease as your mother was." Sobriety returned to his eyes. "I hate the idea of you going under a knife for no reason, honey, you know that, but if it's what you want, I'm here for you."

Guilt threatened Logan with the words, because she knew exactly how much he hated surgery, particularly that which didn't ease or cure an ailment. Her mother had gone through a number of operations in an attempt to get all of her cancer. In the end, nothing had been enough to save her.

As much as she'd loved her mother and hated knowing the pain she'd gone through in her final months, Logan wasn't her. God willing, she had sixty-plus years ahead of her, and she wanted those years to be as enjoyable as possible. Being horny in a way her vibrator could only temporarily placate was not enjoyable.

Refusing to cave to the guilt, she squatted to kiss her father on the cheek. "Thanks, Daddy. It's what I want." Straightening, she righted her ball cap, which she wore as much to keep her hair out of the way as to shield her eyes and face from the sun when working outside. "I'm leaving early to finish packing."

Logan was nearly to the door of the garage staff area when an unfamiliar man's voice called her name.

"You Logan?" he questioned, this time from directly behind her.

"I am." She turned toward him and nearly laughed in his face.

One thing about working on an island flooded with convention hotels, you never knew who your next customer would be. Though the guy looked like a Vulcan fresh off the *USS Enterprise*, with his blue and black bodysuit, silver bracelets, whitish green face paint, and matching pointy ears, more likely it was time for the annual Star Trekkicon.

"Rob there said you might be able to help me out." The Vulcan wannabe pointed to the other side of the garage, where a late twentysomething, dark-blond-haired Cuban in coveralls that matched Logan's own checked the oil on a red Miata.

She took advantage of Vulcan Man's head being turned and made a face at Rob—he knew damned well she was trying to leave. In return, he sent her the sexily amused smile that, along with the killer way he filled out his uniform, had given her high hopes of ending up in his bed.

"Shortly after I drove off the ferry," Vulcan Man said, "my 'Vette started acting funny whenever I shifted. The last time it jerked so damned hard, I thought I was gonna fly through the windshield."

Logan brought her attention back to him. Thoughts of the sex she'd never had with Rob, or any guy in eons, had her giving him a better look. Past his pointy ears, face paint, and the glove-tight bodysuit, he was actually quite good-looking. Sandy brown hair and hazel eyes. Nicely defined facial structure. And, then again, that bodysuit might not be such a bad thing. It made blatantly clear the impressive size of his package.

Maybe he stuffed. And maybe he was attractive enough for her to look past his Star Trek fetish and find out firsthand whether the bulge in his bodysuit was *au naturale*.

As fetishes went, his wasn't even that bad. She liked the long-running sci-fi show just fine. Had spent more than one lazy weekend in her teens tossing back chips and soda and watching a Trekkie marathon with the guys. Well, except most of the time she'd done as much watching of the guys as of the episodes. Not that any of them had noticed. Hell, most of them probably still hadn't figured out she was female.

"So, what do you think? Can you check it out, or is it outta your experience level?"

Logan frowned. Had she fazed out there, or what part of the conversation had she missed for him to think she wasn't up to the job? Or hadn't she missed anything? Was this because she was a woman?

Her hackles wanted to rise. She kept them restrained to ask, "What do you mean?"

"You look and sound pretty young to know all that much."

Okay, so not about her gender. Still, he was questioning her know-how, and that pissed her off nearly as much. Enough to forget about leaving early. "I'm not that young. I'll take a look right now."

"Yeah, you probably aren't." Vulcan Man's eyes glazed over as his mind seemed to drift to some far-off time.

He actually looked better that way. Definitely not old enough to be thinking back too far. His face didn't have the slightest wrinkle. Just a straight nose, strong jawline with the first traces of five o'clock shadow, and lips full and soft-enough-looking to suggest she would enjoy pressing hers against them. A few brushes of mouth against mouth, a little teasing with her tongue, and then she'd go for the kill, licking her way into his mouth and, soon thereafter, his bodysuit.

"Hell, I remember when I graduated from high school. My voice was softer than yours, and it took me another two years before I shot up to six foot. Your time's coming, kid."

Logan's daydream burst on a barely suppressed gasp. Did he

imply what she thought he'd implied? That she was a guy! Silently seething, she jerked out her hand, palm up, and spoke none too gently, "Keys."

Vulcan Man appeared oblivious to her tone, giving her a three-thousand-watt smile that a few seconds ago probably would have had her wet. He handed over the keys and followed behind her as she went outside to where his metallic blue Corvette was parked. She started the engine and popped the hood.

"Hey, thanks," he said, all but breathing down her neck, making her want to slap the ridiculous pointy ears off his head. "I appreciate you squeezing me in. Sure, I can catch an island taxi if I need to go more than a half mile, but that doesn't exactly shout *impressive* to the women."

Her temper shot up. Yeah, he definitely thought she was a guy. Just for the hell of it, she pitched a little bass into her voice. "Sounds like you're going after the wrong type of women if they judge you by your transportation."

He gave a snorting laugh. "I'm on vacation, kid. They got a nice rack, they're my type."

If that didn't alternately make her blood boil and prove how right she was in getting a boob job, nothing did.

Shutting out the cling-on looming behind her, Logan worked in silence. She enjoyed a nice long inward laugh when she discovered his problem wasn't repairable—at least, not tonight. Straight-faced, she broke the news to him. "I've got bad news for you. Your transmission's shot. Looks like you'll have to pick up the sort of rack—I mean, woman—who doesn't have a problem with a taxi."

Vulcan Man looked ready to streak his face paint with tears. Biting back her smile, she handed him his keys. "Don't forget to pay the cashier."

She tugged off her ball cap as she headed back for the garage, letting her nearly waist-length dark brown hair fall free as she gave her best attempt at a provocative sway of her hips. The sound of the dickhead's breath catching when he realized his mistake did wonders for her ego. But that was nothing compared to the way it would soar in a month, when she had a rack of her own and beefcakes brawling for a spot in her bed to show for it.

"Remember to look up Tanner when you're on the island," Rob called to her just before she made her escape into the staff bathroom to shower and change.

"I mean it, Vage. Viv says it's a tradition, and, hell, you're way overdue for an *orgasmo* that isn't thanks to a vibrating chunk of plastic."

Logan sucked in a breath. For a moment, she was torn between crossing the garage and beating the shit out of Rob for calling her Vage—short for "grease monkey with a vagina"— and beating the shit out of him for bringing up her sex life within listening distance of customers, let alone her father. He'd said *orgasm* in Spanish, but like adding a little accent and an *o* to the end of the word did anything to camouflage its meaning.

In the end, Logan skipped the beating and gave him the finger. After all, she couldn't be too hard on him. Not when it was all his doing she would be naked and sweaty and huffing and puffing on the verge of climax with the Don Juan of orgasms in less than twenty-four hours.

Unless Tanner was already occupied with another lucky guest of the week by the time she arrived.

But hell, no. That wasn't a possibility. She would be spending the time until her surgery catching up on all the orgasms she missed out on these last years. And it would be with Tanner, resort tradition and all-around fantasy man. Any other outcome was unacceptable.

2

Logan stiffened self-consciously with the knock on the consultation room door. Totally ridiculous considering she was about to let the doctor doing the knocking fondle her breasts. Okay, not fondle, but hands-on examine them.

"Come in," she called.

The door opened, letting in a guy who could easily grace the cover of *GQ*. His dark hair curled an inch or two over the collar of his navy polo shirt, which encased broad shoulders that shouted "perfect for gripping." His friendly smile cut gorgeous creases around the corners of his mouth, and his light green eyes held a wounded edge that made her want to jump off the reclining chair and soothe him with her tongue.

Remembering where she was and why had Logan forgoing a tonguing to cover her chest with her hands. The front split in the white and yellow terry-cloth gown was tied shut, covering her as much as a shirt would, but the material wasn't close to thick enough to hide the suddenly erect state of her nipples.

"This room's occupied."

His smile grew, warming his eyes and moistening her panties. "I see that."

"So, then, uh, shouldn't you go?" Or could she be lucky enough to learn he was a complimentary part of her resort package? Hers to use and sensually abuse as she pleased. Mmm . . . the possibilities.

He moved into the room. Her surroundings had surprised her in that, aside from the stiff white paper covering the lower half of her chair, nothing came close to resembling an exam room. Exotic local artwork and lavish furniture filled the insides of the buildings, and Conch-style architecture, which blended Old World style with New World comfort, constituted their outsides. The entire resort looked more like a . . . well, a resort than a hospital facility. The staff was 100 percent professional, though, at least those employees Logan had met in the few hours she'd been at Private Indulgence.

"Not unless you've changed your mind about the implants." Stopping within touching distance, he extended his hand. "Dr. Grey. I'll be performing your surgery."

She felt her mouth fall open but couldn't do a thing about it. "Oh, my God. I expected your father."

"You'd have to go to Hell to find him."

"I mean you don't look old enough—" She stopped short to frown. "Did you just tell me to go to hell?"

He laughed. "I guess I did. I meant Hell, Michigan, where I grew up and where my parents still live."

Her belly zinged with warmth. What a wonderful laugh. Full-bodied. Deep. So masculine. Like the guy himself. And he was her doctor. The man who would be feeling her up shortly, for completely medical reasons.

Damn. Life was so not fair. "Your picture wasn't on the brochure with the rest of the aesthetic surgeons."

"You must have an outdated copy. I joined the resort medical team over a year ago." He pulled a wheeled stool out from under a massive oak desk on the opposite side of the room and sat down less than two feet away.

Though Logan would place his height right around six feet, the stool had him at a disadvantage. If he leaned forward, his mouth would be at breast level. In his line of work, he had to be an expert at nipple stimulation. One suck of his warm, wet mouth and she was bound to be squirming. Or maybe it wouldn't take that much, since she found herself squirming just thinking about his full, sensual lips latched onto her nipple. The paper beneath her crinkled with her shifting.

He lost his smile. "If you would rather work with someone older, Ms. Delaney, that's understandable, but I can assure you I'm more than accredited to do your surgery. I did my residency and fellowship in plastic and reconstructive surgery at the University of Michigan, then spent three years on the surgeon's team there. I'm certified by the American Board of Plastic Surgery and do hundreds of augmentations each year. Should I go on?"

Just because he was a lot younger than she'd expected and sent her va-va-voom meter soaring didn't mean he wasn't the right man for the job. "No. You shouldn't have had to say that much. I'm sorry I second-guessed you."

"Don't be." The right side of his mouth curved up, revealing an endearingly sexy lopsided smile. "I would have told you my credentials even if you hadn't asked. I want my patients to be as comfortable as possible."

Logan almost laughed over the irony of his words. If he wanted his patients comfortable, he should seriously consider doing something about his appearance. Like not washing his hair for a couple weeks and wearing clothes suited to a doctor.

Where was his long, white, totally shapeless coat, for cripes sake? "Could you put your glasses on?"

He gave her an odd look. "I don't wear glasses."

"Right." Perfect vision. Perfect face.

He stood and went to the desk, grabbing her patient folder from beside a small potted cactus situated off to the right-hand corner. Her mouth watered over the way his tan slacks pulled taut across his firm backside, and her hormones all but did a standing ovation.

Perfectly graspable ass.

He turned back, his groin coming into view. Her pussy contracted with her wondering if his cock was perfect, too. Something told her he would be a slow and thorough lover, petting and stroking every inch of her, ensuring she was trembling with need before he slid inside her wet body and saw to both of their pleasures with the pumping of his hips.

Logan resisted the urge to shift a second time. This man was her doctor, not a viable lover candidate. Of course, it would be a heck of a lot easier to remember that if someone killed the seductive bedroom melody floating down from the overhead speaker system.

Sheesh, this was the Caribbean—didn't they have any Bob Marley or some similar upbeat island music?

He returned to the stool and rested his right ankle over his left knee. He set her folder across the side of his bent leg and opened it, scanning over the gazillion questions she had to fill out in preparation for the consultation. After jotting a few notes, he asked without looking up, "No allergies?"

Good. He was all business. She could be, too. "No."

"And you don't smoke?"

"Not unless I'm really pissed off at someone." She could be *mostly* all business. He'd been asking for that bad pun of a response.

He looked up, his frown back in place. "Does that happen a lot? I have to warn you, smoking can have serious side effects. Not only is there the potential for delay in the healing process, but it can cause your skin to die, leaving bad scars."

Either the pun was worse than she thought, or he had no

sense of humor. Logan went with the latter. *All the better to resist fantasizing about you, my dear.* "I didn't mean that kind of smoking. I meant like out of my ears." The way he just sat there looking at her suggested he still wasn't getting it, so she let it go with a shrug. "I don't smoke. Ever."

Finally, he gave an appeased nod and returned to the Q&A. Logan relaxed a little more with each question, until she almost forgot how hot he was. Then she did forget, as the one question she'd been dreading popped into her head.

He stopped midsentence to give her a concerned look. "You look like you want to say something."

She fidgeted on the chair, not caring how much the paper crinkled. All she could think about was her father's stricken expression when she'd first told him she would be having surgery. "Um, yeah. I know there's a small chance of death with any surgery. What are the odds I'm going to die?" The low pitch of her voice reflected her nerves, so she added lightly, "Because I have to tell you, Dr. Grey, that would really suck."

"Call me Tanner, and yes, that would suck, wouldn't it?" His eyes flashed with playful teasing; then he was Mr. Medical again, responding in a humorless but confident tone, "You're right, complications can arise in any surgery, particularly where anesthesia is involved. However, I have a zero mortality rate, and I plan to keep it that way as long as I'm practicing."

Logan breathed a sigh of relief . . . and then nearly fell off her chair when his first name caught up with her. Words gasped out before she could stop them: "Holy shit!" Belatedly, her hand flew to her mouth.

Tanner sat forward, looking ready to pull her into his arms and rescue her from whatever horrible thing had overtaken her thoughts. "What's the matter?"

Something huge. Something that could only happen to her. This lip-smackingly good-looking man, this doctor who was about to touch her breasts in a totally clinical fashion, was

Tanner. *The* Tanner. The guy who dominated her fantasies. The guy whose name had screamed from her lips with every orgasm for weeks now.

She'd guessed Tanner to be a groundskeeper or something similar. Not a plastic surgeon with the looks and, undoubtedly, the money to have whatever woman he wanted.

He still looked ready to be her white knight, so she placed her hand in her lap next to its mate and forced a nonchalance she couldn't begin to feel. "Nothing. I just . . . realized I forgot to eat lunch."

His expression said he wasn't buying it, but he let it go with a nod. "We should only be another twenty minutes or so."

"Good." Now that she knew who he was, her hormones were jumping around so wildly it was like she'd discovered a buffet of masculine virility waiting for her to indulge in by taking a bite.

One bite would never be enough.

With Tanner, Logan would be a glutton of the worst kind, wanting to bite and nibble and consume him whole. Only with Tanner, none of that would be happening. Not now that she knew what a huge conflict of interest it would be sleeping with him.

"How big are you hoping to go?"

"What would turn your head?" Damn. That was the absolute last thing she should have said.

For a guy who supposedly slept with a new woman every week or two, he looked surprised by the question and maybe even a little uncomfortable. He shifted on the stool, straightening his bent leg, forgetting that her patient folder lay across it. He caught the folder just before it hit the carpet and belched out the bulk of her life history. Folder secured in his hand, he asked, "On you?"

Had she been mistaken on who he was? Or how did Rob's

friend fail to mention Tanner of the oh-so-skilled hands and legendary cock had all the finesse of a walrus? "Yeah."

His gaze slid to her breasts, his eyes narrowing as he studied her chest so intently it was as if he could see through the terry cloth to the itty-bitty titties beneath. Only, he didn't seem to notice their microscopic size. Or if he did, he didn't mind. As close as he sat, she could see the subtle darkening of his irises, the slight dilation of his pupils. She could hear his heightened breathing. Then Logan realized it wasn't his breathing but hers.

She was the one all but hyperventilating, the one with rock-hard nipples and a growing ache in her pussy. All from a look.

Oh, yeah. He *had* to be the right Tanner.

She sighed quietly. How was she supposed to view him as her doctor when all she wanted to do was relive her every screaming, quaking fantasy of him in the flesh?

He continued to study her breasts through the thin robe, his gaze caressing her more thoroughly than any past lover had managed to accomplish with their hands and tongue combined. Before it got to be too much, before she would have given in to her damp, deprived body by saying to hell with their doctor/ patient relationship and begging him to pick her as his next lucky resort guest lover, he looked away.

"You look amazing to me just the way you are." His voice was deeper, thicker.

She might have been the one breathing hard, but the signs of arousal she'd witnessed in his eyes were genuine. He'd definitely been affected. How affected?

"Your build is on the petite side," Tanner continued, his tone back to factual, "so a small C cup would look the most natural. At the same time, I've seen up to three sizes larger done where a natural result was attained and the patient was very happy they went with that size." He flashed a tight smile. "Not much help, am I?"

More than he would ever know in the getting-her-hot department, but otherwise not really, particularly since he thought she was amazing as is.

Yeah, right. That had to be his dick talking. Though, even his dick liking her as is was a start . . . and totally irrelevant to the conversation. "I guess I'll go with the small C."

"This isn't a decision to make lightly, Ms. Delaney," he scolded, sounding like her father to an eerie perfection.

"Call me Logan, and I know. I didn't mean for it to sound that way." Her mind just wasn't fully engaged on the discussion.

Focus was needed here. To remember why she came to the resort and not the part about doing her fantasy man either. Rather, to earn her a lineup of hunks all eager to get their hands on her grade-A rack. "I want huge Cs that scream *female*."

Tanner's eyes narrowed a fraction, and he glanced down at her paperwork. He scanned it a few seconds before looking back at her. "You didn't fill in the reason for surgery."

"It seemed like a moot question. I want bigger ta tas."

The lopsided smile made an appearance, budding the delectable creases at the corners of his mouth. "The question is actually *why* do you want them?"

Because she could imagine how incredible his mouth would feel running over them. And that was officially the last time she was going to think about him and her and sex. "Because I'm tired of looking like a popsicle stick minus the popsicle."

"You feel the surgery will boost your self-image?"

"And get me laid." Whoops, had she said that out loud?

His face revealed his shock. Then his gaze was sliding along her body, from head to toe and back again, lingering on all those parts that weren't supposed to be thinking of him, but oh, boy, were they ever.

Tanner's eyes met hers, his saturated with a sensual interest she would have to be dead to miss. "I find it hard to believe you have a problem in that area."

Logan wanted to be good, she really did. But when he was looking at her that way—like she was an honest-to-god alluring woman even without noticeable breasts, snug-fitting clothes, makeup, or any of the other crap so many women relied on—it made being good so hard. And not even close to desirable. Being naughty sounded much better.

She'd spent the entire consultation sitting up. Now she reclined back on the angled chair, allowing her hands to slide downward until her fingertips dipped between her narrowly parted thighs and brushed against her crotch through her cotton shorts. Her pussy had been moist from nearly the moment Tanner walked into the room. That one little touch was all it took for her sex to flood with cream.

"The last time I had a man-induced orgasm"—she sounded breathy, sexy, nothing like herself and absolutely perfect for this moment—"was nearly three years ago. If it wasn't for vibrators, I would've forgotten how to come."

Color rose into Tanner's cheeks. His fingers curled around the sides of her patient folder, which seemed to be sitting a little higher on his lap than before. Was his legendary cock trying to make an appearance?

He cleared his throat. "Yes, well, um . . ."

"How much bruising should I expect?"

He gulped audibly. "Bruising?"

Logan barely resisted snorting out a laugh. He thought she was talking about rough sex. Well, if she'd ever deserved a spanking, now was definitely it. Her ass tingled with the prospect of his fingers swatting against it. No doubt it would be an experience to fantasize about for years to come. Or come over for years as she fantasized.

Since she really did want to know the answer to her question, she shut out the delicious tingling of her backside and straightened in her chair to clarify, "Following surgery."

Tanner visibly relaxed, as if switching back to doctor mode was all that saved him from ravishing her. God, what a heady thought. "My hematoma rate—severe bruising—is two to three percent; the industry average is five to eight percent. A lot of it depends on your skin type, how smoothly the surgery goes, and where we go in at. In general, I prefer going through the underarm."

He stood from the stool, setting her patient folder back on the desk. The tingling in Logan's ass raced to her breasts when he pumped soap into his palm and used the sink built into the counter near the door to wash his hands. She held her breath, knowing even before he said it they'd reached the examination part of the visit.

Tanner went to the door, opening it and calling a female nurse into the room. Logan assumed the striking blonde was a nurse anyway. Her hair and makeup looked more suited to a club setting, and her lavender silk blouse clung to high, full breasts that suggested she'd taken advantage of the employee discount. On second thought, maybe the blonde wasn't a nurse. Maybe she was a female heavyweight here for the purpose of holding Logan back in the event she could no longer control her lust and attempted to throw herself at Tanner.

Her tension relaxed a little with the absurd idea, and still her hands shook and her pulse sped as she disrobed. She swore she could feel his gaze lock on her bared breasts. But when she glanced over, his attention appeared to be completely engaged on whatever he discussed with the blonde.

Another fifteen seconds of talk and Tanner crossed the room to stand a few feet away. He didn't even glance at Logan's breasts, which mildly annoyed her, before introducing the blonde as Melinda, a registered nurse studying to be a plastic surgeon. Any annoyance Logan felt vanished in the next instant, as Tanner's attention went to her chest, visually inspecting her nearly nonexistent breasts.

With the other woman standing guard, she shouldn't feel stimulated, but Logan did, maybe even more so, as twisted as that was. Her nipples jabbed toward Tanner's hand, silently begging for his touch.

Heat rose into her cheeks over her totally inappropriate response. She feigned a shiver. "It's a little cold in here."

"I can heat you up."

"*What?*" And did she hear Melinda snicker?

"I can turn the heat up," Tanner said.

"Oh. That's okay. I'm your last client today. No sense in turning this place into a sweatshop just for me." Yet another bad choice of words. It brought to mind a vision of Tanner naked, steam rising up around his leanly muscled body, perspiration glistening on his tanned skin. His cock huge and hard and filling his hand. His skilled surgeon's fingers stroking from tip to base, spreading the pre-cum that seeped from the meaty head—

The real-life Tanner's fingers moved over her breasts, and Logan nearly arched her hips in reaction. Sighing out, "Oh, my . . ." wasn't much better.

He ceased the poking and prodding, which felt much more like rubbing and stroking. "Sorry. Are my hands cold?"

More like sizzling. "No. I . . . my nipples are sensitive." That time she definitely heard the nurse snicker. Tanner wasn't snickering. He actually looked a little annoyed.

Really, who could blame him? He was being the consummate physician, and she was being hot and bothered.

"You may lose some sensitivity in them following surgery. In most cases, it comes back after a few months, but it can take up to a year or so."

"I love having my nipples pinched." Logan bit her tongue. Jesus, why had she said that? Next, she might as well suggest he go ahead and give 'em a pinch.

For a second, as his eyes lifted to hers and she discovered it wasn't annoyance in his but desire, Logan thought he might do exactly that. Then her stomach let loose with a loud rumble, and he lifted his hands from her breasts and stepped back.

"Sorry," she said, half relieved, half wanting to do bodily harm to her damned stomach. "Like I said, I skipped lunch."

He glanced at his watch. "I didn't realize how late it is. Anyway, you look perfect—like a perfect candidate for surgery. You'll need to call in the morning to schedule an appointment with my assistant to have before-photos taken and confirm the implant size." He inclined his head at the nurse. "Melinda will help you try on some sample implant bras now to give you a better idea of the size you're after. Unless you have further questions for me, you and I are all set."

Tanner was suddenly talking at warp speed, which pretty much suggested he would rather stab out his own eyes than stay in this room and answer her questions.

"Nothing at the moment," she said.

"Good." He backed toward the door. "Call if anything comes up. Otherwise, I'll see you Friday morning. Remember, no alcohol forty-eight hours prior to surgery, and nothing to eat or drink, period, after midnight on Thursday."

"Or I'll start multiplying and pick up all sorts of nasty habits." Nice. She already had him running from her, and now she had to go and be extra corny. "Never mind. Bad humor. See you Friday, Dr. Grey." Only, Logan knew better. Even using his doctor designation wouldn't be enough to stop her from seeing him tonight, hot and hard and fucking her in her fantasies.

"Since when is helping a patient select her implant size my job?"

With Melinda's question, Tanner pulled his attention away from his office window, where a fast-falling rainstorm pelted the turquoise water of the Caribbean Sea. Watching the tide crash against the white sand shoreline had always done wonders for his nerves. Tonight, it didn't do a damned thing. He was tense as hell, and it had everything to do with the flat-chested brunette Melinda questioned him over.

Though he could guess she knew exactly why he hadn't wanted to spend more time with Logan, he swiveled in his chair and dismissed Melinda's question with a shrug. "I figured you would appreciate the experience."

She smiled knowingly. "You like her."

Shit, he wanted to lie, to tell her he didn't know a thing about Logan so how could he possibly like her? But Tanner and Melinda had been friends for nearly thirty years—neighbors both back in Michigan and on the island—and he knew Melinda would see through his words in a heartbeat. "She's different."

Her smile turned smug. She pulled out one of the patient chairs in front of his desk and sat down, crossing her arms and plumping the double Ds he'd personally given her, until they threatened to spill out of her shirt's low-cut neckline. "She worries you."

Tanner looked at her breasts. Why couldn't he get aroused over Melinda? They would make the perfect couple. Instead he had to spend the duration of Logan's consultation fighting off a hard-on that had as much to do with her intimate admissions as her quirky personality. "She doesn't worry me."

"All right, then she threatens that little vow you made to yourself. You know, the one about remaining celibate until a woman you can potentially see a future with enters your life?"

He swore under his breath, because that much she was right about. "Don't you have somewhere to be?"

After giving him a displeased look for keeping her late, she stood, smoothing her hands down her short black skirt with an inborn sensuality. "I had somewhere to be half an hour ago. By now, Jaelin's probably figured I stood him up and has his dick pressed up against some beach bimbo."

Though she was over a decade older than him, in her late forties, Melinda didn't have a line on her Botox-injected face, and her body was better than that of most twenty-year-olds. She was one hot number, and he couldn't see a guy letting her go that easily. "Then he's an idiot."

She laughed huskily as she made her way to the door. "He's a male, sweetie. That much is a given."

Where the bulk of the male population was concerned, Tanner would agree. But since he probably fit into that bulk right now, he stood up for the team, saying darkly, "Good night, Mel."

"Night." She closed the door behind her as she left his office, only to pop her head back inside less than a minute later. "Just thought you should know your patient's still in the building, so don't lock her in." She grinned naughtily. "Unless, of course, you plan to stay in with her and offer to heat her up again by performing a more thorough exam."

Tanner's cock jerked with the suggestion as she made her exit. And he hated that. Goddamned hated himself for not being able to contain his libido around Logan.

Even if she did interest him more after an hour than most of his previous lovers had after a week, she wasn't going to end up in his bed. For one thing, she was his patient—he'd slept with numerous resort guests before making his vow to take sex more seriously again, but never with one of his patients. For another thing, Logan lived in Miami. He had a long-distance relationship once, and considering its bitter end was the reason behind his recently forgotten Lothario ways, he wasn't even going to consider going down that road.

Just because he wasn't going to screw her didn't mean they couldn't be friends.

Mentally calming his cock as he walked, Tanner went in

search of her. He found her in the waiting area, eyeing a wall collection of before-and-after breast shots. He'd done most of the surgeries in the collection and hadn't felt even slightly aroused. Hell, he'd never felt aroused over one of his patients, period. But watching Logan eye those breasts . . . It made him think thoughts that weren't close to professional.

He cleared his throat to let her know he was there, asking when she looked his way, "Did you have more questions?"

A flush crept into her cheeks, as if she suddenly found the objects of her attention as erotic as he did. "No. Just checking out some pictures to see what I might look like afterward."

"Not like a Gremlin."

Humor glistened in her soft brown eyes. "You got that, huh?"

"I got that." Though he was surprised she remembered the *Gremlins* movie. Her file said she was twenty-six, which would have made her three when the sci-fi film about furry little creatures who multiplied when exposed to water and turned evil when you fed them after midnight came out in theaters. And him . . . too damned old for her. Eleven years separated them—just another reason he should cease all future thoughts of her naked for purely pleasurable reasons. "And the bit about steam coming out of your ears when someone pisses you off. I'm heading out for the night."

"You need me to go so you can lock up."

Exactly the intent. Only, his mouth seemed to have other ideas. "I'm not in that big of a rush."

"That's okay. I was about to leave." Logan grabbed a small stack of pamphlets from the seat of the chair near her thigh and started for the door. "See you Friday."

"Good night." *Sweet dreams*. Tanner refrained from tacking on that last part. Not because it would make him sound like a pansy. But because from the moment she turned and flashed her compact little ass at him, he knew he wouldn't stop at suggesting she have sweet dreams. He would end up planting some fantasy in her head that amounted to sticky, hot, dripping wet dreams starring her and him and her tight behind.

His cock gave an anxious twitch over the thought. Logan disappeared out the front door, blessedly taking her sweet ass with her. Time for him to leave as well. Go home to a cold beer and a colder shower.

Ah, fuck, who was he kidding? It would take a hand job to erase the effect of her unexpected appeal. A hand job he wouldn't be receiving via her slender fingers no matter how much the idea had his body throbbing and his heart rate skyrocketing.

3

If she knew what was good for her, Logan would keep walking, get back to her bungalow before the rain seeped through her tennis shoes the way it was quickly doing to everything else she wore. Unfortunately, she'd waited beneath the clinic's front canopy too long, in the hopes the rain would slow. Tanner's curses had alerted her to his presence seconds after she set off down the sidewalk. He must have come out a staff exit, because when she turned back, she discovered him forty feet away, standing in the parking lot before the raised hood of a Grand Cherokee. Obviously, he had Jeep trouble. Even more obvious was the fact that she couldn't walk away.

Vowing to behave, especially now that she knew he had a sense of humor, she joined him at the front of the vehicle. "Problems?"

He visibly jerked. Glancing at her, he narrowed his eyes. "I thought you left."

She should have been turned off by his glare, considering she'd risked the rain's wrath for him. If anything, it upped his appeal, knowing he wasn't the emotionless doctor he'd tried to present himself as, but rather the expressive man from the waiting area who'd eyed her as if he couldn't get her naked fast enough. The man Logan would not be getting naked with— fast, slow, or ever. She had had her moment of naughty fun; it was time to put things right. "I had, but then I heard the sound of a helpless vehicle in distress and couldn't keep walking."

"Won't turn over." Tanner leaned over the engine, touching parts here and there before jiggling the battery cables. He looked back at her and laughed self-deprecatingly. "I don't know what the hell I'm doing. I never took auto shop."

Perfect. If there was a guaranteed way to turn a guy off, it was showing him up in an area considered masculine. A quick fix to his car and their doctor/patient status would be secure.

Ignoring the disappointed flutter of her sex, she gave his elbow a shove. "Move over." She'd been working on cars for nearly a decade and spotted his problem right away. She drew it out so he wouldn't feel completely emasculated. After a good minute, she tightened the loose coil wire. "Give it a try now."

Tanner climbed into the Jeep. A few seconds passed, and the engine sputtered once and then roared to life. He came back around to the front of the vehicle. "I'm impressed."

What he was was appetizing as hell with his drenched overlong hair pushed back from his face as if he'd run his fingers through it when he'd been in the Jeep. Logan didn't dare look lower than his neck. His wet clothes would be plastered to his body, outlining every inch of delectable flesh and muscle.

She closed the hood to distract her mind from thoughts of one muscle in particular. "Don't mention it. It's fixed for now, but your coil wire's starting to corrode. Get it into the shop to have it looked at soon or you'll need to replace the plug wires, cap, and rotor. You might anyway." He was looking at her like Rob did right before he called her Vage. Exactly what she'd hoped for. And it irked her to no end. "I better go before I get any wetter. Not that it's possible; even my underwear feels squishy."

Tanner looked away, as if talk of her underwear made him uncomfortable, probably because he'd deduced her as the grease monkey she was with her quick engine fix and felt disgusted with himself for momentarily being attracted to her. "Which of the villas are you staying in?"

"The third bungalow off the pier." What was the harm in telling him now? It wasn't like she had to worry over him slipping inside and ravishing her. Logan tried to keep her moroseness from her voice. "I thought it would feel more like a vacation that way."

"They're nice, and over a mile from here." He nodded at the Jeep. "Let me give you a lift."

"I'll catch the bus." If she'd known it was pouring, she would have called for a pickup at the clinic's front door. But she hadn't and the nearest bus stop was far enough away she'd be too drenched to bother with a ride by the time she reached it.

He looked back at her. "It's the least I can do after you saved William."

"William?"

He smiled sheepishly. "My Jeep."

The rain had started to cool her, despite the salt air still being balmy. She wasn't cool anymore. One flash of his smile and it didn't matter what Tanner thought of her; she was warm right to the bone, not to mention damp in a way that had nothing to do with the rain. And, damn, on top of being sexy as hell, he had to go and say something quirky.

Logan sighed. They could have been so perfect together . . . if he wasn't her doctor . . . and she hadn't fixed his Jeep. "Most people name their vehicles after women."

"I've always had a soft spot for Shakespeare." He rounded to the driver's door, eyeing her over the roof. "Stop thinking about what a dork I am and get in."

"I wasn't thinking about what a dork you are." She was thinking proximity could be an evil bitch of temptation. Enough for her to forget he'd lost interest and make a move. "It's a sweet name and so was your offer of a ride, but like I said, I can't get any wetter. In fact, I think I'll skip the bus and walk to my bungalow."

"Get in the car, Logan." His gaze turned steely. "I can't do the surgery if you're sick."

Commanding her would get him nowhere. The comment about her not being able to have surgery if she was sick, however, was a valid point. Against her better judgment, she climbed inside. "So you're sweet and like to play dirty," she said, fastening her seat belt and trying to ignore his nearness and the way the rain on his skin made him smell deliciously earthy and extremely male. "Anything else I should know—like do you have serial-killer tendencies?"

Tanner snorted to himself as he pulled out of the clinic parking lot and onto the resort's service drive. She had the "he liked to play dirty part" right anyway. With her clothing soaked all the way through to her squishy underwear, he couldn't think of much else but playing dirty.

He shouldn't have offered to give Logan a ride, but he owed her, both for fixing William and for not rubbing in what an easy fix it had been. She'd played it off like the problem wasn't overt, but he was trained to note the details, and he knew she'd seen the trouble nearly the instant she looked under his hood.

Hell, he shouldn't be thinking about her looking under his hood either. Or him pulling back hers so he could suck on her clit for a while.

He groaned. For over two months he'd been celibate, waiting for the right woman to come along to share in meaningful sex with the potential to lead to a commitment of the marital kind. Less than an hour with Logan and he wanted to say to hell with his vow, stop the Jeep, and screw her here and now.

"Something wrong?" she asked.

Tanner wasn't about to risk looking at her rain-kissed face

with her long, dark hair sexily disheveled all about it. He concentrated on adjusting the wiper setting. "I just remembered I left a report on my desk I wanted to read tonight. Nothing I can't do in the morning."

Logan seemed to buy the lie because she didn't say anything more until they reached the pier a couple minutes later. With a rapid, "Thanks," she pushed open the passenger's door and jumped out of the Jeep like her seat was on fire. He climbed out just as fast, grabbing his umbrella from the floorboard between the seats and popping it open as he rounded to her side.

She didn't look impressed. "Let me guess, Shakespeare taught you chivalry isn't dead?"

"No, but the island directory taught me the pier's twelve hundred feet long, and your bungalow's more than halfway down it." He moved next to her, seeing they both got the best coverage from the umbrella as possible. It was a mammoth-sized golf umbrella, which meant he was closer than he needed to be, but she felt warm and smelled good, and since this was as intimate as things between them were going to get, he allowed himself to indulge. "I know you're hungry, so let's get moving."

Logan's hip brushed against his outer thigh with every few steps. Tanner never realized what an arousing sensation such a subtle brush could be. His groin tightened reflexively. Silently damning his libido, he turned his attention to the handful of resort guests walking along and fishing off the pier. An L-shaped breakwall created a channel between the sea and the shoreline, trapping the tide water that would otherwise crash over the pier and drench them far worse than the rain.

"Have you walked a lot of women down this pier?" Logan asked when they'd nearly reached her bungalow.

He glanced over at her. Was she suggesting he used the rain as an excuse to get inside her place and put the moves on her? Her expression didn't give anything away. "A few."

"Been inside the bungalows much?"

He looked over again. Still no expression and her voice was equally impassive. "I've stayed in them before."

"Then you know how to get the bed out of the wall?"

Tanner almost laughed with his relief. The odds she would want his help lowering her bed stopped him. He could be a good boy and resist temptation. Though, sticking that temptation by a bed, when her clothes were dripping wet and just asking to be stripped off, was pushing it. "They can be a bear to work. There's a lever hidden in the side of the mattress. You have to unzip the mattress cover to reach it."

Logan didn't speak again until they reached her bungalow. Unlocking the door, she moved just inside and turned back to smile. "Thanks for the umbrella. It was very gallant of you."

"Want me to be extra gallant and show you how to go down in your bed?" *Or stick my tongue in your pussy and have a little predinner snack?*

Christ, what was wrong with his mouth today? It was like her presence alone knocked a good forty points off his IQ. Turned him into a bumbling idiot whose only thoughts were of sex, sex, Logan, and more sex.

Surprise flickered across her face. Or was that interest? Whatever it was, she grabbed hold of his shirtfront and yanked him inside, umbrella and all. The umbrella was too big for the doorframe, and the spokes caught, sending it flying back outside and Tanner hard up against her warm, wet body.

He grabbed hold of her arms out of instinct, and then all he could do was stand and stare down at her. She had a petite build, but her height was on the average side. Her lips were slightly parted and not all that far from his own. Full and glistening and letting out sexy little puffs of hot air, they more than made up for her chest. Not that he had a problem with her small breasts. His cock was hard from the mere thought of taking them back into his hands and pinching her big, dusky nipples the way she loved.

"I think I heard you wrong over the rain." Her voice was low, throaty.

He lifted his gaze to find her eyes hazed over with lust. He spoke carefully this time, afraid one more wrong word choice was all it would take to break his vow by turning his patient into his lover. "I asked if you want me to show you how to get your bed down."

A wantonly wicked yes filled her seductively soft brown eyes. Thank God she was smart enough not to voice it. "No." Logan stepped back into the bungalow. "I don't think that's a good idea. Because I'm sure you're hungry, too."

She whirled away from him, glancing around the combined sitting area and kitchen, finally grabbing a thin resort booklet off the small, round kitchen table. "I just remembered there are directions on how to work the bed in here." She thumbed through the booklet, stopping on a page he could guess didn't mention a thing about the bed. "Yep. Right here," she said without looking up. "Thanks again for the ride. See you Friday."

"Friday." Four whole days from today. More than enough time to pull his head out of his ass. "Sweet dreams," Tanner added, then just managed to stop his tongue from painting a verbal scenario where it wasn't his head up his ass, but his tongue on her ass, licking away.

After closing the door, he grabbed the umbrella. He didn't bother holding it over his head as he hustled down the pier to the parking lot. Between his rapid pace and the rain's cool nip, he hoped to ease some of his frustration over his stupidity.

Tanner's frustration was still going strong when he reached his Jeep and climbed inside. Worse than his frustration was the raging-hard state of his dick. If he got into an accident, the air bag was liable to break it off.

Folding his arms over the steering wheel, he rested his head against them and cleared his mind. Several minutes passed before he had control of his body again. He straightened in the seat and turned the key in the ignition, the Jeep gunning to life in an instant thanks to a quirky brunette he wasn't going to think about. He backed out of the parking spot and made it almost thirty whole feet before a tight, round derriere in soaked cotton shorts caught his attention from the sidewalk that ran alongside the service drive.

He would recognize that ass anywhere. Apparently, so would his cock, as it stirred to awareness all over again.

He should pretend like he'd never seen Logan, let her take a walk in the rain as she seemed determined to do. But he really didn't want her getting sick. And he really did want to spend more time with her, if only to discover some facet of her personality that majorly turned him off.

Tanner hit the button for the passenger's side window and pulled up next to her. "You know, it wasn't just after midnight you didn't want to get a Gremlin wet. It was any time. Get in before you start multiplying."

A shudder snaked through him with the thought. Considering what a hard time he was having resisting one Logan, God forgive his behavior if he had to contend with multiples.

"Forget something at the clinic?" Tanner asked after Logan climbed inside the Jeep's passenger's side.

She hadn't forgotten anything at the clinic, but she'd apparently left her brain on Cristos to be back inside this temptation mobile. Now more tempting than ever because she knew he was still attracted to her, even after she'd threatened his male ego with her mechanic skills.

Back in the bungalow, the desire in his eyes had quickened her heart. The press of his hard cock against her belly had drenched her pussy. Saying no to his offer of bed help had been a pop quiz for her willpower. If he'd repeated what she knew he said the first time—an offer of oral sex—she would have purposefully failed the test.

Her sex pulsed with the imagined stab of his tongue inside her wet folds. Logan clamped her thighs together and cleared her mind. "I didn't forget anything."

Leaving the Jeep in park, Tanner glanced over at her. "Then what were you doing out in the rain again?"

"Getting dinner. I figured I was already so wet why bother taking the bus?"

"I'm on my way to get something. We can eat together."

Now there was a good idea—getting their first date out of the way. Yeah, right! "I don't like what you're having."

Amusement shone in his eyes, but he spoke seriously. "Then you can pick the place. The island isn't all that big, but the other side hosts a cruise-liner port, so there are quite a few restaurants and ethnicities to choose from."

"Mexican. I'm in the mood for some good gassy food."

This time he didn't bother to check his amusement but let out a hearty laugh as he slid the Jeep into drive. "One gut bomb coming up."

One nutcase pulling into traffic.

Tanner had to be nuts to still be attracted to her after a comment like her last one.

Logan really had skipped lunch, and the closet restaurant was a mile from the pier—a mile that seemed much longer with the continued onslaught of rain. For the sake of keeping her health and, therefore, getting her new breasts as scheduled, she gave in to the nutcase and fastened her seat belt. The soft *snick* as the lock mechanism grabbed hold didn't make her feel the least bit safe, but like she was trapped in a vehicle headed to nowhere good and everywhere she'd been fantasizing about going for weeks now.

* * *

"You're from Miami?"

Logan looked at the one place she'd avoided since sitting down at a corner table inside Castillo's—across the table at Tanner. Allowing his hair to dry naturally had produced a head full of rebellious curls that glistened even in the low lighting.

She was a sucker for curls. They made her want to grab hold of his dark, shiny locks and drag him across the table and onto her lap. She wouldn't need to wait for her wet burrito to arrive to sate her appetite. She could fill up on thick juicy cock.

His words reached her then. "I am?"

"That's what your patient folder says."

Obviously, she hadn't paid attention to the address area when they'd asked her to check her information for accuracy at the clinic today. That could have something to do with the fact that she'd been anxious as hell to see the doctor. She probably would have wet herself with excitement if she'd known that doctor was none other than the Don Juan resort tradition himself.

Logan considered explaining she'd been living in Miami when she decided to have implants and had relied on the post office to forward her nonfinancial mail after her abrupt move back to Cristos. But inevitably Tanner would want to know why she returned, and that would mean talking about her parents and making their relationship more intimate than it already was.

Instead she opted to sound like her few drinks of cabernet had gone straight to her head. "No, I was saying that like 'I am,' you know, agreeing with you. I like it there, lots of pretty, green palm trees." She lifted her wineglass and took a sip. The bold flavor was surprisingly light on her tongue. "This is good. Slightly tannic. Sharp with a smooth finish. I don't drink wine often, but when I do, it's always a red."

"The woman knows her way around an engine and wine,

too." The heat flaring in his eyes said what he hadn't. That he was truly impressed on both accounts.

Crap. She'd been holding out hope she could still turn this trip to fantasyland around. Thanks to her bigmouthed response to that last drink, the gas pedal was stuck to the floor.

Logan took another drink, this time draining the glass. Getting obnoxiously drunk had to be enough to throw the brakes.

Tanner grabbed the wine bottle and refilled her glass. He flashed a lopsided smile as he set her glass down. "Good thinking. Enjoy all you can tonight, since you won't be able to drink after tomorrow."

She wanted to scream, though she couldn't decide which thing to scream over—how completely his smile affected her hormones or how he seemed to think she could do no wrong. Given the odds that screaming would get her kicked out of the restaurant with her belly still empty, she settled for acting bitchy. "Tell me, Doc, do you wine and dine all your patients?"

"You're the first."

Narrowing her eyes, she laughed sardonically. "I bet."

The wounded look she'd noted in his eyes at his office returned. "I'm not saying I've never taken a resort guest out to dinner, just never one of my own patients. The whole doctor/ patient thing has a tendency to get messy fast."

For a second there, with the emergence of his hurt look, she'd felt guilty. Now, Logan felt like pouting. Immoral as it was, deep down she hadn't wanted to put the brakes on. She'd wanted him to like her so much as is that he was aching to take her back to the bungalow and show her how to go down on her bed. "I don't look like the type to make a mess?"

"You saved William. I owed you."

In other words, he hadn't really meant to offer to go down on her. Maybe he hadn't even said those words. Maybe her horny little head had imagined them.

Her head couldn't have imagined the impressive length of his cock against her stomach. Unless he was that big flaccid. Not that she would ever find out. Because he wasn't attracted to her. Probably only went for the type who wore buttloads of makeup and dressed in itty-bitty clothes precisely for his viewing pleasure.

The bastard.

The server arrived with their food before Logan could tell Tanner what she thought of his narrow-minded ways. Dressed in a cleavage-thrusting, gold and magenta uniform top that looked stunning against her dark brown skin and wearing makeup that made her nearly black irises seem huge while drawing out the rise of her cheekbones, the woman probably fit his dream-girl image to a T.

Or maybe not, considering he didn't even look the server's way. He just thanked her for the food and smiled at Logan. "*Apetito bueno.*"

Okay, so maybe he wasn't such a bastard. Maybe he was just a nice guy, with a really bad Spanish accent, who wanted to thank her for fixing his vehicle by buying her dinner. Maybe she should enjoy her food and stop thinking altogether.

"What the . . . ?"

She looked up from stabbing her burrito to death in the hopes her arousal would die with it. "What's the matter?" Had he realized what a grave error he made in not wanting her?

Tanner nodded toward the front of the restaurant. "Either I'm seeing things, or we're being invaded by aliens."

Nope. No error. Damn.

She looked at her plate and gave the burrito another death stab. Pale brown cheesy beany blood oozed everywhere. The dish smelled like heaven, but her stomach suddenly wasn't up to it. "You're not seeing things. The annual Trekkie convention's on Cristos this week."

"And you know this because you're a fan?"

"I know it because I live . . ." Logan looked up quickly, realizing what she'd almost said. Even if he wasn't attracted to her, she didn't want to go into depth about her personal life. "My dad lives there. I spent last week visiting and had the misfortune to cross paths with an asshole of a Spock impersonator. He thought I was a guy."

Tanner stilled a forkful of food midway to his mouth to look across the table. His gaze drifted from her face to her neck to her chest to areas hidden from view by the table. He gave a low whistle. "Now there's a bad joke if I've ever heard one—you being considered manly."

Her heart beat faster. Her pussy clenched excitedly. She resisted the urge to give her mangled burrito an apology hug.

Maybe he did want her. Maybe after another three or four glasses of wine, she would be bold enough to stop wondering and ask him outright. For now, she stuffed a forkful of wet burrito between her lips and watched his succulent mouth engage in the erotic act of mastication.

"Thanks for dinner." Now would he like to come inside and have some fresh cream for dessert? Logan wanted to say the words so badly, but she still wasn't positive he wanted her.

Tanner leaned against the doorjamb of her bungalow, his arms crossed leisurely over his chest. The rain had blown over, leaving behind a warm, salty breeze that toyed with his hair and made her fingers curl against her palms in jealousy.

He smiled, cutting those lickable creases around his mouth. "Thank you for fixing William."

She smiled back, daring to give his arm a gentle stroke. "Thank you for walking me to my door."

He came away from the doorjamb, stepping a foot into the bungalow, inches away from her. "Thank you for complimenting my taste in wine."

Something shifted in his mood with the words. His smile

went from closed-lipped languid to openmouthed sensual. She could just see the tip of his tongue past his teeth. Just imagine how amazing it was going to feel licking her pussy. And he *would* be licking her pussy. That shift in his mood made Logan feel sexy in a way she never thought possible with her tiny tits. It guaranteed he wanted her.

Heart pounding, she closed the space between them, not stopping until her breasts rubbed against his torso and her nipples spiked to instant hardness. She tipped her head back, eyeing his lips, parting her own. "Thank you for giving me a good-night kiss."

Tanner's hands came around to her back, sliding lower torturously slow to cup her ass. Her hips shot forward, and he thrust his against her, pivoting his groin at the last moment. Her pussy swelled with arousal. She felt light-headed in a way that had nothing to with the three glasses of wine she'd drank and everything to do with the size of his hard cock.

The real thing lived up to its legendary status . . . at least in magnitude. In ability, she was about to find out.

"You did do a great job of fixing William." He bent his head. "He purrs just like a kitten. Do you purr like a kitten, Logan?"

Yes. And she wouldn't mind a bit if he petted her pussy to find out.

His hold on her ass went from gentle to firm. His fingers kneaded the flesh of her buttocks as he slanted his mouth over hers, nibbling at her lips a few seconds before Logan parted them and demanded he come inside immediately with a low growl.

Tanner's tongue pushed into her mouth, licking over her teeth, her gums, and then against her own tongue. She licked back with relish, savoring his masculine flavor underlain with the taste of cabernet. Her body hummed with every caress. Her cunt grew wetter with every squeeze of his hands around her ass.

Leaving her panting, he pulled from her mouth and turned his wicked lips on her neck, nipping at the sensitive skin, laving her flesh until goosebumps rose and she shivered with the thrill. "Meeow!"

Grinning, he returned to her mouth, loving it long and hard and thoroughly as he ceased the kneading of her bottom to lift her up his body. He carried her through the bungalow, not stopping until he laid her on the couch. He didn't follow her down but jerked at the button of her shorts, sighing loudly when it gave way. He unzipped her shorts and had them and her wet panties down her legs and tossed aside in seconds.

Sitting at her feet, he lifted and bent her legs, exposing her intimate flesh past her mound, which she'd waxed in preparation of meeting and doing him. Apparently, he still couldn't see enough of her for his liking. Using his fingers, he separated her labia and eyed her cunt with such intense desire Logan felt like the most stunningly appealing woman in the world.

Tanner looked like he might say something. No words made it out before he took her thighs in his hands and pushed them wide open, his broad shoulders spreading them farther as he brought his mouth an inch from her sex.

He blew on her moist folds, and she squirmed on the couch, wanting, needing his tongue on her hot, wet flesh pronto. She didn't have to say the words. His mouth covered her pussy in the next instant, his tongue licking the length of her slit, circling her swollen clit and finally stabbing into her center.

Sizzling heat raced from her sex to her chest to her face. Her breasts ached with heavy want, her nipples pressing painfully against the thin lace of her bra. Her pussy flooded with cream. Just as she'd fantasized him doing for weeks, he ate her out masterfully, licking the walls of her cunt with an alternating fast and slow tempo.

Orgasm built as a hot ball of sensation deep in her core. She arched up with the delectable pressure, twining her fingers in his hair. The silky softness of his curls took her that much higher. "Still paying me back for saving William?"

Tanner pulled his tongue from her body, brushing his nose against her juicy opening, making her quiver with ecstasy. "I love that Jeep."

With lightning-fast precision, his tongue shoved back inside her. No alternating slow and fast licks this time. Just fast, furious tongue-fucking that had Logan's blood pumping madly and her pussy aflame.

The hot ball of sensation burst. Shards of sensual heat blistered her body, fanning outward until even her toes felt on fire. "I'm going to come!"

One of his hands lifted from her thigh. Fingers brushed over her clit, pinching the tight pearl as orgasm caught her in its throes. His fingers pinched harder, and she couldn't stop her mindless shouts for more. He gave her more, another raging, quaking climax on the tail of the first. Both blowing the top well off her va-va-voom meter.

Tanner's fingers left her clit. His tongue pulled from her sex, returning quickly to lick her folds clean.

With a last playful tug of his teeth on her labia, he released her thigh and stood from the couch. The unchecked lust in his eyes as they met hers had her pussy freshly moist. He could slide inside her with ease.

"Thanks for dessert." He stepped back toward the door of the bungalow. "Good night, Logan."

Inhaling sharply, Logan rose up on her elbows and eyed him through the vee of her thighs. He was *not* leaving. If that was his idea of chivalry, getting her off without worrying about his own pleasure, he was sorely mistaken. He was her first official hunk in a soon-to-be long line of them, and she would show him as much carnal bliss as he'd shown her.

"See you Friday." He continued his retreat. "At the office."

Her belly clenched with disappointment. *At the office.* As in, they were back on doctor/patient terms. As in, he probably regretted what he'd done. Well, damn it, she probably should regret it, too, but she wouldn't. She also wouldn't throw herself at him and demand he allow her to repay the favor by giving him a blow job. No, she would torment the hell out of him instead.

Logan lay back on the couch as gracefully as she knew how, angling her thighs so he couldn't help but look back at her sex. She slipped a hand between her legs, petting her hairless mound, and then sunk a finger inside her opening. She gasped with the entry, a little louder when she began a slow thrusting.

"Night, Tanner," she breathed. It was the first time she used his name to his face. And it felt good. Really good. Or maybe that was the feel of her finger fucking her pussy while he watched. "I'm here for you . . . if William has any more problems and needs a good stroking to get him going again."

4

Tanner had to stop ending up like this, with his head rested against his folded hands on the Jeep's steering wheel while he willed his dick to calm down enough to allow him to safely drive home.

Something told him no amount of deep breathing and visualization of cold, snowy places would ease the ache of his hard-on tonight. Nothing would erase the knowledge Logan was inside her bungalow finger-fucking herself.

His cock pulsed with the memory of her slick pussy gobbling her finger all the way to the last knuckle, and he groaned.

He had no right kissing her. No right at all giving her oral sex. No right or brain, apparently, since he was considering retracing his steps down the pier and finishing what they started.

Sleeping with Logan would go against Tanner's professional ethics, but it wouldn't break his vow, at least not completely. She didn't come across as too young for him, and he could see himself with her beyond a few days, engaging in meaningful sex if only because loving her stayed with him long after the act itself ended. They had no chance at a future, given where she lived and his abhorrence for long-distance relationships, but two out of three weren't such bad odds.

He lifted his head from his arms and looked down at his crotch. "All right, you win."

With a snorting laugh, he climbed out of the Jeep and started back down the pier. Logan had gotten to him good for him to be talking to his penis. He hadn't done so since he'd been a cocky shit of a teenager.

It seemed an eternity before Tanner reached her bungalow. As he was considering if he should knock or just walk in and continue with his voyeurism as if he had never left, the door pulled inward and there stood Logan, wearing nothing but an impish smile that said she knew he would be back.

The sight of her nude, aroused body and the smell of her stimulation on the sultry air had another holdover from his teenaged years coming out of his mouth—the name of his cock. "I should be on my way home, but William has a problem."

Her smile gave way to a frown. "Your Jeep won't start?"

He wasn't sure if she was disappointed over not fixing his vehicle better or not making him want her enough. He'd had dozens of women go out of their way to impress him into their beds, so Logan possibly being upset about her mechanic skills had him liking her all the more.

Of course, she wouldn't have to worry over the value of her mechanic skills for long. He had some serious body work for her to see to and had every faith she would do a superior job.

"Not that William." Tanner stepped through the doorway. He closed the door and nodded at the sizeable bulge at the front of his slacks. "This William."

Amusement gleaming in her eyes, she let out a throaty laugh. "You *do* have a soft spot for Shakespeare."

"Trust me, there's nothing soft about it." He wanted to pull her into his arms and rub up against her to show her exactly how hard she had him. First, he needed to make one thing clear.

"I have never slept with one of my patients, Logan. I was serious when I said that at dinner."

"But?"

She looked so unabashedly hopeful he had to mentally command his hands to stay at his sides. "But I want to help you put the bed down and then help you get the sheets wet."

"I wish I could let that happen."

She *what*? Had he read both her behavior and expression wrong? Or where the hell had those words come from?

Reminding himself he was a professional and it was likely that part of him which warranted her rejection, Tanner reached behind him for the doorknob. "I understand. I just couldn't go home without telling you I want you. Any man who doesn't realize how lucky he is to have you is a blind fool. You don't need big breasts to get laid. You're a knockout as is."

He started to turn for the door and a night of jerking off. She was on him before he could move more than a couple inches. Her arms came around his neck, and her mound brushed the back of his knuckles. "Keep up the compliments and you'll be lucky to get the bed down before I jump you."

His cock jerked with relief, or it could have to do with the continued rubbing of her silky sex. He shifted to bring her flush up against him, then rewarded his hand for its earlier patience by moving it between her thighs and caressing her damp slit. "What happened to not letting it happen?"

Logan's breath caught as he took one finger deeper, lightly entering her hole. "I was talking about getting the sheets wet. I don't have the patience to put them on the bed. If I don't fuck you immediately, I'm liable to come on the floor just thinking about having you."

Around his finger, her pussy quivered. He recalled her candid admission in the consultation room, how long she'd gone without a lover, and he had no doubt she was serious about orgasming right where they stood.

Watching her climax again was liable to be more than Tanner's control could handle. He didn't have any desire to live out more of his teenaged years by coming in his pants, so he kissed her quickly on the mouth, letting his tongue spill inside to stroke her warm wetness for seconds. Then he released her and hurried to the far wall of the two-room bungalow. Yanking the cleverly disguised medical bed partway out of the wall, he unzipped the mattress cover near its foot and groped for the re-lease latch, swearing when his fingers came up empty time and again.

The more he thought about how long she'd gone without a lover, the more desperate his cock grew to push inside her tight pussy. His fingers came up empty for the latch again, and he glanced at the blue-green carpet. Not exactly comfortable and burns were likely to ensue, but then desperate times called for desperate measures. "Did you say it's been almost three years since you've had sex with another person?"

Logan's arms wrapped around his waist from behind. Her pelvis nuzzled the lower half of his ass, and his sphincter mus-cles tightened. "I did and I wouldn't recommend it." The warmth of her breath taunted his earlobe, sending shivers rac-ing down his spine and tightening his balls. "You're liable to make inappropriate remarks like telling your hottie of a doctor you like to have your nipples pinched."

Another time, he would have laughed. Now he grappled like a madman for the release, nearly praying when he finally found it and the bed lowered to the floor with the subtle hiss of hy-draulics. Tanner didn't waste time on prayers but swiveled in her arms and drew one big, stiff nipple between his thumb and forefinger and squeezed. "Hard enough?"

She whimpered. "Almost." He pinched harder and her eye-lids flickered partially closed on a moan. "Ooh . . . yeah . . ."

Ooh, yeah, was right. One more moan like that one and she wouldn't be alone in coming on the spot.

Logan didn't moan again but opened her eyes fully and pressed her palms flat against his chest, pushing him back on the narrow bed. He went gladly, lying at an angle across the mattress.

She climbed up and over him, her legs straddling his upper thighs and providing a tantalizing view of her sex. Her feminine lips were plump again, juicy again, and his tongue was eager to be back inside, devouring her cream. He lifted his attention to her breasts. Small, he couldn't deny, but also appealing as hell. Her long, dark hair swayed erotically against them, teasing their blood-reddened peaks. "Christ, you're so sexy."

Disbelief passed through her gaze, and then it was lust alone darkening her eyes as she sucked her full lower lip between her teeth and wrenched at his polo shirt.

"Let's see how sexy you are." The shirt tugged from his slacks. Her hands were on his abdomen instantly. Warm and explorative, they moved up his torso, short nails skimming along muscles and bringing every nerve in his body to screaming life. "Not bad, but I need more to go on."

Logan's hands moved back down his body, stopping at his belt buckle. She made quick work of unhooking it and pulling it through the loops of his slacks. Reclining back on his thighs, she cracked the belt into the air. "This could come in handy."

Tanner's cock jumped with the primal sound. He should have guessed someone who enjoyed having their nipples pinched so hard would be in to kink. He wasn't complaining a bit. "Will you let me swat your ass with it?"

"That depends—are you worthy?" She tossed the belt aside and grabbed his shaft through his pants. Her eyes widened, and she released him to undo his pants and get her hand inside his briefs. Her lips curved in a Cheshire grin. "Legendary indeed. Makes a girl wish you really were a Gremlin."

Something about her word choice bothered him—maybe that she'd referred to his dick as legendary, maybe that she'd hinted she would like to get it wet and produce multiples, as if one cock wasn't enough for her, as if she had the same morals as the faithless twit he'd caught fucking another guy behind his back because she claimed his visits were too few and far between. He couldn't say which, since Logan chose that moment to pull his shaft free of his briefs and lick it from base to tip.

She swiped her tongue over the pre-cum glistening at the eye and let out a throaty *mmm*.

His heart rate shot through the roof with the damp, velvety swipe. His cock pulsed. He curled his hands into fists and fought for restraint. "Good?" he asked tightly.

She licked the head of his penis again, slower this time but with more pressure, all but forcing his control past the snapping point. "Very."

"Then you can suck me all you want later. Now we end your celibacy streak." Only, now he couldn't end her celibacy streak. That last lick had him ready to explode. One thrust inside her hot pussy and he would be going off.

With a short detour in mind, he pulled her against him and rolled them over. Trapping her on her back with the weight of his body, he reached to the panel built into the side of the bed. Pressing the first button made metal side rails rise up on either side of them, and Tanner returned her taunting words with a wolfish grin. "These could come in handy."

Logan wasn't sure what Tanner had in mind for the side rails, though it obviously involved sex and the two of them, and at the moment that was all she cared about.

He moved down and then off the end of the bed. His gaze went to her cunt, lingering there hot and heavy, and her urge to come was almost more than she could bear.

"Finger-fuck yourself the way you were doing when I left."

There was no questioning the words were an order. Normally, she didn't do orders. But then, normally she didn't sleep with her doctor.

Logan's clit tingled with the prospect of finally feeling the hard, human cock of a certifiable hottie rubbing against it. Only, despite what Tanner said moments ago, it didn't sound like he planned to immediately enter her. "What happened to ending my—" He lifted aside the hem of his shirt to take his meaty cock in hand, and the words stilled on a gulp. "Never mind."

"Like watching?"

She could hear his amusement, but she didn't look up, couldn't steal her attention from the slow, rhythmic stroke of his fingers along his shaft. Wanting him every bit as enthralled, she gave in to his request, parting her thighs to sink a finger inside her tight passage. "What's not to like?"

"Good point." The words came out raspy. His thumb moved to the head of his cock, swirling over the glistening fluid, making her tongue throb with the need to taste his silky essence. "Put your feet up on the rails. I want to see everything."

She sent an uncertain look at the rails on either side of her and quite a good distance apart. "I'm not a contortionist."

"The bed's four foot wide at most. Your legs are plenty long. Spread 'em."

Okay, so maybe she did do orders. Or at least she should start. The rough edge of command in Tanner's voice spiked delicious tremors in her core. Tremors that turned to quaking waves of pleasure as she planted her feet on the side rails, spreading her pussy lips wide open. His hand fisted white-knuckled around his cock, his throat working visibly.

Preening with satisfaction to know she had him so keyed up, she played with the folds of her labia, rubbing and pinching the aroused flesh, taking herself as close to the brink as she dared to go. "Like giving orders?" Her breath panted out.

"What's not to like?"

"Good point." Logan brought her attention back to his cock, deliciously bared while the rest of him was clothed. She would have to insist on the same erotic attire for all future office visits, give herself something to think about other than her impending surgery. For now, she wanted him naked and ready to mount. "Strip for me. I want to see everything."

Hesitation passed through his eyes, but then he started moving. She thought he would push his pants and briefs down his legs, step out of them and his socks and shoes and call it good. Instead he planted his palms on his ass and started thrusting his hips in the direction of her face. Between his bad-boy grin, his ginormous cock jerking toward her and his fingers sliding beneath the rear of his slacks to lower them slowly down, he could have easily been a real stripper.

Remembering her end of the bargain and that it had nothing to do with using her teeth to stuff his briefs with dollar bills, Logan resumed her fondling. Her hips shot off the mattress with the first brush of her finger against her clit. Her pulse stampeded and she gasped aloud.

Tanner swung around and bent over, wagging his ass at her face while he removed his shoes and socks. He pushed his pants and briefs the remainder of the way down his thighs, and his balls peeked out from beneath his butt cheeks. His pants and briefs came to his feet. Tossing aside the pants, he held on to the briefs and swiveled back around. The quick move had his shirt falling over his cock, producing a tentlike effect. He twirled his briefs on one finger and then sent them flying. His hands free again, he slid them up his torso, dragging the shirt upward until his dick sprang free of its hiding place.

Logan's pussy fluttered, clenching around her finger, with her first unrestricted look at his groin. Oh, boy, had her fantasies fallen short. His erection appeared huge against the backdrop of chestnut pubic hair. Staying on the bed and out of touching distance took almost more willpower than she possessed.

His penis undulated as his hips started back into a slow circling dance. The polo shirt came over his head. Her tongue went wild in her mouth, licking over her teeth and gums with the need to get on his scrumptiously muscled chest.

One large hand returned to his cock, fisting over the granite-hard flesh. The other hand went to his balls, massaging the arousal-reddened sac. The gyrations of his hips grew faster. She increased her thrusting in tandem, imagining it was his finger pumping inside her moist pussy, the way she'd fantasized so many times before.

His carnal dance brought him to the side of the bed. The rich scent of his musk filled her nose and bombarded her senses. His pelvis pushed forward, and the weeping head of his cock rubbed along the sole of her foot, wetting it, wetting her cunt beyond measure. Sizzling heat unfurled in her belly, raced up to her breasts, and singed her cheeks.

Tanner's hips stilled. His shaft moved away from her foot, and she whimpered at the loss of contact. "Don't tell me that's the end of the show."

Sensual promise filled his eyes and curved his lips. "Just changing routine. Got a condom handy?"

A couple dozen of them she bought last week with him in mind. Purchasing the magnum size had been enough to get her hot and bothered; watching him roll one on was liable to be the next best thing to feeling him thrusting inside her.

Shuddering with anticipation, Logan pointed to the small oak coffee table in front of the couch. "I stashed a couple in there."

He started in on a new dance that did wonderful things to his ass and even more wonderful things to her body as he made his way over to the table. She brought her free hand to her nipples, pinching each in turn, thrilling in the resulting stab of pleasure deep in her pussy.

Tanner's laugh had her releasing her nipple to look back at him. His hand was heaping with condoms and his eyebrows raised Logan's way. "A couple?"

"I had a lot of time to collect them."

"Nearly three years?"

"Nearly three years." How long had it been for him, even a full week since he'd last had sex? She shouldn't want to know. No, she didn't want to know, because it didn't matter. She'd known his track record coming in—it was the reason she picked him as her first hunk to do. With luck in the form of new breasts, she would be able to match his record one day soon.

He returned to the foot of the bed, sheathing himself in a show of expert skill as he moved. "Prove worthy and I'll help you burn through every last one of them."

Logan noticed how well he played to her quirky side by tossing so many of her words back at her. Then all she could notice was how amazingly better a real cock felt filling her than a plastic one as he climbed onto the bed and pumped into her with a single, smooth thrust.

Sliding his hands beneath her ass, he groaned. "William just found his new home. Now let's hope he doesn't come so fast, you evict him on the first night."

She puffed out a sharp breath as heady tension licked through her. If William did come fast, he wouldn't be alone. Her feet were still up on the rails and between Tanner's size and her utterly open body, his shaft impaled her to places she was certain no man or machine had gone before.

Cupping her ass in his hands, he lifted her hips off the bed and moved inside her with graceful strokes that had her eyelids fluttering closed and her pussy contracting with wild wonder. He increased the tempo, his fingers nipping into the soft flesh of her bottom, eliciting more luscious tension.

She groped for the side railings, wrapping her fingers around the cool metal, desperate for a staying point if she was going to keep her feet on the rails. "Definitely not a walrus."

"Definitely not a popsicle stick."

She wasn't even close to feeling wooden right now; Logan would give him that. His hips started the pivoting thing they'd done on his imaginary dance floor. Each circling had the rigid side of his shaft hitting against her aroused clit, the thickness of his cock stroking into her pussy.

One hand left her ass. Seconds later, two fingers found her nipple. Pinched hard. Harder. Her eyes flew open as wicked heat rocketed to her core. Carnal pressure flooded her body. His cock pressed up against her clit once more. Once more than she could handle without giving in.

Logan cried out as her cunt spasmed and exploded with a deluge of juices. Tanner's eyes narrowed, his lips firmed into a tight line of control. He pushed into her twice more, gave the other nipple the same delectable pleasure-pain pinching treatment, and then came with a shout of satisfaction.

Resting the bulk of his weight on his elbows, he lazily nuzzled her neck. She brought her hands to his sweaty back, loving the firm play of muscle, and took her feet from the rails to run along his crisp leg hair. His breath fanned warm and fast near her ear. She closed her eyes, savoring the raspy sound and the reality that this time when she opened her eyes, her fantasy wouldn't burst to reveal a vibrator filling her.

The weight of his lower body lifted slightly. Her breath hitched and her eyes snapped open. It wasn't time for him to leave. Not yet.

Tanner lifted his head to eye her soberly. "You do realize I can't be your doctor anymore?"

Fine. Just so long as he could still be her lover. "During my consultation, you said I could have someone else do my surgery if I wasn't comfortable with you. I'll use one of them. Though, for the record, it's not because I'm uncomfortable with you."

With a naughty grin, Logan squeezed her feminine muscles around his softening cock. "I'm very comfortable."

Fresh desire gleamed in his eyes, but he kept his tone professional. "It will probably mean waiting an extra day or two if you use another doctor."

She traveled her hands to his ass and gave the cheeks a squeeze. "I'm sure I can find someone to do to fill the time."

"Or you could not have the surgery. I didn't just say you don't need big breasts for a guy to want you, Logan. I meant it. You're an amazing woman as is."

She sighed. "You sure you aren't my father in disguise?"

His smile finally appeared as he glanced down at their joined bodies. "For both of our sakes, let's hope not."

Tanner's lopsided smile affected her as always, getting her damp all over again. This time she wouldn't cave to her hormones. Logan pushed at his chest until he rolled to the side of the bed and frowned at her.

She lifted a leg and ran her hands along the calf. "Chicken legs." She moved her hands up to her thighs. "Zero thighs." She slid her hands all the way up to cup her barely there hips. "Total lack of hips." Total lack of anything feminine. How she managed to get him into her bed was a mystery. "What I need is a whole-body implant."

He moved off the bed, disposing of the condom in a tissue from the box on the coffee table. Lying back down beside her, he came up on an elbow. "Do you have any idea how much women pay and how much pain they go through to have hips and thighs that look like yours? They aren't lacking. They're slender and fit you perfectly." He reached over, caressing the subtle arch of her breast. "Just like these succulent breasts do. I wouldn't change a thing."

Hell, he sounded so sincere. Too sincere. Logan laughed, because she desperately needed to lighten the moment. "Nice try, but *I* would. You might like me as is—itty-bitty titties and zip for curves—but most men won't even look twice."

He hesitated a few seconds, looking anything but happy, but then gave in with a nod. "All right. I'll talk with Gilbert Lasa tomorrow. His schedule's pretty booked through the end of the month, but he's one of the best and owes me a favor."

Good. Now that they had that taken care of . . . She came up on an elbow, mimicking his stance, and walked her fingers down his torso and into the thick, dark hair surrounding his cock. "What do I have to do for you in exchange for using this favor?"

Tanner's smile reappeared, warming his eyes and creasing the corners of his mouth. He pounced on her, getting her flat on her back again. He tongued her nipple until it ached with awareness, making her *ooh* and squirm beneath him. "You don't have to do anything, sexy lady. Just lie there and let me have my way with you."

5

Tanner looked up from his computer monitor with the knock on his office door. He glanced at the wood wall clock. Ten after five. Most of the clinic staff would be gone for the day, which placed odds on the knocker being Melinda, dropping by to see if he wanted to join her for dinner. The answer was "hell no." She would sense something was different about him and immediately attribute it to the brunette she left in the clinic with him last night. He *was* different today, relaxed in a way only hours of great sex could accomplish.

The knock came again, and he accepted Melinda wasn't going to go away. Not a problem. He would turn her down, then usher her out the door on the pretense he had work to wrap up. "Come in."

The door pushed inward, and Tanner's body shot to instant awareness. Not Melinda, with her perfect hair and makeup and tits. Logan, with her hair in a long, straight ponytail and no makeup and very small tits that he wanted to rush across the room and suck into his mouth.

It wasn't right how she charmed him without even trying. "What are you doing here?"

She frowned. "I just got done having my boobs filmed and noticed your name on the door as I was leaving. I was going to say hi, but obviously you're too busy." She turned to go.

He pushed back his wheeled chair and came to his feet. "Don't leave. I wasn't aware your appointment was today. That doesn't mean I don't want to see you."

She looked unconvinced, so he went to the door and pulled her inside his office by the waist of her plain white T-shirt. He wanted to close the door and kiss her senseless. Ah, fuck, no, he didn't. He wanted to close the door, strip her naked, and bang her brains out until she got it through her head she didn't need implants to impress a man; he was impressed as hell already.

Tanner didn't do that, because it wasn't him she wanted to impress. It was all the other men she planned to lure into her bed by way of her new breasts. Initially, when Logan reminded him of her reason for wanting implants last night, he'd been pissed. Then he remembered she wasn't a woman whose morals he had a right to question, just someone he planned to have meaningful sex with until her surgery prevented it.

He closed the door and gestured to the chairs in front of his desk. "Have a seat." She moved to a chair and sat down a little stiffly, as if she didn't know how to act around him now that it was a new day and they were both dressed.

He considered taking his shirt off to make her more comfortable but then remembered he had serious matters to discuss with her before his dick took over. Sitting down behind his desk, he slipped into doctor mode, hoping it would be enough to keep the displeasure from his voice over her continued desire to have augmentation surgery for all the wrong reasons. "I spoke with Dr. Lasa. He can fit you in for surgery Saturday morning."

"You guys don't have weekends off?"

"We take weekends, just not the typical Friday night to Monday morning ones you have in mind." Tanner's weekend had officially started at five. He would save that information for later, when he revealed the bigger of his two surprises for her.

"I don't work regular hours either." Logan's eyes widened, and she clamped her mouth shut.

Clearly, she hadn't planned to bring up her profession, which made him eager to know all about it. "What do you do?"

She came to her feet swiftly. Planting a jean-shorts-clad hip on his desk, she leaned across it and grabbed a handful of his hair. Her lips parted inches from his. Warm air curled into his face with her breathy, "Wanna play doctor?"

Tanner's cock pressed hard at the fly of his trousers. She angled her head and swiped her damp, pink tongue seductively over her full lower lip. The end of her ponytail slipped over her shoulder with the move, teasing along his jawline and making his shaft ache to feel her silky hair wrapped around it.

How in the fuck could she think she wasn't sexy?

"Yes." He wanted to play immediately, but she stoked his curiosity with her avoidance of his question, and he knew it wouldn't rest until he had her answer. "First, I want to know what you do and why you're embarrassed by it."

Logan's lips closed on a sigh. She released his hair and dropped back down on her chair, all trace of desire gone. "I'm not embarrassed. It's just not a glamorous job."

"Like being a doctor?" Could she feel inferior to him?

"Being a doctor isn't glamorous." He must not have looked pleased, because she smiled reassuringly, adding, "It's a very respectable job, though. You should be proud of yourself."

"I am. So, what do you do?"

Her smile vanished. She studied the short, unpainted fingernails of her right hand in an awkward way that suggested she never bothered to check them out before. "They call me Vage."

Had he misunderstood her quiet words, or what exactly was Vage supposed to mean to him? "I'm not following you."

"It's short for *vagina*," she admitted in the same low tone, still not looking at him.

If another woman had whispered the confession, Tanner would have been apt to leap to conclusions. With Logan, he was clueless. Unless she'd lied to him about her celibacy streak. No, he'd felt the tightness of her pussy milking his cock. She couldn't fake that. "Up until last night, you hadn't had a lover in close to three years, which leaves me to believe you either take phone sex calls or get paid to do strip and masturbation shows over the Internet."

That had her looking back up at him to snort out a laugh. "My voice isn't nearly seductive enough to get guys off over the phone, and you're the only stripper in the room."

"You don't give yourself nearly enough credit. Your voice is very seductive, and you already know how I feel about the rest of you."

She gave him a look that said he would find her next words appalling. "I'm a grease monkey with a vagina. Female mechanic. Not glamorous or sexy."

Maybe not glamorous, but the sexy part she was seriously mistaken about. "I hate to distort your vision, but I was ready to go home to a cold beer and a solo hand job last night; then you came along and fixed my Jeep. There was no chance of my going home after that. At least, not alone."

"Tightening your coil wire gets you hot, huh?"

"No, but bending over my engine and sticking your compact little ass in my face while you work your own brand of magic does something to my dick that isn't fair."

Her eyes warmed with her laughter, her lips parting into an oval. "You're a goof. I like that about you."

Tanner liked too much about her to mention without worrying them both. He concentrated on the shape of her lips, the perfect oval they formed, how his cock felt sliding into that lush, wet oval. His blood heated and he called a silent end to their professional dealings.

It was time to play doctor.

He opened his bottom desk drawer and pulled a long black tube of gel from a bag inside. "You're tense." He rounded the desk to stand behind her chair. "Let me do something about it."

Logan glanced over her shoulder as he squeezed the clear gel onto his palm. "Is that what you fill implants with?"

"No, what I use to seduce my patients." Her gaze went wary and he chuckled. "Kidding. Besides, you're not my patient anymore, and it was your idea to play doctor."

He set the tube on the desk and worked the gel on his hands. Its coolness was soon replaced with heat that had his fingers tingling. Though she hadn't truly been tense before, she tensed now as he eased her forward a few inches on the chair and pulled her T-shirt up to expose her back. Her rigidity vanished the moment he put his hands on her bare skin. He unhooked the back clasp of her bra and palmed her sides, bringing his thumbs together to knead along her spine.

She wriggled with the first circling of his thumbs. "Oh, God! My entire back is . . . I don't know. Hot. Cold. Stinging in an incredibly good way. What is that stuff?"

"Warming gel with love dust. I picked up a few things on my lunch hour in case you decided to bestow me with your presence."

Logan stopped her wriggling to look back at him, her eyebrows knit together. "Bestow you? Most people don't talk like that, Tanner. What's the deal with you and Shakespeare?"

He continued massaging her, working his hands from nape to tailbone, awakening every sexual neuron in her back before turning his touch on her front half. His hands came over her breasts from behind, his fingers closing around her nipples, squeezing the erect nubs. She jerked forward in the chair with a whimper.

Grinning, Tanner resumed his sensual assault, his cock hardening a little more with each of her throaty sighs, every one of her heightened breaths. "My great-great-great-grandfather was his lover," he finally responded. "Took it in the ass every night for twenty-three years."

She gasped. "Are you serious?"

He laughed. "No, but hearing your reaction was worth the lie." He skimmed his hands down her flat belly, teasing his fingers above the waistline of her shorts, and then slid them beneath. She sucked in a sharp breath when his gel-coated fingers stroked over her naked mound. "I had to do a report on *Romeo and Juliet* in high school. Thought it was the shittiest assignment ever, so I put off reading the story until the last minute, which meant skimming the pages in between watching the football team try for a playoff spot. Laura Damien caught me reading it, complimented my taste in literature, then pulled me behind the bleachers and gave me my first blow job."

Logan's laughter was thick with lust. "Laura was hot stuff, huh?"

"Laura was the love of my life—for about two weeks, when she found out I didn't know Shakespeare from Dr. Seuss and dumped me. Shakespeare and I have been close ever since."

She tipped her head back, shooting him a naughty, upside-down smile. "You seem to get Shakespeare now, so how about a taste of Dr. Seuss? Bestow me right and I'll blow you all night. Or maybe you prefer, do me good, Doc, and I'll suck your cock."

Tanner's groin tightened, his fingers stilling their circling over her mound. "Somehow I don't think we're talking about the same author, though I do recall reading a page or two out of your author's latest book. It went something like, sit back and relax and I'll give you a climax."

"Ooh. That sounds like a best seller."

"More like a best yeller."

She laughed in a way that could only be called giggling. He hadn't heard a woman giggle in ages; it made him feel good even before he pulled her chair away from the desk, went down on his knees, and pushed her shirt out of the way to draw her nipple into his mouth. The warming gel on his tongue made him feel good, too, just in a completely different way.

The gel did more than give off an icy-hot feeling; it seeped into the pores and warmed the blood. The scent was loaded with pheromones and claimed to be among the most powerful of aphrodisiacs. As rock hard as his dick was, Tanner believed it.

"I don't think we'll be needing this." With a little twist of her wrist, Logan pulled the T-shirt over her head.

He sat back to take in her disheveled appearance, from her loosening ponytail to the flush of her cheeks to the straps of her white-lace bra resting against her arms and the cups pushing out to expose her disproportionately large nipples.

He'd never had sex in his office. He intended to remedy that tonight.

She relaxed back in the chair and closed her eyes on a blissful sigh. He palmed her thighs and returned his mouth to her breasts. Taking a swollen nipple between his teeth, he twisted and bit, applying the pressure he knew she craved, the pressure he was quickly becoming addicted to supplying her.

The gel responded to moisture, and the dampness of his mouth was obviously just what Dr. Seuss in the form of Logan ordered. Her fingers dove into his hair. Her thighs jumped beneath his hands. "Holy shit, yes! That stuff is freaking incredible. I swear I'm about ready to come."

Tanner lifted his mouth from her nipple to give her a cocky look. "I'd like to think I have a little to do with it."

"You have *everything* to do with it." She pushed his head back down to her breast. "Now suck me."

With an inward laugh, he dragged her nipple back into his mouth, sucking hard on the straining tip while he fingered its mate, pulling, tugging, pinching with enough force to have her fisting his hair and crying out, "It hurts . . . sooo good."

His next suck had her breathing heavily in his ear, her thighs tensing beneath his hands. Her short fingernails clawed at his scalp. He lifted a hand from her thigh and pushed it between her legs, stroking her pussy through her clothes.

Even with those layers, he could feel the heat rising off her sex. The open leg of her shorts invited him to move beneath. He slid his fingers inside and beneath her panties, found her folds wet and hot, her clit standing at attention. He caught the stiff pearl between his fingers and pinched it and her left nipple in tandem, while his teeth attacked her right nipple.

Logan's hips arched up. Spasms racked her body. Heat rolled from her cunt followed by her ecstatic shout of "Va-va-voom!" and the warm rush of cream.

Tanner coated his fingers with her juices. He lifted his mouth from her breast to suck his first finger between his lips. He was just about to tell her how much he loved her taste when a flash of movement past Logan's head had him looking up. Melinda stood in the doorway, watching with rapt interest.

"Whoops. Didn't realize you were working on a patient."

The female voice had Logan crashing down hard from the throes of orgasm. Flinging her hands over her breasts, she spun in the chair to find Melinda smiling at her like she knew some dirty little secret.

Did that secret have to do with Melinda's reaction to catching Tanner giving her an orgasm? He'd told Logan he didn't sleep with his patients, had gone so far as to remove himself as her doctor because they had slept together. Melinda's word choice made Logan wonder if that hadn't been the real reason.

Melinda's gaze shifted to Tanner, who had come to his feet

next to Logan's chair. "I guess you don't want to have dinner tonight?"

"Thanks, but I was having it when you walked in."

She let out a decadent laugh, while Logan wanted to crawl under the desk. She thought she was beginning to get a sense for who Tanner was, but the Tanner she had in mind would never say something so ribald in mixed company.

Logan laughed to herself over the irony of her thoughts as Melinda made some crack about them having a good night and closed the door. *Of course* the Tanner she knew would say something like that. Just like he would sleep with a different resort guest every week or two, maybe even lie to her about not sleeping with his patients. His endearingly goofy side and the sneak peeks into his life had momentarily allowed her to forget who he was, but that wouldn't be happening any longer.

He was the Don Juan of orgasms. A resort tradition. The first hottie in a long line of them to get her sheets wet. And she owed him a blow job.

"Sorry about that," he said, sounding as if he truly was. "I should have locked the door. I figured when Melinda didn't stop by right at five, she'd already taken off."

Who was Melinda to him that he'd expected her to stop by with an offer of dinner? A fuck friend for those weeks when the resort guest list ran low?

Never mind. It didn't matter. Logan had three whole days before her surgery. Three days and one night she would spend engaging in fantasy sex with Tanner.

She gave a thought to locking the door, but then chalked it up as pointless, given the only other person still in the building had already been witness to her climaxing. She stood from the chair and poked a finger into the middle of Tanner's chest. "You owe me, buck-o."

He gave her an apologetic look. "Does it help knowing I have a surprise for you?"

"Nope. The only thing that's going to help is stripping from the waist down and having a seat on your desk."

"If the plan's to embarrass me in front of my colleagues, you should know they're already gone for the night."

"I don't want to embarrass you. I want to blow you."

His expression went from repentant to stunned to elated. He toed off his shoes, then shucked his trousers and briefs. "If I'd known it would have that effect on you, I'd have had Mel stop by earlier."

Wonder over who Melinda was to him threatened to resurface. Logan erased it by looking at his groin. Her so recently satisfied cunt thrummed with arousal and she sighed.

Would just looking at his legendary cock ever cease to make her wet?

Tanner hopped up on the front edge of his desk. Her mouth went dry with the bobbing of his heavy penis. She went to him, sliding between the vee of his muscled thighs and taking his dick in hand. It was almost scary how natural it felt being there, holding him this way, so she dismissed that thought as well to concentrate on his seduction.

Pressing her bare breasts against his chest, Logan worked her fingers up the length of his cock. "You liked making me orgasm." She tipped her head back and hungrily eyed his mouth. "Licking my cum off your fingers. Getting caught in the act."

"Guilty." His upper half leaned forward. His lips parted slightly, eliciting warm air, inviting her to come closer, to have a taste.

Logan pulled her chair forward and sat down on it before temptation became too much to resist. He would get his kiss, but first he would get his punishment.

"You'll like this even better." Gripping the base of his cock, she gave him her best seductress's smile, which probably wasn't all that good, but then he seemed to have Mary Poppin's syndrome where she was concerned, capable of noticing only her finer points, so he probably found her smile hot as hell.

She certainly felt hot as hell. One suck of the deep-pink head of Tanner's cock and her pussy flooded with heat. One taste of the pre-cum seeping from the tip and her nipples throbbed for attention. And what a luscious taste that was.

She'd licked his dick last night, had it between her lips for a few seconds, but then he'd stopped her from going any further, saying it was time to end her celibacy streak.

There would be no stopping her now.

Pumping her hand along his length, she lapped at his silky fluid, greedily dipped her tongue into the hole it pearled from in demand for more, and then sank her lips around the meaty head.

She loved the head of his cock, sucking it in and out of her mouth while her fingers went to his balls. One of Tanner's hands wound its way into her hair, yanking the ponytail holder free. The tresses came down, tickling against her cheek. She took the ends of her hair into her hand and stroked them against the section of his cock she had yet to get her mouth on.

His hands went to the desk, his fingers gripping its edge. "Damn, are you good at that." His voice was strained, intense, rough with desire, just how she loved it. "Makes a guy wish you really were a Gremlin."

"Smart-ass," she murmured against his hot flesh.

He laughed; the sound cut off short as she sank her mouth down his length, torturing him with the lash of her tongue against the sensitive underside of his cock.

Looking up at him revealed his face taut with restraint, his eyes closed. Perfect. She grabbed the warming gel from near his hip. The cap required two hands to unscrew, so she increased the pressure of her mouth, working his cock faster, licking him with purpose while she released his balls, uncapped the tube, and squeezed gel into her palm.

The icy-hot sensation wasn't as powerful on her palm as it had been on her nipples, but it still got to her, heated her belly with sensual warmth and had her pussy fluttering.

And there was no questioning it would get to Tanner.

She slid her mouth upward, sucking on just the head of his penis, so her fingers had plenty of room to wrap around it and share the magic of the gel.

Three seconds passed before his hips shot toward her face and his erection pushed so hard into her mouth, Logan nearly swallowed her hand. "Jesus Christ!"

"Ain't that nice?" Now wasn't the time for erotic Dr. Seuss rhyming games, but she hadn't been able to resist.

"Goddamned amazing," he agreed, his cock filling her mouth once more, his hips pumping toward her face without relief. "Keep it up and soon I'll be blazing . . . a hot trail of cum right down your throat."

Damn, she couldn't think of a single thing to rhyme with *throat*. Then again, since her mouth was awfully full, it was probably just as well.

Fondling his balls with both hands, she attacked his hyper-sensitized cock with her mouth, licking, lashing, biting with enough pressure to send mild pain shooting through his dick and straight to his balls.

Tanner clearly shared her affection for pleasure-pain. His body went rigid, his cock stilling in her mouth only to start pumping again with his guttural groan. His shaft pulsed between her lips. Hot, salty fluid shot into her mouth and coasted down her throat. She sucked him hard to the last drop and then kissed the head of his cock and sat back in her chair with a satiated smile. "Mmm . . . Good to the last drop."

He eyed her through heavy lids, his chest rising and falling rapidly beneath his shirt. "You've more than earned your surprise."

"I don't normally get into surprises, but you make me want to be bestowed."

He stayed in place, sucking in deep, restorative breaths in a way that made Logan's ego soar. If she could destroy his control so completely with itty-bitty titties, just wait until she had a grade-A rack. Of course, it wouldn't be Tanner's succulent cock in her mouth then.

The thought did nasty things to her belly. Fortunately, those nasty things didn't last too long. Tanner slid off the desk to round to the opposite side, flinging her back into the moment. Giving her the lopsided smile that made it seem he'd just been caught with his hand in the cookie jar, he pulled out the drawer the warming gel had come from. Her sex contracted with the wonder of what goody he had in store for her next.

"I saw this and thought of you." He held up a Y-shaped string of silver she could identify from doing Internet research in the hopes of improving her fantasies. Two foot-long chains led to rubber-tipped nipple clamps accentuated with red ladybug weights. A longer chain met where the two shorter ones connected. The lobster-claw clip connected to the end of the longer chain had her clit tingling with prospect.

"You probably already have a drawerful just like it."

"Not even close." Logan joined him on the other side of the desk. She took the Y-clip from him, ogling the clamps that were going to feel so incredible on her body. "When your favorite fuck is your vibrator and your second favorite fuck is your hand, there isn't a lot of need for accessories."

"I didn't know when your surgery was going to be when I bought it on my lunch hour, so I thought the nipple clamps would have to wait. But since your surgery isn't until Saturday, you have a couple days to try the whole thing out without fear of residual inflammation."

Hearing the expectation in his voice, she looked up at him.

His eyes were sage green with arousal, and a glance at his crotch revealed a fast-returning hard-on. "Were you hoping I would model it, by any chance?"

"If you want to give me a show when we get to your other surprise, I won't complain."

She looked back at his face, shocked he would bother with so many gifts for the small amount of time they would be together. Normally, she really wasn't one for surprises, but for his surprise, particularly after how exciting the last one proved, she was anxious as hell. "What's my other surprise?"

He grabbed hold of her arm and spun her around. She planted her empty hand against the edge of his desk to keep from losing balance. His finger shoved up the back of her shorts leg. Her pussy was soaked from blowing him and her thoughts of modeling the Y-clip. The slick sound of her wetness as he pushed his finger inside her hole had her sex on fire. That was nothing compared to the blaze in her core when his rejuvenated cock brushed up against her ass and he commanded, "Bend over and I'll tell you all about it."

6

Tanner opened his front door prepared for the gut-punch of lust he felt whenever Logan graced him with her presence. The gut-punch was there, but so was shock.

Gone was the natural beauty with her makeup-free face, long straight dark brown hair, and casual clothing. In her place was a woman he barely recognized. Skillfully applied makeup brought out the gold flecks in her soft brown eyes. Hot-pink lipstick made her lips appear seductively swollen. Waves of loose, lustrous brown curls streaked with lighter shades of brown and dark blond framed her face, giving her a freshly fucked aura.

And her breasts . . .

She had cleavage. So much cleavage the edges of her areolas peeked from beneath the plunging neckline of her neon pink, body-hugging catsuit.

Tanner found his voice to gasp out, "What happened?"

Logan grinned so widely the edges of her mouth almost disappeared beneath her mile-thick hair. "I started my transformation process early. Like it?"

On another woman, yes. On her, not one damned bit.

He'd done some thinking on it and realized he liked her so much because she was natural. She didn't fake who she was but let her God-given appearance and personality shine through.

Being oneself was a rarity these days, in both men and women—an extreme rarity around Private Indulgence. While Logan wouldn't be with him in the long run, he still wanted to prove to her how naturally appealing she was. His plan for doing so had been to take her on an overnight excursion to a clothing-optional hotel and nightclub on a neighboring island. He thought to show her that men couldn't stop ogling her hot body. Only now, with her totally unnatural transformation, Tanner didn't want other men looking at her. Hell, he didn't want to look at her himself.

He resisted the urge to scowl, but only because Logan's smile made it clear she finally felt sexy. It was also clear she waited for a response. "It's . . . different."

Her grin turned to a forced smile. He'd tried to hide his censure but had obviously done a shitty job. Telling her how he felt about her makeover was liable to do more than bring an end to his surprise getaway before it began—it was likely to hurt her feelings.

He wouldn't hurt her feelings. Instead he made himself look like an ass by leaving her standing at his door while he made his way through the foyer and toward the bathroom, saying as he went, "I need to finish getting ready."

Logan appeared outside the bathroom door a half minute later. He expected her to tell him to go to hell. Instead she came into the bathroom, grabbing his hand before he slid it into his damp hair and attacked his pain-in-the-ass curls with straightening gel.

She implored him with a batting of mascara-coated lashes. "Don't style the curls out. I like it better natural."

Tanner wasn't sure what turned him off more, her tacky behavior or how goddamned hypocritical her words were. "Going natural has never gotten me laid."

Insult passed through her eyes; then her lips curved in a siren's smile, and she rubbed up against him. "It will tonight," she vowed in a breathy voice. "I have on the Y-clip beneath this catsuit and nothing else."

Her outward appearance might be a turnoff, but beneath the layers of makeup and hairspray and skin-tight nylon lay the natural Logan. It was *that* Logan who spoke to him now, *that* Logan who had his dick bobbing to rock-solid life so fast he feared it might be permanently stuck that way.

"Fine. I won't put the gel in my hair." Tanner attempted to sound unaffected, but his arousal was clear in the roughness of his voice. He set her back from him to finish packing his travel toiletries case. "We need to get going anyway." Before he forgot he wasn't happy with her and took her up against the bathroom sink. "I made dinner reservations for seven. Between riding time and checking into the hotel, we'll already be cutting it close."

"Do I get any more hints on where this hotel is located? Considering we're in the middle of the Caribbean, 'on an island' doesn't say a whole lot."

He'd given her that much information last night, thinking to save the rest for today in the hopes she would kiss and grope the details out of him. But today he didn't want her mouth or hands anywhere near him. Today, he couldn't stop thinking about what brought her to Private Indulgence. The same reason she was dressed the way she was. "Somewhere you're guaranteed to have dozens of men anxious to fuck you."

How could Tanner be successful at his job when he spent so much time trying to convince patients not to have surgery?

Logan had spent the last hours attempting to forget his mocking remark about how he never got laid looking natural and his obvious disapproval of her transformed look. But that was damned hard to do when she'd spent the morning at a day spa on the other side of the island, being buffed and plucked and dyed and styled expressly for his viewing pleasure.

Okay, so it hadn't been expressly for his benefit. She'd wanted to discover how sexy she could be. Once she'd gotten past the masochists disguised as salon specialists, the makeover process had gone from painful to pleasurable.

Pulling on the nylon catsuit with its built-in water bra cups had made her feel incredibly naughty. Closing the nipple and clitoris clamps over her sensitive flesh had her tingling with raw ache from the top layer of her skin to the deepest recesses of her pussy. And when the snug nylon brushed against the clamps, she was lucky not to have come on the seat of the bus she caught to Tanner's house.

Or maybe not so lucky, given the low odds of her coming with him tonight.

He'd been surly as hell from the moment she arrived at his house. Not even reaching his surprise destination—a clothing-optional hotel and nightclub—had been enough to turn his black mood around. Dinner worsened things. Every time a naked male diner walked past, Logan couldn't help her innate urge to check out their equipment, and Tanner couldn't seem to help his disgusted snorts over her ogling.

He acted like he felt threatened by her new look, afraid some other guy would show an interest and she would want him more. What a laugh, considering in another few days she would be on a no-sex diet, and he would be on to his next resort guest lover.

Would he surprise that woman with gifts and shower her with compliments, too? Would he make her forget all they had together was a handful of days, the way Logan had forgotten yesterday?

She was letting Tanner guide her across the sand from the

seaside hotel to the nightclub, but she wasn't in the mood to go clubbing. The ache that started in her belly with the idea of him sleeping with another didn't help. She wanted to forget the club and return to the playful fun they'd been having in his office yesterday afternoon before Melinda walked in.

Judging by Tanner's rigid posture and the fact that they'd barely spoken a handful of words all evening, that playful fun was a thing of the past, so she continued on wordlessly beside him, across the sand and through the front door of *Extasis*.

They cleared the long, dark hallway that kept those outside the club from viewing the actions of those inside. The pulsing, sweaty, blatantly carnal atmosphere of the black-light brightened nightclub gripped Logan in its throes so quickly and completely, she didn't give her actions a second thought, just said to hell with Tanner's crappy mood and flung herself at him.

Wrapping her arms around his neck, she tipped back her head and rotated her pelvis. The lobster-claw clamp shifted on her clit with the press of their bodies, and her loudly spoken words came out half moan, half pleading. "Dance with me."

He remained motionless, his eyes narrowing. "Try out your new look on some other guy."

"Do you really want that?" She added a thrust to her rotating and felt his erection against her belly. Moody he might be, but he was also anxious to do her.

"Yes." The words growled out.

Logan stopped the circling of her pelvis to return his glare. "I get that you hate the way I look, maybe even feel threatened by it, but you have no reason to be." She softened her look, rising on tiptoe to flick her tongue against his ear. "I only want to sleep with you tonight, so stop acting like a Gremlin on a mean streak and dance with me."

"The last thing I feel is threatened." Tanner's voice was hard. His touch even harder as he spun her around and pushed her into the teeming sea of bodies on the dance floor.

The noise level was deafening here. The air sweltering with the sexual heat and musky scent of an orgy in process.

Jerking her against him, he palmed her breast. His fingers curled beneath the edge of the nylon, taunting her aroused nipple by pulling at the ladybug weight descending from the clamp. His hips pistoned against her back, pressing his cock against her spine with each hard pump. Ceasing their taunting his fingers squeezed her nipple, pinching harder than he'd ever done before, harder than she dared to set the nipple clamp for its premier voyage.

That Tanner was pissed at her was clear. That he was trying to punish her even clearer. What he didn't seem to realize was how completely his punishment was failing. Every angry squeeze of her nipple shot excruciatingly sinful pleasure-pain directly to her core. Every pump of his cock had her pussy that much wetter.

Rocking back against him, Logan took in the crowd. Men with their dicks exposed and pumping into their own hands as they danced or slamming into the person nearest to them, be they male or female. Women pleasuring their bared breasts with their fingers, pleasuring the breasts of other women. Her gaze locked on a blonde on her knees between the legs and gripping the thighs of a full-figured brunette. The brunette was naked aside from a white silk scarf wrapped around her waist, her ample tits jostling with the circling of her hips.

The circling turned to thrashing as the blonde captured the ends of the scarf in her fist and sank the silk between the glistening folds of the brunette's pussy.

The rapturous look on the blonde's face as the pristine scarf disappeared inside the brunette's cunt was the most erotic sight Logan had ever seen. Her own pussy thrummed, juices streaming down her thighs, dampening the crotch of the catsuit. The blonde pulled the scarf free, replacing it with the lash of her tongue, and Logan's legs nearly gave way with her overwhelming excitement.

The ache in her sex and the heaviness of her breasts growing with each lick of the blonde's tongue, Logan brought her hand over the one Tanner used to torture her breast. She urged his fingers to punish her further, for him to fuck her in any way he desired, because she already knew it would feel more amazing than anything she'd experienced.

The pumping of his hips slowed, and he turned her in his arms. The lust blazing in his eyes and curving his lips in a wicked grin was palpable. Releasing her breast to place his hands at the small of her back, he bent his knees until he was cock level with her pussy. He thrust up against her with a hard shove. She screamed with the riotous sensation of the clamp tugging at her tight, aching clit. He shoved against her again, angling his shaft to slide between her thighs at the last second. The clitoris clamp tugged down with the move, the silver chains attached to it yanking at her nipples and shooting pleasure-pain so achingly intense through her that her entire body shook with impending orgasm.

Digging her salon-supplied fingernails into the front of his shirt, Logan panted for air. One more push of his cock. Just one more . . .

Tanner's hands lifted from her spine to join hers at the front of his shirt. She thought he would follow the move with his next thrust. Waited for it with held breath and a desperately pulsing sex. He didn't thrust against her again but plied her fingers from his shirt and stepped back.

His mouth moved. She registered the word *drink*, or maybe it was *dink*. He deserved to be called something a hell of a lot worse for the way he turned and disappeared into the crush, leaving her in the middle of the dance floor, surrounded by flashing lights and naked, sweaty, grinding bodies, with her pussy on the verge of exploding.

Seconds passed as she considered what to do. Turn her hands on her own body and give herself the orgasm he failed to provide, or leave, both the nightclub and the hotel? She would much prefer spending the night getting herself off in her pier-side bungalow than dealing with Dr. Moody.

A hand slid around Logan's waist from behind. A hand the black light revealed to be large and wide and completely masculine. An unmistakable erection pressed against her ass. She spun around, hoping Tanner had gotten over his mood and returned to her. It wasn't Tanner dancing up against her, his bare, stiff cock brushing her belly with each shift of his pelvis, but it was a hunk. A tall, dark, delicious hunk. The kind of man she dreamed of wanting her for years. The kind of man she was getting implants to aid in luring into her bed.

She had no doubt she owed his attention to the buttloads of makeup and sprays and her dirty little catsuit and its water bra cups that made it seem she actually had cleavage. That was the way the world worked. It was time she remembered it and her reason for being here: sex and sex alone.

She would have sex before the night was through, with Tanner or this hunk or some other hottie who caught her interest. Who fucked her no longer mattered—it was all about the when.

Tanner felt guilty as hell over leaving Logan on the dance floor. Really, though, he had no reason for guilt. She wanted to attract strangers for the sole purpose of sex, and alone on the dance floor, she would attract more strangers than she knew what to do with. They wouldn't need a bed to screw her either. They would do her right where they stood, so long as she was agreeable.

Would she be?

Though it was ridiculous, considering she was nothing more to him than meaningful and short-term sex, testing her faithfulness was the real reason he left her alone in the midst of an orgy. If he was going to get over his dislike for her new look and end this night with her in his arms, he had to know she was serious about wanting only him tonight.

Tanner waited another couple minutes, then gave up on the drink line that never seemed to get any shorter and headed back to the dance floor. Logan's neon-pink catsuit appeared Day-Glo beneath the black light, zipping his attention to it. Her actual face and body he couldn't distinguish. He pushed his way through the swarming crowd, stopping abruptly on a sharp inhale when she came into clear view, along with the man who held her around the waist while he pumped his naked dick against her. The guy was barely taller than Logan, and where Tanner's cock had pressed along her spine, this joker's rammed directly against her ass.

Bitter ache twisted Tanner's gut. Two-and-half-year-old memories pressed at his temple.

Son of a bitch, he thought he finally managed to cast aside his bitterness over walking in on his girlfriend screwing some other guy and was ready to try at a meaningful relationship again. Maybe he had. Maybe it wasn't memories pressing at his temple and splintering as rage through his body. Maybe the fury eating at him was all because of Logan and her lie about wanting only him tonight.

He should leave her on the dance floor, let her be fucked by every guy who approached her. But, goddammit, he couldn't. She was right. He *was* threatened by her new look. Threatened and envious as shit of the guy who held her.

Tanner shoved his way to the center of the dance floor, smacking away a hand when it tried to grope him in passing. He didn't stop until he reached Logan, and then only long enough to jerk her away from her dance partner's arms to drag her toward the club's rear exit.

He was acting like a Neanderthal. Shakespeare had to be rolling in his grave. Too fucking bad.

He shut out the looks of the bouncers and the passersby as

he hauled her out the doors, past the club's back parking lot, and onto the beach. Shut out the almost fearful look on her face as he pulled her into the moonlight-brightened blackness that lapped at the water's edge.

The foreboding hiss of his zipper as he unzipped his khakis had his cock pulsing. As he yanked the front zipper down on her catsuit to unveil her nude, sweaty body and the sexy-as-hell Y-clip, Logan sharply inhaled making him nearly come on the spot. He fisted the silver strands where the three chains met, ready to make her pay.

"Hand her over or die, Joriff of Vulcan!"

The irately shouted words came from somewhere down the beach and stopped Tanner's hand midtug.

"Holy shit," Logan whispered, "what if he's serious?"

He almost laughed with her words—not scared or pissed or anything else they should be for the way he was acting. No, she sounded aroused, stimulated in a primal way that said he could have plunged into her the instant he freed his cock, and she would have come with his first thrust.

Because she was wet for him, or for her dance partner?

It shouldn't make a difference, so he forgot the question to focus on the argument happening a short ways away.

If the guy was serious, Joriff was liable to be dead by the time Tanner could return inside the nightclub and get help. Hoping like hell he didn't regret it, he took Logan's hand and pulled her along the beach. "Let's check it out."

"By whose hand, Brisban?" a hard male voice returned, cold humor ringing in his words. "Yours are tied and your beloved Marjie would rather see to my pleasure than pain."

Tanner and Logan hurried along the shoreline, using the man-made sand dunes, the palms, and the darkness of night for camouflage. A glance around the edge of the fourth short dune revealed a woman and a man standing with their backs to Tanner while a second man kneeled in the sand. The second man's hands were tied submissively behind his back, while his upturned face revealed a sneer and a deep wrinkle-embedded forehead that extended to the top of his head and could never be human.

"What the hell?" Tanner breathed as the first man came to his knees in front of the shackled one. His profile was to them now, and it revealed pointy ears and thick, bushy white eyebrows that slashed up toward his temples.

Logan shook free of Tanner's hand to stand beside him. "Trekkies," she whispered. "The guy with his hands behind his back is a Romulan, and the other one's a Klingon. They're probably acting out a battle scene."

His shaft had deflated with the idea of encountering a murder in the making. The heat of her breath against his ear had his body hardening all over again.

Forty feet away, the Klingon grabbed the Romulan by the shirtfront, jerking him to his feet. Tanner held his breath. His attention returned entirely to the scene on the beach, as if a murder was truly occurring. Then he realized the only death happening out there on the sand would be a little death when the Klingon's hand dropped to the Romulan's zipper and jerked it down.

The Klingon turned, flashing a wickedly corrupt smile at the woman. "Show him how traitors are punished, Marjie."

Marjie did as she was bade, grabbing hold of the sides of the Romulan's pants and yanking them and his underwear down to his ankles.

Tanner's body went taut in expectation of the woman taking the man's hard-on into her mouth. Instead she stepped back, and the Klingon went to work, fisting the other man's dick in his hand and pumping while the Romulan begged for mercy.

The Klingon tossed back his head, letting out a rough laugh. "You had your chance to confess, Romulan. Now you will suffer by watching your woman fuck another."

As if she was waiting for the words, Marjie fell to her knees, pulled the Klingon's penis free of his clothes, and greedily sucked it between her lips. The Klingon kept up the pumping of his hand, petting and stroking the other man's balls while Marjie sucked the Klingon's cock.

Beside Tanner, Logan's breathing grew intense. She was obviously affected as strongly as he was by the show, rapt in a way that wouldn't allow them to end their voyeurism.

"Enough!" the Klingon shouted after a minute or two had passed. "No more pleasure for you. It's time to die." Marjie's lips slipped from his shaft as the Klingon rounded on the Romulan and slammed his dick hard into the man's ass.

The Romulan howled. Marjie fisted the base of his cock and took him deep into her mouth. Tanner swallowed hard as the three began moving in tandem, the Klingon thrusting into the man's ass, Marjie sucking his cock, and the Romulan writhing and screaming his ecstasy in the middle.

"I'd say beam me up," Logan said thickly, "but I have a feeling you already are up."

He pulled his attention from the trio on the beach to face her. The moonlight revealed her brown eyes rich with lust. She hadn't bothered to zip her catsuit before they made the trek down the shoreline, and her nipples stabbed from the circle of their clamps. The scent of her arousal lifted on the warm, salty air. Hot. Musky. Delicious. He growled in the back of his throat with his renewed desire to grab hold of the Y-clip and use it to torture her.

A glance at her dripping pussy and back to her heavily lidded eyes told Tanner there was no reason to deny himself. He gave in to his desire, fingering the thin silver chain that led from her left nipple to join with the other chains.

"I'm rock hard, but it has nothing to do with them." He gave a tug, and she yelped out a cry. "All right, it does. But I was hard long before we came out here."

"I've been ready to come since you left me for a dink."

He frowned. "I said *drink*."

"Maybe, but you acted like a dink."

What about the way *she* acted?

Asking the question would only start an argument. He didn't want to argue. He wanted to torment her with the Y-clip and then take her in a way that guaranteed she would never forget him.

7

Logan had tried to convince herself it didn't matter who she slept with tonight, so long as it was the sort of hunk she could never get without cleavage, feigned or otherwise. It hadn't worked. As hot as her dance partner had been, the feel of his cock pushing against her rear hadn't gotten her wet the way Tanner's mere smile did.

She wanted only Tanner tonight, wanted him to tug on the silver strands extending from her nipples to her clit until she was insensate with need. Beyond tonight would be a waste of thought.

She looked down at her body. The glove-tight catsuit was undone from where the zipper started at her navel to midway down her thigh. His fingers gripped the chain leading from her left nipple, his thumb stroking the flesh beneath with languid circles.

Those lazy circles were a lie.

The roughness of his voice, the unstoppable heat in his green eyes, and the swell of his cock where it escaped his zipper spoke of his want to go wild on her. Any moment now, he would start to move. Unleash the same feral cries from her as those sounding from the trio just beyond the sand dune.

Logan shuddered with anticipation. The warmth in her belly, which had started as a slow burn the moment they'd entered the nightclub and turned into a sizzling blaze while watching the threesome, intensified. Cream leaked from her sex, rolling along her inner thighs.

Thickly, she asked, "Do you like the Y-clip?"

"Very much." Tanner's thumb idled and he gave the left chain a tug. "Do you?"

Wicked sensation erupted in her throbbing nipple. Restless want blasted to her core. She arched against the heavily building pressure in her breast, sighing, "Oh, yeah . . ."

He pulled her toward him, spinning her in a semicircle. She landed with her body plastered against his, much the way it had been on the dance floor. Only now, his erection wasn't pressing up against her spine. Now, he clearly bent his knees, as his rigid staff thrust between her thighs from behind, cruising along the aching, wet folds of her pussy.

The head of his dick contacted the lobster-claw clitoris clamp. They moaned in unison. "Do you like that?" His voice was rough, coarser than she'd ever heard it.

"I like everything you do, Tanner."

The heat and hardness of his body left her. The swat of his palm against her ass seconds later was unexpected and erotic as hell.

Logan's blood sizzled. Her overly aroused pussy lips pulsed in a way that shifted the clamp a little, more than enough to have her shouting, "Yes! I like that! Love that! Do it again. Please."

His hand returned to her stinging flesh, spanking her ass with a whack that echoed in the night as the breath cruised between her lips. Her entire body trembled. His hand returned, striking her buttocks lower, his last finger coming into contact with the rear of her cunt and making her squirm with ecstasy.

The clitoris clamp shifted again, harder this time. Much harder as Tanner's fingers regripped the silver chain.

His yank was severe. Punishing.

Logan whimpered. Her nipples vibrated with delicious pain. Sweat slicked her skin and beaded along her forehead with the exertion of her harried breathing.

His free hand shoved between her thighs from behind, his fingers petting her trembling sex once and then grabbing the weight attached to the clamp and giving it a hard tug. He repeated the tug with his other hand, the action jerking her clit in the opposite direction, her nipples downward.

The tension was exquisite. The pressure blindingly intense. Beyond intense as his hips joined the foray, pumping against her ass while his fingers continued their sensual assault.

Logan turned her fingernails on his hips, digging them into his skin as she rocked back against him. Her pussy contracted wildly, and she fought for air. Then she gave up on breathing as Tanner's hips reared back only to return with his cock guided straight to her opening.

She came violently with the shove of his dick into her sheath. Her pussy gripped him with uncontrollable spasms, the clitoris clamp caressing his hard flesh with each of his thrusts until it wasn't just a device for her pleasure, but for his, too.

The push of his hot fluid deep in her core made her own orgasm that much more powerful. She sank her nails deeper in his hips, riding out the soul-blistering climax, only too happy to stay joined together forever.

That there was no forever for them resurfaced a half minute later, when the remnants of Logan's orgasm died away. Tanner was the only man she wanted tonight and for the remainder of the time left before her surgery, but her wants would change once she left Private Indulgence.

His arms wrapped around her middle, his breath rolling along her ear. "It will never feel that good again."

Shuddering involuntarily, she attempted to diagnose his meaning. If she believed he was truly threatened by her new look, she would assume it was jealousy talking, suggesting no other man could make her feel as good. But she knew better than to think such a thing.

Understanding dawned with a flicker of annoyance. She unwrapped his arms to pull away from his body and turn to glare at him. "You mean after surgery?" They were back to the "convincing her she didn't need bigger boobs" game. Or maybe there was no "back to" about it. Had that been his intention all along?

Increased annoyance heated her words. "I thought you said sensitivity comes back after a few months or so?"

"Sometimes, but just as often you never get it back as good as it once was. Melinda had her surgery a year and a half ago, and she still can't feel much of anything around her left areola, and her nipple only responds to the kind of pain that has nothing to do with pleasure."

Who the fuck was Melinda to him? A client and friend, or a reoccurring lover? She had cast aside the questions in his office last night because she knew the answers wouldn't matter. She forced them aside this time as well, though doing so made her belly churn.

Logan told Tanner at her consultation she smoked only when she was pissed, and right now she was certain steam shot from her ears. "I want the surgery, Tanner," she bit out. "If I lose nipple sensation, it will be worth it for the added pleasure for the rest of my body."

"Right. From all the guys your new breasts help bring into your bed." He snorted in the same derisive way he'd done over dinner whenever she'd checked out another man's package. Then, suddenly, the frustration was gone from his expression, and he was back in professional mode. "I just want to make certain you're as knowledgeable as possible."

Damn it, this was not a time to be professional! "Is that why you gave me the Y-clip, to make me knowledgeable? Or were you hoping it would be enough to convince me not to have surgery?"

"I saw it and thought you would like it. Your *pleasure* was all I had in mind."

He spoke so seriously it made Logan want to believe him. She couldn't. Not when his cum was sliding down her thighs and soaking the crotch of her catsuit.

She ought to rip him a new one for coming inside of her. But she'd started on Depo-Provera weeks ago, in preparation for her trip to Private Indulgence and the hopes of running into the Don Juan resort tradition. And, too, it made her feel incredibly sexy to think he'd been so far gone with desire for her, he hadn't thought of contraception.

Desire for her truly, though, or would any woman have done?

"I don't believe you." So long as she was accusing . . . "How many other women have you bought presents for in the hopes of dissuading them from having implants?"

The wounded look entered Tanner's eyes. He fisted his hands near his hips. "I don't like what you're implying. I told you I've never slept with one of my patients."

"Then why me?" Or was she pointing fingers she had no right to point? Was the fault her own for all but throwing herself at him during her consultation? Had none of his other patients been so tacky?

His gaze slid over Logan's body, from her overstyled hair to her slightly stinging nipples to her shimmering mound. When his eyes met hers, they didn't hold arousal but an appreciation that appeared to go well beyond the physical. "You're different. Naturally appealing in a way most women couldn't pull off if they tried. You're going to lose that by having the surgery."

"I don't want to be natural!" She didn't want him sounding

so sincere even more—it made her question her decision to have implants. But, no, she wouldn't question that choice, because only Tanner found her natural appearance attractive, and he would soon be out of her life. "I want to be sexy in a way more men than just you appreciate."

The words had their intended effect. His expression closed off, and he focused on straightening his clothes. Without looking at her or the sky, he said distantly, "It looks like rain's coming in. I'm not sticking around and getting caught in any more storms."

Fresh from a shower that hadn't done a thing to cool his frustration, Tanner opened the bathroom door. The hotel suite opened up directly outside of it, and from his vantage, he could see Logan curled up on the two-man couch.

She *was* Logan again.

He let her take a shower before him, and when she'd emerged from the bathroom, the only remnants of the transformed version of her were the highlights in her hair and her long pink fingernails. His gaze slid to her hands, which held her knees tucked up under her chin while she watched TV.

He didn't mind the nails. For one thing, she could grow them long naturally. For another, they felt like his own personal nirvana biting into his hips.

"I'm going to watch a movie, if you want to join me."

Tanner jolted with the sound of Logan's voice, not realizing she'd known he was out of the shower. He moved into the suite's living area. She sounded like she was trying to get past their words on the beach, and he wanted to do that, too. "Anything good?"

"*Bravehea* . . ." Her reply stalled as her gaze fell on his naked body. She blinked and tried again. "*Braveheart*. I know it's an older movie, but I really like it."

Did she? Or was it his body she really liked?

He probably should have put clothes on, but he figured it rather pointless given how often she'd seen him naked. He corrected that mistake now, going into the bedroom and pulling on a pair of canvas shorts, not bothering with underwear.

He returned to the living area and sat down on the couch beside her as copyright information flashed on the television screen. She quickly hit PLAY, like she couldn't get her head into the movie fast enough, and the movie started up. Not with a scene of a young Scottish boy in a kilt, but of a guy around Tanner's own age walking through a field of heather, wearing a kilt and nothing else.

A woman appeared on the screen, a plaid wrapped around her body, long bare legs peeking from beneath the wrap. She shared a smile with the guy, and then she gave him a much bigger smile as she tugged at the plaid, and it fell to the heather to reveal her nude body. The scene went to a side profile, showcasing the tented front of the guy's kilt and then his mouth as he pulled the woman to him and closed his lips over a plentiful breast.

Tanner's cock stirred. "I thought you said this was *Braveheart*?"

"I thought it was." Logan went to the TV. She bent down to open the cabinet beneath it and pulled out a DVD case. "Whoops. Guess it's actually *Bravehard*. Should've known an X-rated hotel wouldn't carry regular movies. Do you want me to turn it off?"

When her shapely ass was in his face, all he wanted to do was slip inside her body. His shaft hardened further with the memory of swatting her tight backside. The only way it would have been better was if the lighting had allowed him to see the pink left behind. "It's up to you."

For a few seconds, she stood facing the screen, where the

man now pumped his dick between the woman's tits; then she turned back to reveal her cheeks flush with desire. "I've always been a slut for a man in a kilt." Her gaze dropped to his groin, where his hard-on rose against his shorts. "Or a man without a kilt but a sexily lopsided grin and a big, hard cock."

With a raspy laugh, Tanner flashed the grin in question. He opened his arms to her, and she returned to the couch, dropping down on his lap with her knees bent and her thighs wrapped around his waist. She leaned forward, flicking her tongue against the corner of his mouth.

"I'm sorry for being a dink. You looked hot today. Not hotter than you look naturally, just in a different way."

Logan reclined back. She lifted her right hand in the Vulcan peace sign, her first two fingers and last two fingers separated in a vee. "I come in peace."

"No, you don't. You come all over my lap."

As it turned out, Tanner was right. Logan thoroughly enjoyed coming all over his lap while moans and groans and sighs of rapture played out on the screen behind her.

She sank against his sweaty chest and listened to the wild tattoo of his heart as her own beat rapidly. His arms came around, his fingers stroking the length of her spine.

This felt good. Right. Stupid.

There was no future for them. She had plans to notch her bedpost. Even if she didn't, he was a "by the week" kind of lover. Why? "Have you loved another woman since Laura?"

"I wouldn't exactly call my high school experience love, but, yeah, sure I have."

Logan lifted her cheek from his chest to give him a disbelieving look. "Sure you have, like it's not a big deal?"

The wounded edge was in his eyes stronger than she'd ever seen it. "It was a big deal . . . until I surprised my girlfriend with a visit and found some other guy screwing her."

"Ouch. That's rough." And explained a whole lot.

"I'm over it." The words rang with a conviction that seemed to surprise him. He paused a few seconds, the wheels all but noticeably spinning in his head. His voice and expression both lighter, he continued, "She cheated on me because I moved to the Caribbean to take a job at Private Indulgence, and she stayed back in Michigan. The funny part is, she was the one who pushed me to take the job. I envisioned moving down here and having her join me when I got settled. She never came down, and I could only get up there once a month for a day or two."

Tanner's expression went blank, his fingers lifting from her back. "Long-distance relationships aren't worth it. There isn't enough love in the world to make them work."

Long-distance relationships aren't worth it.

Tanner's words from the night before rang in Logan's head as she lay awake the next night, dreading the day after tomorrow. Tonight, she slept at his house, in his bed and arms. Tomorrow, they would probably go on as they had today, as if there wasn't a mountain of tension between them.

That tension was there and she hated it.

Hated even more reflecting on the way her spirits had felt crushed with his admission last night, because it meant all that stood between them and the demise of their relationship was another thirty-two hours.

She should be happy her surgery was so close. Truthfully, she was thrilled at the prospect of finally getting her new cleavage, but that it came with the price of losing Tanner sucked big-time.

Would it make a difference if she told him she didn't live in Miami but on a neighboring island, so he could see her even after her time at Private Indulgence was up?

Of course it wouldn't.

He took his lovers a week at a time, for valid reason it seemed, now that she knew of his hurtful past experience, and soon she would be taking hers the same way. Logan could only hope all those future hotties were as appealing to her mind as they were to her body, the way Tanner was.

8

"What hat are you doing here?" Logan asked, finding Tanner standing outside her bungalow at seven o'clock on Saturday morning, her shock clear by both her stunned look and tone.

She probably figured she wouldn't see him again after he left her following dinner yesterday with a reminder not to eat or drink after midnight. He probably shouldn't see her again, but she deserved to have someone familiar by her side before and after surgery, even if that someone still wasn't all that keen about her having surgery.

His attention went to her natural breasts. She didn't wear a bra beneath her loose-fitting, button-up shirt, and her nipples tented beneath his gaze, forming perfect circles against the thin white cotton. He wasn't allowed to touch, both because her breasts shouldn't be stimulated this close to surgery and because he cut himself off from her body eleven hours ago, but damn how he wanted to.

Shifting his attention to the safety of the kitchen area, he jingled the Jeep's keys. "Driving you to the clinic."

"I planned to take the bus."

The coolness of her voice brought Tanner's gaze to her face—makeup-free and too inviting for its own good. "Most people bring someone with them to surgery for moral support. Besides, you need someone to bring you back here after it's over."

"Which is the main reason I chose to have my surgery done at this resort." She crossed to the couch and slid her bare feet into the backless white canvas shoes lying on the floor in front of it. Picking up the brush from the small coffee table, she ran it through her hair. "The brochure said I'm supposed to have a health and wellness care provider assigned to me for forty-eight hours following surgery, then on call through the end of the first week."

Tanner glared at the couch. Once she checked out, he should advise someone to burn the thing. Just knowing it existed would be enough to keep the memory of her masturbating on it fresh in his mind. His body wanted to react to the thought. He killed that want by thinking of all the other men who would soon experience the same erotic show.

For the next several days, there would be no others. Just Tanner and Logan, who would undoubtedly be in so much pain, she wouldn't even have sexy thoughts. "You are and do. Me."

She stopped brushing to flash him an incredulous look. "What about your work?"

"I had vacation time coming. I already split my surgeries between the three other aesthetic specialists on staff, so there's no point in telling me no."

"But you don't even *want* me to have surgery."

"Who cares what I want? A week from now, I won't be anything more than a memory. A month from now, you'll have so many men vying for a spot in your bed, you won't remember my name." Though it was asinine, Tanner held his breath with his want for her to deny him by saying she wouldn't forget him, in a month or ever.

His breath whizzed out slowly with Logan's dismissive shrug. She gave her hair a few more strokes, then dropped the brush on the table. She grabbed her driver's license and resort patient ID from next to the brush, sliding them into the pocket of her shorts as she stood. "Okay, then. Thanks for driving me."

Logan loved her responsive nipples.

While lying on a hospital gurney, being prepped for surgery, wasn't the time to debate the potential loss of her nipples' sensitivity. It was the time to pull in deep breaths and pray that Dr. Lasa—who, with his graying hair and time-lined face, looked much more like the doctor she had in mind when scheduling her surgery—had the same zero-mortality rate as Tanner.

She hadn't questioned it because Tanner recommended him. She couldn't see him steering her wrong on a life-and-death matter. Honestly, she couldn't see him steering her wrong on any matter. He was one of the good ones, better than she'd even realized to show up at her bungalow this morning and to be here now, looking on as the anesthesiologist fed her sleepy-time medicine through the IV in her hand.

An hour or two long nap was all that was in store for her. A chance to catch up on the sleep she hadn't gotten last night for her tossing and turning, thinking about this surgery and about how empty her bed felt without Tanner in it. The extent to which she'd missed him was the reason she'd been so cool with him this morning. It wasn't his fault, and she spent the last hour feeling like complete crap because of it.

He took her hand, giving it a squeeze. "Relax. You'll be fine. Gil has never lost a patient, and I plan to make certain he doesn't start today."

"You're going to help him?" That explained why he'd left her long enough to don green scrubs a short while ago. But why would he want to help with her surgery when he was so against her having it? Did it all come down to his being a nice guy?

"Not help, but I'll be in the operating room, breathing down his neck. At least until he points out he has over a decade more experience with augmentation surgery than I do and orders me to get the hell out of his way."

Logan tried to laugh, but it came out sounding like a gurgle. "Thank you," she managed groggily.

His face blurred a little as it came closer. His lips looked fuzzy. Still, she knew their intention even before they came over hers, brushing so gently, so tenderly.

Why did he bother? She blinked when her tongue felt too thick and cottony to help enunciate words.

Tanner smiled. "For luck, sexy lady."

She wanted to respond, to apologize for her attitude toward him this morning. She never had the opportunity before the anesthesia rendered her unconscious.

Tanner stood from a visitor's chair in the recovery room with the subtle sound of Logan shifting on her hospital bed. Her eyes opened slowly. She blinked and blinked again. Pain contorted her face, and she cried out in a low, throaty voice, "I want my mommy."

He'd been witness to enough of his patients' post-op pain to know she was sore as hell. He went to the phone mounted on the wall near the door, looking back at her with a sympathetic smile. "Tell me her number and I'll get her on the line."

"She died of ovarian cancer three years ago."

His stomach clenched for her loss. He should have known of the death through the question on Logan's patient form that asked if there was a history of cancer in her family. Only, he'd been too distracted by her behavior to get that far on her charts during the consultation phase and, shortly thereafter, had handed her case over to Gil.

Tanner moved to her bedside. He wanted to take her hand as he'd done before surgery but was unsure how she would react or even if that light touch would add to her ache. "I'm sorry. I had no idea."

"Of course you didn't. Telling you that kind of stuff would make us too close. Her death's the reason I was worried about dying in surgery. Daddy couldn't handle losing me."

He frowned. She generally seemed to say what was on her mind, but something told him she wouldn't be quite so candid about keeping information from him, even now when they couldn't have sex. The morphine had to be loosening her lips. "Do you see your father a lot?"

"Such a goof. I live with him."

She *what*? The clenching of his stomach returned, much more intensely. "You said your father lives on Cristos."

"He does."

"So, you're not from Miami?" She actually lived an island away? Twenty minutes by boat. Why had Logan lied to him?

"Nope," she said, far too cheerily. The morphine was clearly working its magic.

Tanner could use some happiness-inducing drugs himself.

He spent last night convincing himself they weren't meant to be. He wasn't up to another long-distance relationship, and he wouldn't ask her to move here for him. Not that she would want to move for him. If she wanted to be with him beyond the time they shared this week, she would have told him where she lived. If not in the first place, then the other night, when he commented on how long-distance relationships weren't worth it.

"You just told me that so we wouldn't get too close?" The words sounded as wrung out as he suddenly felt.

"Yep." Logan let out a huge yawn, then shrieked when her

arms lifted a couple inches off the bed with her stretch. She closed her eyes. "I'm going to sleep now."

"Yeah, you sleep." While he attempted to find a way out of his commitment to be her care provider. He couldn't stick himself in that bungalow alone with her, not knowing how he felt and knowing how she felt and how far apart those two feelings were.

Logan opened her eyes slowly, afraid even that much movement would be too much for the miserable state of her body. The breasts hidden beneath a stretchy bra and bandages better be grade-A-plus for how damned badly her chest hurt.

"Feeling better?"

She moved her head very slowly toward the sound of Tanner's voice. He sat on a chair beside the bed, a small smile curving his lips. "Than roadkill?"

"Than you did when you woke up following surgery."

"I woke up before?"

His smile faltered. He looked like he wanted to say something important, but then just shrugged. "Several times."

"I remember being woken up once in the OR where I was freezing to death, and then getting dressed and leaving the clinic to come back here, but that's about it."

"Between the pain and the morphine, I'm not surprised." He stood and went to the kitchen area.

"Thanks for staying with me, Tanner. It's sweet."

"That's me. Sweet Tanner who you don't dare get too close to."

"What?" Had he said what Logan thought he said, or was that still the morphine in her system? Or, more likely, the Vicodin. Right before she'd fallen asleep, she begged him for a handful of them. The good-intentioned bastard had given her only two.

"Nothing." He returned to her bedside, a bowl of something in his hands. "Ready for some soup?"

She eyed the bowl warily. "You expect me to move enough to get a spoon to my lips?" Or eat, for that matter—just the thought of soup made her feel nauseous.

"I expect you to drink it through a straw." From somewhere near the wall—she wasn't about to try and see where—Tanner produced a straw. He stuck it in the soup and brought the bowl in front of her, holding the straw before her lips. "I know the last thing you want to do is eat, but you need to get as much down as you can. Nourishment is critical to the healing process."

She managed a weak smile. "You sound like a doctor."

"I'm glad you brought that up." His tone went from clinical to detached. "One of the specialists I handed my cases over to came down with the flu. I need to handle the surgeries after all. I'm sorry, but I won't be able to be your care provider."

"Oh." Logan attempted to suck down more soup, but her stomach suddenly felt beyond volatile. One more sip and the little bit she had gotten down would be right back up. She clamped her lips shut. "I can't."

His hands moved near the wall again and then came back empty, his expression even more vacant. "My replacement will be here in a half hour. Do you need anything before I go?"

For him to stay. They couldn't be lovers any longer—not even if she wasn't fresh from surgery—she got that, but she wanted Tanner by her side. With him in the room, she still felt like shit, but it was a nicer kind of shit than she was bound to feel like with his replacement.

He'd already done too much for her. She couldn't ask him to risk his job now, so she settled on, "A Mocha Frappuccino."

He smiled. "Sorry. The closest Starbucks is on Cristos."

"I know."

Gone went the smile. "Of course you do."

Logan jerked a little with his snide tone, nearly shrieking with the resulting pain that ripped through her body. She closed her eyes and willed the hurt to pass, wondering over his tone all the while. Or had his voice not really sounded that way? Could hearing things be a side effect of Vicodin?

"Bye, Logan. Good luck with your implants."

She opened her eyes to find Tanner almost to the door. Her belly roiled in a way not even the soup had accomplished. That good-bye had sounded like forever. "Will I see you again?"

"You know where I live."

But he wouldn't be coming by her bungalow anymore. This was it. The end she'd always known was coming. How come she hadn't known it would feel so horrible? His leaving hurt almost more than her breasts, and that was saying something.

"Thanks." She tried not to sound as gloomy as she felt. Not that it would matter if her unhappiness came through; he would assume it was a result of her pain. "It's been fun. But now it's done."

Damn, she hadn't meant to add that last part, to remember the other time she'd been botching Dr. Seuss. But then Logan was glad she'd done it. It earned her a last lopsided smile before Tanner walked from her bungalow and out of her life.

9

"Have fun tonight, honey."

Logan rose up on the toes of her dangerously high heels to kiss her father's cheek. Sarita was coming over for a movie date night in the living room, and Logan hoped they had fun of their own. Her father was falling in love with the woman, and Logan couldn't be happier. Her mother would always be in both of their hearts and memories, but it was time to move on.

"Thanks, Daddy. You, too," she said, her thoughts already on her own plans to move on via the fun in store for her tonight. Lots and lots of fun of the screaming, quaking, raging-orgasm variety. It was the first flight out for her new beautiful, bountiful, warm-to-the-touch and just as exciting breasts, and her date was the man of her dreams.

Okay, so the man-of-her-dreams part was a lie.

Another man still filled her dreams and fantasies, but that would change tonight. A honk outside told her the hottie who would change it had arrived. Logan waited a minute for him to come to the door, then realized he had no such intention.

Mildly annoying and not even close to chivalrous, but then she wasn't looking for a Shakespeare wannabe—just a guy who set off her va-va-voom meter to screw for a week or two. The blond hunk waiting in the convertible in the driveway would do nicely.

She grabbed the tacky little orange purse that went with her even tackier and, quite possibly, littler dress, and hurried out the door and into the passenger's seat of the convertible. The wind was going to play hell with the hair she'd spent hours trying to get perfect just so Hottie-Man could mess it up for her, but such was life.

"Hi." His attention zoomed to her breasts, the tops of which were exposed by the skintight dress's low-cut bodice. "You look great."

My face is up here, buck-o, she wanted to say but managed to refrain. After all, she not only purposefully dressed to flaunt tonight but also paid good money and endured a buttload of pain to have him ogling her tits.

Two hours later, Logan wondered why she'd bothered with her hair and makeup, or even coming on this date. She might as well have sent her implants solo, because Hottie-Man couldn't keep his eyes off them. That was supposed to be good. Only, it didn't feel good. It felt a lot like he was having visions of titty-fucking her. And that should have been okay, too. Maybe it would have been if it didn't remind her of watching *Bravehard* with Tanner.

Tanner might like to titty-fuck her, too, but he wouldn't spend all of dinner making the fact blatantly obvious by never taking his eyes off her chest.

He would engage in conversation. Tell her how impressed he was with her mechanic skills. How he appreciated her taste in wine. The bozo across from her had ordered cabernet for her, too. Something about the way he pronounced the word with a hard *T* and guzzled his glass down ruined the effect.

"Ready for dessert?" he asked her boobs.

"Yes. They are. And they'll be having it with my father." That didn't come out quite right, but frankly Logan would rather have incest on her mind than thoughts of fucking this loser, no matter how big of a hunk he might be. She stood and dropped her napkin onto her plate. "Thanks, but this isn't quite what I had in mind."

He glowered. "Hey, this is one of the nicest restaurants on Cristos."

"I wasn't talking about the restaurant."

What was she talking about? Just the way this date had gone, how he seemed to favor looking at her breasts over her face? Or did it go beyond that?

Of course it did, Logan accepted as she made her way to the front of the restaurant and asked the concierge to call her a cab. It went to the heart of the matter, which was the fact that she didn't want to share dessert with her father tonight either. She wanted to lick it off Tanner's scrumptious chest and then let him do the same to her.

Except Tanner wouldn't want to lick her chest, or titty-fuck her, she acknowledged on a sigh. Not now that she had full breasts. He liked her with barely there boobs, warm to the touch and, in his mind, very exciting.

Would he even be attracted to her anymore?

It wasn't supposed to matter. He wasn't supposed to still be in her mind. But he was and in a way that involved much more than living out her fantasies. In a way that said he'd been right about her not getting a boob job and so much more.

Only, he hadn't been right about her not getting a boob job as a whole; merely her reason for wanting one had been off. Logan shouldn't have done it to get laid, but she was glad she'd done it. She liked the way she looked now. Felt comfortable in her skin in a way she'd never before known. Tanner deserved to hear that, to know she was finally happy.

All right, so the happy thing in general might be a bit much. But as far as her breasts went, she was ecstatic.

"I need you!"

Tanner had dreamed of having a woman charge into his house and speak those words for almost two months now. He hadn't envisioned the woman wearing a thigh-length, red silk robe and, by the looks of things, nothing else, but it was a nice touch. Or it would have been, if the woman in question was Logan instead of Melinda.

She rushed over to where he sat sacked out on the couch in his underwear and pushed the robe off her shoulders to reveal she wasn't completely naked. She wore matching panties that exposed more than they concealed.

He should try to work up a little excitement. He hadn't had sex since before Logan's surgery, and doing so now was liable to help out in the forgetting-her department. But he'd never been attracted to Melinda in a sexual way, and even seeing her essentially nude didn't make a difference. "Sorry, but I don't like you that way."

"Jesus, you're such a typical man. I'm having a life-and-death moment, and you're stroking your ego." Worry weighed down her gaze as she palmed her breasts. "I think I broke one of them. I was practicing for my tango class in the kitchen when I lost my balance and landed on my chest on the tiling. I heard a noise, like a popping sound."

Tanner stood from the couch, forgetting the television show he hadn't been able to get interested in to feel her breasts. "What the hell do you expect a guy to think when you rush into his house and take your clothes off?"

"I see your point, but c'mon, Tanner, I used to babysit you."

"Wouldn't know you were old enough, looking at your body." Despite her babysitting comment, she clearly basked in his words, enough to have her nipples tightening. He hurried to finish the exam, afraid Melinda might change her mind about not wanting him. She dumped Jaelin last week and was on the prowl for a new man. "They feel fine. You probably imagined the pop or heard one of your bones making noise. They do that when you start to get old."

Her eyes narrowed, and she opened her mouth to make what he guessed would be a nasty retort. Another female voice accused, "I knew you two were lovers," before Melinda could say a word.

Tanner jerked his hands from Melinda's breasts with the sound of Logan's voice. He could imagine how badly it looked, his examining Melinda while she wore next to nothing and he wore only briefs. He turned to find Logan standing just inside his doorway, a distressed look on her face, and his heart pounded with the wonder of what she was doing here. "Then you knew wrong. Mel fell on her chest and thought she heard a pop. She rushed over to make sure she hadn't damaged her implants."

Logan glanced at Melinda. "Rushed over?"

Melinda grabbed her robe off the floor, sliding it on as she nodded. She sent him a conspiratorial wink, then started toward Logan. "I live next door. According to Dr. Grey, I'm fine, so I'll be going."

Tanner waited until she closed his front door to ask Logan, "Why are you here?"

Logan's distressed look was replaced with anxiety. "I realized I didn't have surgery to get laid. I did it for me, to make myself feel more confident and comfortable in my skin."

"You came all the way from Miami to tell me that?" He wasn't buying she'd even come from as close as Cristos for that purpose, when she looked so nervous. Dare he hope she was here for the same reason he considered setting aside his ego and going to her place: to plead to give them a chance beyond a handful of days?

She moved into the living room, standing a few feet away, looking like she wanted to be closer. "I don't live in Miami."

"I know."

"You do?" she gasped.

"You told me you live on Cristos with your father when you were in the recovery room following surgery. You also told me you didn't want me to know that because you didn't want me getting too close."

She shook her head, bringing his attention to her long, loose ponytail. She still had her highlights, but a glance at her hands showed the fake nails were gone—likely for the sake of her job—and her clothes were the casual kind she'd worn the day they'd met. "At first I might have felt that way, but then I kept quiet about it for the sake of protecting my heart. I knew you didn't want me beyond a week or two."

Tanner jerked his gaze back to her face. Was he asleep during one of their conversations, or when had he suggested anything like that? Hell, the last couple days they spent together before her surgery, he'd already been acting like a jealous boyfriend. "What makes you say that?"

Logan's look suggested she couldn't believe he had to ask. "Your reputation."

"My *what*?"

Color tinged her cheeks, and she glanced away to say, "It's not exactly a secret you sleep with a different guest every week or two. You're a resort tradition. The Don Juan of orgasms."

"Where the hell is this coming from?" he shot back, sounding unintentionally fierce.

She looked at him, her eyes anxiously searching his face. "Vivian . . . I don't know her last name."

Neither did he, though Tanner could guess she was one of the many resort guests he'd slept with during his Lothario streak. "You got this information from a stranger and believed it?"

"She's a friend of a friend." She continued to search his face, the hope in her eyes making him believe it was denial she sought. "Are you saying it isn't true?"

"Not the way you make it out to be. I'm sure as hell no resort tradition." The idea Logan had only slept with him because of his supposed reputation registered. Anger gripped him hard. He'd been more open with her than with any woman in years, had developed feelings for her despite his best efforts not to do so. How the fuck could she not see that? "You're the only person I've slept with in months."

"I didn't realize."

"A lot of stuff apparently. I have to work so—"

"Do you? Or do you just not want to be around me?" After standing across the road from his house for over an hour, working up the courage to knock, only to find herself running blindly inside when she caught Melinda entering his home in a scanty robe, Logan wasn't leaving without answers.

Tanner scowled. "I have to wor—shit." He pushed a hand through his hair. "I just don't want to be around you."

Her belly tightened. Well, what had she been expecting? For him to bestow her with his undying love? Bad word choice. It made her want to smile over all the times he'd used the word. "Is it because of my breasts? I'm not natural any longer."

His scowl let up with the shake of his head. "I didn't want you getting implants because your reason was all wrong. It sounds like you've since worked that out."

"Then why don't you want to see me?"

"Because I don't want to fuck you."

Logan cast a woeful look at her breasts. Such a nice rack. She caught so many other men checking them out. Checked them out herself each morning when she gave them their daily wakeup massage and hug. None of that mattered when the only man she wanted hated them. "They *do* turn you off."

"They *don't* turn me off. Your body gets me hot, but it's what's inside that matters."

Her self-pity let up a bit. Not entirely, though, because she wasn't touching him or seeing his sexy smile. She really wanted to touch him. See his smile. Lick his smile. Lick him from one end to the other.

She forced a small smile of her own. "That was sweet. I miss it."

Tanner sighed loudly. "What are you doing here, Logan?"

She'd forgotten about the bag in her hand until now. After hearing his exasperated sigh, she wasn't sure she wanted to give him its contents, which she brought along on a hopeful whim. It would probably make her look desperate. But then, what was pride for if not sacrificing? "Giving you this." She pulled the Y-clip from the bag and held it out to him. "And asking you to put it on me. I'm sorry I lied about where I live, though actually it was more of a misunderstanding since I used to live in Miami."

"Before your mother passed away."

"I told you about that, too?" He nodded, and Logan's smile felt incredibly brittle. "I miss her, but I can't get her back." She glanced at her outstretched hand. "Can I get you back, Tanner?"

"On what terms? Like I said, I don't want to fuck you." He stepped a foot closer and finally, finally, the lopsided smile she'd been fantasizing over for months appeared. "I could be convinced to make love with you." He closed another foot. "I might even be convinced to start seeing you on a permanent basis." He came the last foot, lifting the Y-clip from her hand. "Push a little harder and I'm liable to admit I love you."

Logan sniffed back her tears. How would it look for a mechanic to be crying all over the place? Then again, knowing Tanner, he would think it was the perfect response. Not much she did seemed to bother him, at least not more than what an apology or a few quirky words would fix. "Makes a girl wish you really were a Gremlin." She leaned into him, her sex going moist the instant their bodies touched. "I'd come all over you, get you juicy wet until I had a house full of you talking about loving me, big boobs and all."

Tanner brought his arms around her, stroking them over her back as he bent his head and brushed her mouth with his. He caressed her lips for a long while, soft subtle touches that heated her blood, and then sank his tongue between and ravished her mouth. She ravished his right back, their bodies quickly picking up the pace, moving against each other in a blatantly carnal rhythm that had her pussy dripping and her nipples stiff as nails.

He lifted from her mouth, breathing hard while he flashed that smile she adored. "I'm not a Gremlin, but I'd be willing to let you come all over me,"—he held up the Y-clip—"after I put this on you."

Breathing just as hard, she beamed back at him. "I love you, Tanner. Now get the Y-clip on me. My nipples aren't as sensitive as they used to be,"—at least, she hadn't thought they were until he started kissing and rubbing up against her a few minutes ago—"but I have faith that if you touch them enough, they'll be as good as new one day soon."

He moved his hands beneath her T-shirt and then her bra. "Just touch?"

She squirmed with the delicious warmth of his hand and the knowledge of what was to come. "Pinch."

His thumb and forefinger closed over her nipple, applying pressure. "Hard enough?"

"Harder," she whimpered, moaning with the increased pressure. "Ooh . . . yeah . . . perfect."

Just like he was. Perfect vision. Perfect face. Perfectly graspable ass. And his cock . . . yeah, that was perfect, too, and all hers.

Logan claimed her territory, pushing her hand down the front of his briefs to grab his cock, not letting go until he had her naked and the Y-clip attached. Only then did she let his shaft slip from her fingers to embed firmly inside her warm, wet body—right where her fantasy man belonged.

Join Jami Alden for a
PRIVATE PARTY!

On sale now from Aphrodisia!

1

Julie Driscoll was, without a doubt, the most beautiful bride Chris Dennison had ever seen. Her strapless ivory gown left her arms bare, and, if he closed his eyes, he could imagine how silky her skin would feel against his fingertips. Though her veil obscured her face, he could vividly picture wide, long-lashed eyes the color of the Caribbean sea at sunrise; her small, slightly upturned nose; and full pink lips. Her breasts swelled tastefully against the bodice of her dress, though even that was enough to make his mouth dry and his palms sweat. With the wide, poofy skirt her wedding gown nearly spanning the entire width of the aisle of San Francisco's Grace Cathedral, she reminded him of a luscious dollop of whipped cream, tempting him to lick her up with one lusty sweep of his tongue.

His chest got tight as she approached, his stomach twisting in knots as every step led her closer to the altar. She was really going to go through with this. He'd had eighteen months to mentally prepare himself, and still the realization hit him like a fist in the gut. He clenched his hands into fists, took a deep, calming breath, and willed himself not to turn tail and run from the church as fast as he possibly could. He'd made a promise, and unlike some men in his family, when he gave his word he kept it.

"Who gives this woman in marriage to this man?"

Chris watched, a sour ache building in his stomach, as her father, Grant, lifted her veil to reveal a nervous-looking smile that didn't quite reach her eyes.

"Her mother and I do," Grant replied, and Chris swallowed back the curse screaming in his brain as Julie's groom, Chris's older half brother Brian, stepped forward to take her trembling hand.

"Where in the world is he? It's time to cut the cake."

"I'm sure he'll be here any minute," Julie Driscoll Dennison attempted to soothe the frazzled wedding planner. "Why don't you have one of the ushers check the bathroom, and I'll see if he's out in the lobby."

Honestly, you'd think Brian would know better than to disappear in the middle of the reception.

"Everything okay?" Wendy, Julie's maid of honor sidled up alongside her and asked.

"I can't find Brian. He probably needed a moment to himself."

Wendy quirked a brow. "Right . . ."

Okay, so Brian wasn't exactly the introspective type, but still, it was his wedding day. God knew Julie was all but overwhelmed by it all. "I don't suppose you've seen him."

Wendy shook her head. "Where's his brother? I thought it was the best man's job to keep tabs on the groom."

"He left right after he did his toast," Julie said. She smiled a little when she thought of Chris's toast. So practiced, so polite. So unlike him. Chris wasn't the kind of guy who worried about what people thought of him, especially not the stuffy, overly self-important crowd attending her wedding. His easygoing, casual style made him stick out in this crowd, even as he tried to fit in.

Unlike Brian, who could have been a GQ cover model, Chris's dark brown hair was always a little shaggy, his big, muscular body always looking a little too big for his clothes. But he had looked absolutely delectable in his tux, the white shirt a seductive contrast to his skin, burnished from the strong Caribbean sun. Chris had always been gorgeous in a rough around the edges kind of way, and he'd only improved in the five years since she'd seen him last.

She closed her eyes, trying not to imagine the acres of tanned muscularity he had hidden under that tux. She'd thought she'd gotten over her silly teenage crush on Chris a long time ago, and her wedding day to his half brother was no time for her to resurrect it.

She mentally slapped herself. Today was her wedding day, for goodness sake. All of her months of hard work and planning had finally come to fruition, and now was not the time to revisit her long-dead infatuation with her fabulous groom's black sheep of a younger brother.

She exited the ballroom and made her way down a hall, stopping to chat politely with guests along the way. As she neared a utility closet, a thump sounded from behind the door. Then a giggle. Then a moan.

A decidedly masculine moan.

Her stomach somewhere around her knees, Julie had an awful premonition of what she would find behind that door.

"You son of a bitch." Her voice sounded very far away, like it came from the end of a long, echoing tunnel.

She squeezed her eyes so tight her eyelids cramped. This could not be happening. It simply couldn't.

But there was no mistaking Brian, frozen mid-thrust as he

nailed another woman against the wall, who was gaping over his shoulder at her in a way that would have been comical under other circumstances.

She spared the other woman a quick glance. Ah, of course, the lovely Vanessa, Brian's newest assistant. She had suspected Vanessa's employment had more to do with her mile-high legs and oversized chest than her secretarial skills, and she kicked herself for stupidly giving Brian the benefit of the doubt. But the last time she'd caught him cheating he'd sworn to God, on his grandmother's grave, and the title of his prized Ferrari, that it would never, ever happen again. He'd promised that the next time he would have sex would be with Julie, on their wedding night. And with their wedding plans forcefully in motion, it had been easier to believe him than to admit she was about to make the biggest mistake of her life.

"Julie, it's nothing. It doesn't mean anything." Brian fumbled with his tuxedo pants, grabbing at his cummerbund as the trousers slid back down around his ankles. Vanessa had pulled her skirt down and made a dive to retrieve her underpants. The action sent Brian stumbling backward over a mop and bucket, and he landed on his ass in the middle of Vanessa's chest.

Julie had never been sucker punched, but she imagined this was what it might feel like. A sharp hit to the middle of her lungs, a sensation of all the air leaving her lungs, leaving her gasping like a dying trout. Pain radiated through her, accompanied by the icy burn of humiliation. Still, she grasped for control, trying not to let Brian see that she was blowing apart from the inside out, into a thousand tiny fragments. Her mind worked frantically, searching for the appropriate thing to do or say in a situation like this. But there was no sweeping this under the rug with social niceties.

Taking a mop handle and shoving it somewhere extremely painful was probably not the best response, however appealing it was at the moment. "We're supposed to cut the cake now," she said stupidly.

In a daze, she made her way back to the ballroom. How could she have been so stupid? Allowing herself to be hauled to the altar like some sacrificial cow. Sweet Julie, perfect Julie, always doing the right thing for her parents, for her family, for the business. So determined to never make a fuss that she had refused to acknowledge the truth about her husband-to-be.

Barely conscious of her actions, she pushed open the door to the ballroom of the Winston hotel, the crown jewel in the D&D luxury hotel empire. Her father, Grant Driscoll, and Brian's father, David Dennison, had acquired the property just two years ago. Within a year, it was giving the Fairmont a run for its money as *the* luxury hotel in San Francisco.

But she didn't even see the beautifully redecorated ballroom with its elaborate chandeliers and silk wall coverings that conveyed an atmosphere of old-fashioned elegance and luxury. She didn't care about the tens of thousands of dollars worth of white roses that adorned each of the seventy tables that had been set to accommodate the wedding guests. She didn't even care when she stumbled into a waiter and a glass of merlot splashed down the skirt of her custom-made Vera Wang wedding gown.

She moved through the crowd, seeing nothing but blurry flesh-colored shapes of guests as they tried to catch her hands, to kiss her cheeks and offer congratulations. Ignoring everyone, she made her way to the dais at the front of the room currently occupied by the band.

As she reached the first step, she felt a firm grip on her arm. She didn't even acknowledge Wendy as she shook off her grip.

Signaling the band to stop, she grasped the microphone and lowered it until it was at mouth level. It was then that she realized she was shaking. Not just a little tremble of the hand, but a full-body quake. She stared out into a crowd that represented a who's who of San Francisco society. Out of the corner of her eye she saw the mayor hitting on one of her cousins. Her father's business partners, city councilmembers, and wealthy financiers and their spouses stared at her expectantly.

Julie licked her lips and grasped the microphone. Her knuckles were white as she clenched the microphone in a death grip. Glancing to her right, her stomach clenched as two waiters wheeled out the five-tier chocolate raspberry with vanilla fondant icing wedding cake, and positioned it next to her.

"Can I have everyone's attention please?"

The request was totally unnecessary—everyone was staring at her in slack-jawed astonishment.

"I appreciate that you have come here to celebrate what was supposed to be the most special day of my life." A vague, outer-body sensation overtook her, enabling her to see herself as though from across the room. What would the little psycho bride say next? "Unfortunately, my special day has been ruined by the fact that my husband," she gestured to the back of the ballroom, where Brian fought his way through the throng, "decided that his wedding reception was a perfect place to screw his new assistant."

A chorus of gasps and murmurs rippled through the crowd, snapping everything into sudden, vivid focus. Mouths gaped, eyes bulged as people craned their necks to catch a glimpse of the errant groom.

"So, while I encourage you to continue to enjoy the festivities, I'm going to call it a night." She gathered up her full skirts and had barely made it to the edge of the stage when Brian finally reached her.

"Julie, I'm sorry, please, you have to listen." Brian had combed his hair and straightened his tuxedo, and was once again the epitome of perfectly polished masculinity. Grasping her arms so tightly she knew she'd have marks, he said in a pleading voice, "I'm a sex addict. It's an illness. I can't help myself, Jules—"

She wrenched out of his grip, and a surge of rage violently snapped her out of her state of shock. It was exactly the sort of excuse Brian would come up with—one absolving him of all personal responsibility, eliciting sympathy rather than blame. Suddenly, so furious she feared her head might burst into flame, she yelled, "An addict? For an addict you sure haven't had a problem keeping your hands off me!"

Brian walked towards her determinedly, and she backed away and tried to skirt around him. "Can you blame me for trying to avoid a permanent case of frostbite?" he muttered so only she could hear. But for the crowd he said, "How can you turn away from me when I need your support?"

Every eye was riveted to the drama playing out on stage.

"Get out of my way, Brian," She had to get out of that room, away from everyone and everything that had forced her into this public humiliation.

He moved again to grab her, and she instinctively reached behind her, her fingers coming into contact with the smooth surface of the cake. Turning slightly, she grabbed the surprisingly heavy top tier. Using every ounce of strength in her body, she ground it into Brian's shocked face.

"You might want to zip up your fly," she sneered.

She straightened her shoulders, and raised her chin haughtily, as she, Julianna Devereaux Driscoll, the perfectly poised princess of the D&D hotel empire, removed her wine-stained, cake-smeared, wholly enraged self from the ballroom.